I0673199

CONVICT'S CAPTIVE

BOOK THREE

By

PAUL BLADES

Copyright©2013 Paul Blades

Dark Visions Publications
darkvisionspub@gmail.com

All characters and events portrayed in this work are fictitious

Other books by Paul Blades:

The Maddy Saga:

CHAPTER ONE

The tall, shapely, blond woman had been dancing up a storm all night. She had partnered with just about all of the biker boys at one time or another and was downing Jack Daniels shooters like they were going out of style. She was wearing tall, black, high heeled boots with narrow, pointed toes that looked like they could punch a hole in a wall. Her stone washed, designer blue jeans were tight, showing off her rock hard rear cheeks. On top, her breasts pushed out prominently her rhinestone studded, blue denim shirt. Her straw blond hair was long and flew all about her as she laughed and hooted and hollered to the loud, twangy, boisterous country tunes. She looked to be in her late twenties or early thirties and gave off the impression of someone who had dressed down to seem younger and maybe a little less classy than she really was, like some 60's cop show director's idea of a hip, biker chick.

A heavy set, morose looking fellow was at the corner of the crowded, semi-circular bar. He wore a fractured, black leather bomber jacket over a pair of black denims with steel studs down the sides. His large, booted foot was on the gleaming brass rail at the base of the bar and he was nursing a long neck, his gnarled, meaty paw clamped around it tightly. He wore on the third finger of his right hand a prominent signet ring with a ruby red '*R*' on it surrounded by a small, inlaid onyx chain and embedded in gold. His black beard was curly and wild. He had heavy, black eyebrows and piercing eyes.

He had been watching the blond woman all night.

She really didn't fit in. The large bar was crowded, filled with rattily dressed, hulking, bearded and tattooed men and their similarly attired, rugged looking, tattooed female companions. The décor was late log cabin. The state mandated no smoking sign was largely ignored and the place was filled with a bluish gray haze. It smelled of smoke, legal and otherwise, stale beer and sweat. A T.V. mounted from the ceiling in the corner was showing a WWF Smackdown with the sound turned off and a small crowd was attending it, rowdily encouraging their favorites and giving out raucous, loud cheers or jeers at any particularly loathsome or ungentlemanly blow.

No, the woman stood out like a sore thumb. But she was pleasant to look at and easily found partners to gavotte with as she shook what God gave her. A couple of the boys got kind of ornery, debating the fine point of whose turn it was to escort her around the crowded dance floor, but a quick look at the hard, all seeing eyes in the corner convinced the disputants to share the pleasure of the desirable woman's company equitably.

A smaller, mouse faced man, wearing a dark green army jacket over blue jeans, stood next to the man in the corner like an acolyte, attending to his movements like an aide de camp. His long brown hair had receded somewhat, but the cut of his jib made it seem doubtful that anyone ever found any amusement in it.

At about 11:45, the taller man, after watching the woman down another shot, sharing a hoot and holler with her coterie of admirers, said something to the smaller man. The mousy fellow nodded in an understanding sort of way. He sidled off and, when the woman and a lucky companion moved off again to the dance floor, he slinked up to one of the men who had been hovering near her and whispered in his ear. The man looked over to the corner and nodded to the sullen one who lurked there. The mousy man returned to his post.

The next time the woman came to the bar for a shot, the man who had been spoken to leaned over and shouted something in her ear. She looked at him attentively and then over to the man in the corner. She gave out a luxurious smile, spreading her lips widely, revealing a large, eager looking mouth. The man who had spoken to her took hold of her arm and tugged it. She followed his lead willingly.

She was taken to the morose man's side. He turned his back to the bar to greet her. Her escort shouted in her ear, "This here's Ike. He's the owner."

The woman's smile grew broader. She reached out her graceful hand. "Nice to meet y...," was all she got out. The morose man's fist lashed out like a piston and caught her just under the jaw. Her eyes rolled back, her knees gave out and she careened backwards, right into the awaiting arms of the mousy fellow. He gently lowered her to the floor and her escort quickly took hold of the sides of her shirt and tore it open, launching the ivory colored buttons around the bar. Spreading the sides, a set of wires was seen taped to her belly just under her braless, pale, lust inducing breasts. The mousy fellow gently removed it, taking care not to rattle it too much. One of the biker girls came over at Ike's direction and she lifted her shirt, wrapped the tape around her midriff and scooted off onto the dance floor.

It had been done right there in the open. Plenty of people had seen it. Nobody gave a shit. Nobody fucked with Ike and everybody who saw the taped wires being removed from the woman's body understood that the woman was certainly law enforcement. Most of the folks had assumed or suspected as much. Ike's place's reputation was well known and no unescorted female would find herself dead in there unless she were prepared to end the night giving out blowjobs in the men's bathroom, a line out the door.

Once the wires were removed from the woman's torso, a burly fellow, after receiving instructions from Ike, took hold of her under her arms and began to drag her towards the back door of the tavern. The mousy fellow stopped him. He reached down and tugged the fashionable black boots from the woman's feet. He flicked open a switchblade and, after examining the heels carefully, pried one of them open. His face, normally expressionless, exhibited a flit of satisfaction. He showed his discovery to Ike who recognized immediately the GSP transponder taped to the bottom of the boot. The mousy fellow nodded to the man who had hold of the woman's arms and he resumed dragging the unconscious woman to the back exit. Another fellow took hold of her bare feet and assisted.

There were no lights in the back of Ike's place. The night was clouded over and the trio's forms, scooting through the darkness, could hardly be seen. The two men brought the woman to an ancient looking Ford pickup. They lifted her up onto the bed of the truck and put her down while one of them unlocked what looked like a large, rusted, white tool box nestled up against the back of the cabin. He flipped it open.

Inside were several sets of manacles and ropes and other accouterments of submission. The woman was starting to come around and she was moaning lowly. The men went quickly to their task. She was flipped onto her belly and her wrists were fastened behind her. Her ankles were joined. One of the men took a hold of her hair and bent her head back while the other jammed a leather plug into her mouth.

At this, the woman seemed to come alive. She began to twist and turn her body and utter a panicked moan. It was all too late as the gag was fastened securely behind her head and then her ankles were affixed to her wrists.

With a 'heave ho!', the men lifted her body and dumped it into the tool box. She gave out a muffled, unhappy grunt as she landed. The lid was slammed down after her and locked down tightly. The men quickly jumped down off the bed of the truck and hustled to the front, getting in on either side. The engine was soon fired up and the truck slowly and quietly rolled from the back and onto the macadam on the side of the building. Once there, the lights came on and the truck drove across the parking lot out to the highway behind a pair of loud, chopped up bikes, each ridden by a male and female passenger. The bikes roared out onto the highway, heading south. The pickup rolled out behind them and then turned north.

About a quarter mile down the road, they passed a dark brown, late model Chevy Impala parked on the side. There were two men in it. They hunkered down as the pickup passed and then sat straight again once it had gone down the road.

The men were clean cut and dressed in nearly identical business suits with narrow, featureless ties. The passenger was wearing a headset.

"I can't make out a fucking thing in there!" he said to the driver. "It's too fucking loud!"

"Shit, she's probably kicking up a storm while we sit out here and pull our dicks."

"I hate this whole operation," the passenger replied. "I was supposed to be at my kid's recital tonight. My wife is going to kill me."

"I had a date. And she was hot and primed, if you know what I mean. Now I probably won't even be able to get her to answer her phone. I mean, this broad comes in from out of district with orders on high to mount this operation. We don't even get told what it's all about. She's in there drinking and dancing all night and we're out here pulling our puds."

The driver looked into his rear view mirror. The rear lights from the old, rattletrap pickup could still just be seen. He watched them until they faded out of sight.

"I just hope we don't have to wait out here all night," was what he said.

* * * * * * * * * * * *

Miles away, early the next morning, in a small motel cabin high in the Ozarks, Carly lay on the bed, her legs spread wide, her breath still coming deep. The man had just finished fucking her. Her heart was beating strong and her pussy was sloshy and still vibrating. He had fucked her long and hard, starting her out bent over on her knees from behind and then, just as she was about to go over the top, flipping her over and doing her on her back. His cock plunged deep, so very deep within her that it was as if he was trying to drill a hole through her. She screamed and yelled through her gagged mouth as she came. She curled her legs around his thighs and tried to pull him deeper still. He kept going and going and she began to cry and sob, the pleasure was so intense. And when she felt his body tense, heard his grunt and moan, and he began to pound his hips into hers with strong, powerful thrusts that brought her pain, she felt like her whole body was going to be torn apart.

He did not linger long on her. He rose after a short

while, leaving her like this. She didn't dare move a muscle without his permission. So with her legs wide, her shameful, rebellious pussy, so open and so bare, lay still exposed and dilated.

But he didn't tell her that she couldn't close her eyes. She had them shut tight, castigating herself for the lusts that the man brought her. And, even more than that, ruing, ironically, the moment, a moment not too far away, when they would leave this cabin that had been her hothouse of passion for over 24 hours and go back out on the road to her uncertain destiny.

Yesterday had been a roller coaster ride of passion, pain, bliss, fear, desolate unhappiness and even for a brief few minutes, tender communion with the man. But mostly it had been horrid, long, lonely hours of isolation mixed in with periods of intense torment. For even when he fucked her, and her body reacted with joy and celebration of having him within her, wherever it was, her pussy, her rear and even her mouth, her mind knew how terribly wrong it was to have those feelings, so terribly, terribly wrong.

But even despite that, even despite the fact that today, while on the road at least, the man would have limited opportunities to make use of her body, even despite that, she would choose staying here and being subject to his relentless passion, his stern, cruel discipline, the denial of all of her human attributes but her ability to arouse his lusts, rather than bear the uncertainties that walking out the door which lay opposite to the bed would bring her, the door she had stared at so often yesterday hoping that by some miracle she could burst through it to rescue and safety.

She opened her eyes now and looked at it. He had uncharacteristically left her feet unlocked and if by some miracle she could open it now, she could run across the parking lot full of snow, run, run, run until she found a place of safety.

But no, she couldn't do that, she realized. Her wrists were still locked up and crossed high upon her back, a position that had at first produced a painful, humiliating strain, but which now seemed almost normal. The rope that he had tied onto the back of her collar last night when he put her to bed was still attached to the headboard behind her. She couldn't get to her feet even if she could somehow overcome her dreadful fear of retribution from him for even thinking of disobedience.

She bit down on her gag and a wave of bitter unhappiness went through her. There was no room for even the fantasy of escape. The man thought of everything. He left no lock unlocked, never had a moment of distraction from the infliction of his iron will upon her, never left anything to chance. He seemed never to make a mistake.

The air of unquestionable authority he had seemed so natural, as if he had been exercising it for years. She had heard a lot of things about prison, how harsh it was and everything. One thing that always amazed her was the idea that the inmates could still operate their gangs and stuff in there. That was probably where he got it from, she thought. He was a tough guy among tough guys. And he showed it in everything he did.

She could hear him now in the shower, starting off the day right. She wondered whether she would get one. She had done enough sweating and steaming yesterday. And even last night, in the middle of the night, he had awoken her and fucked her again, from behind while on her side and bent at the waist, making her cry with unhappiness and moan with pleasure. She hadn't even known you could fuck like that, but he was able to squeeze his rigid cock into her pussy even though her thighs were jammed tight. He just had to push a little harder to get in, that's all.

There was no way she could adequately describe what it was like to have a cock slipped inside you and not have any ability to stop it or control it. Last night as his cock rasped back and forth, she prayed and prayed and prayed for it to stop, exerted every ounce of her consciousness to will it to stop, begged and pleaded with any force that could hear her thoughts to make it stop. But it kept going on and on and on and on until her orgasm began to grow and grow and grow. It was like some wild animal had been let loose inside her and its gnawing for some reason brought her not pain, but instead, mind befogging pleasure.

It was an almost unreal sensation, as if some dark magic had been performed on her. Logic told her that she should have the ability to close the portals to her body, be able to deny admittance to anyone or anything that did not have her consent. But the raging cock dispelled that logic, revealing how powerless she really was.

And, even more than that, her brain told her that she should be able to control when she felt passion and lust and when she did not. Nobody should be able to bring her pleasure when she didn't want it, especially a man she hated so rabidly. It would have been much more tolerable if she had felt nothing at all, if she could have deadened the nerve endings that the ruthless cock was energizing, derailed the sensations of pleasure that washed through her body, short-circuited the electrical pulses that made her whole being reverberate. It felt so wrong that she couldn't, so unfair. It made the shame and humiliation of being used as a fucktoy so much, much worse.

She did everything she could think of to stop it, thought of mundane things, her apartment, her cat, her job, her childhood. She tried to imagine her hands, so cruelly pinioned up on her back, seizing the instrument, wringing it like a dirty dishcloth, tearing it apart, breaking its rigidity in two. But that ever sawing meat in her cunt would not relent. Little by little it would edge out whatever she had tried to put into her mind to block it and, once it had breached her defenses, the sensations that it was delivering would come roaring back far worse than ever, causing her to moan and groan and her pussy to shimmer and vibrate.

And when her orgasm began to loom, when it had grown inside her and was ready to burst, she cursed herself and her wantonness and then gave in, knowing that further resistance was useless, letting its tendrils of ecstatic joy stream through every ounce of her flesh.

He had fucked her slowly for a while after, desultorily, as his meat slowly diminished. And for a little while, having him softly caress the skin of her buttocks with his large, powerful hands, his warm thighs pressed against hers, felt so soothing, so right. Then, separating from her, he broke the spell. Taking hold of the hair on the back of her head, he made her straighten out and pushed her back on her belly. He refastened her collar to the headboard, caressed her possessively on the ass and thighs, and then rolled over and went back to sleep. She cried for a half hour at least until somnolence finally claimed her.

And then again, this morning. The light was barely shining in through the small gaps in the blinds. What light there was was rosy red, a reflection of the dawn's emerging rays. She hadn't woken when he loosened her ankles. She snapped to consciousness as he was pulling on her hips, lifting them up. His hands forced her thighs apart. She had issued a groan of protest and he slapped her ass hard, three times, making her cry out and sob. Then he insinuated two of his large, implacable fingers along her labial divide. He slid them back and forth gently and slowly, deeper and deeper while her pussy rebelliously began to lubricate. As soon as his fingers could penetrate her hole with ease, he shifted himself, brought his rigid cock to bear and entered her, making her moan.

She had tried to decipher why she was so responsive to him and those thoughts had led her down to some deep, dark places. She realized that it was not merely the sensations of his hands or lips on her flesh. Yes, they were lust inducing, brought on desire, triggered her need, but at a level that she could handle, ignore, resist. No, it was the very thought that she was helpless to oppose the otherwise offensive touching that did it. Something about being unfree to enforce the moralities that she had been taught, the very wrongness of what was happening to her, caused something in her to shift, like a switch that had been flipped. The wrongness became rightness. North became south, east became west, positive became negative. Resistance became need, revulsion became desire, shame became lust, unhappiness became pleasure so exquisite, so purely refined, that it made her feel like she was going to burst.

Whenever he made lusts rage throughout her body, like a firestorm across a prairie, her mind and body seemed to merge into a unity that she had never conceived. It was like his cock somehow traversed the length of her body and pierced directly into her brain, mushing around the mysterious substances inside, her skull a mortar to his pestle. And when he came it seemed like his cum flooded her cranium, coated the inside of her skull, permeated into her mind. It was all so, so wrong, but there was nothing she could do about it.

Now she lay on the bed, her knees raised and spread, his copious cum leaking from her crevasse. She daren't move a single muscle. She knew that she had to remain exactly as he had left her. The switch he had used so cruelly on her yesterday was still leaning up in the corner by the door. She feared its kiss almost as much as she feared his brutal hands which had pummeled her mercilessly each time she had summoned even an iota of resistance to his will or transgressed the slightest one of his demeaning rules.

Although he was in the shower and the thin, interior cabin wall separated them, it was as if he had left behind an evil eye floating somewhere above her, watching her, ensuring the enforcement of his will, guaranteeing that she would not engage in any volitional movement, just as the bindings he had left on her were extensions of his remorseless intent, ever present, like evil spells summoned from the depths of hell itself.

She heard the shower turn off. In a few moments he would be back. Her stomach twisted into sourness as she anticipated with dread the actual return of his presence.

Jack gave out a deep sigh of satisfaction as he stepped from the tub. It was yet another day of freedom begun blissfully by a sojourn into a tight, hot cunt and now topped off with a heavenly shower. Yesterday had been one of the most memorable days in his life. It was as if the fates had bestowed a rapturous interregnum into his desperate flight from captivity. The snow storm had been a godsend. He had spent a luxurious day satisfying his every urge and desire. The girl had been magnificent, another undeserved beneficence. She was pliant and obedient. Her body was soft and smooth and rounded in all the right places. Her mouth was skilled, energetic and imaginative. Her pussy was welcoming, hot and tight. Her rear hole, a clearly previously unexplored path of pleasure, had received him almost willingly, contracting hard like a grasping hand when he made her come.

And she was passionate. He was certain that she had never had her lusts unleashed like he had done to her yesterday. Everything about her when he had first seized her had bespoken demureness, reservation, modesty. She was over all that now. It was too bad that within 24 hours or so, maybe a few days at best, her life force would be extinguished. It humored him to think of what kind of a life she would lead if she was somehow able to survive. She would spend a lifetime trying to recreate the roaring climaxes he had induced in her. She would remember him all her life.

After drying himself, he had a quick shave. Looking at himself in the mirror, he saw a satisfied, pleased face, so unlike the one he had stared at for 12 years in the joint. His few days of freedom had dissolved away the greyness of his demeanor, wiped away the pallid mien he had acquired so quickly after he had been sent up. And if the sparkling eyes that stared back at him were closed forever somewhere along the road today, if he was discovered and had to shoot it out in his own personal Gotterdammerung, it would all have been worth it a thousand times over.

He washed his face and brushed his teeth. He thought of the girl awaiting his presence in the next room. It was too bad they couldn't spend another day here. But he had to keep his eye on the ball. By 1 a.m. at the latest he had to be just outside of a small town called Tularosa, New Mexico. It was coming up to 6:30 now. If he got out of here a little after 7, it would give him about 19 hours. He had looked at the map yesterday and he figured it was about 850 miles or so. If he averaged 50 miles per hour, he would make it in plenty of time. But there was always the unforeseen. So he wanted to get going early just to make sure.

And to average 50 m.p.h. meant the he would have to take some chances. He would really have to push his speed to make up for the inevitable stops. It increased the chances that he would attract the attention of the law. And the FBI, who he knew wouldn't be fooled for a minute into thinking that he had gone north to Wausau after his escape, would have alerts out all the way. The only advantage was that they didn't know what car he was driving, yet. Or so he hoped.

But there was the issue of the girl again. They would be looking for the two of them. Every car that had a man and a woman in it driving alone would receive increased scrutiny. He had two options. He could dump the girl somewhere or she could ride in the trunk. Neither option appealed to him since he was looking forward to having her next to him where he could keep an eye on her delicious flesh and cop a feel of her tits and pussy from time to time. But, like he had said to himself, he had to keep his eye on the ball. There were thousands and thousands of *senoritas* down in Mexico. Never lose your head over a piece of tail. Well, he would make up his mind later. For now, he had to make breakfast and then dig the car out of the snow.

He came out of the bathroom and went to his stash and pulled out a fresh pair of shorts. The girl was where and how he had left her. Good girl. He slipped on the boxers and took a moment to look at her. She was lying there with her legs spread and her eyes closed. She looked so peaceful. Her breasts, belly and thighs bore the traces of the wounds he had inflicted on her yesterday. He felt a little sorry for having done it, but it had given him such a rush. Besides, it had the beneficial effect of increasing her fear of him and therefore her obedience.

He peered at her hairless pussy. It still glistened a little from their bout of passion and he could see where the sheet underneath her was stained from his leaking cum. It was a delectable sight and gave his cock a little twinge of reminiscence. She opened her eyes as he stood there. Her gagged mouth showed no emotion, but her eyes exhibited an exquisite forlornness. They were red lined and brimming with nascent tears. Another day with her here alone and away from the world would indeed be rewarding, he thought. But it was not to be.

He strode quickly to the kitchen area and started a pot of coffee. From the small refrigerator he pulled out the carton of eggs and the leftover steak. There were still a couple of slices of bacon too. He brought out the frying pan and tossed the bacon into it to get it started and then he cut up the steak and tossed the pieces in.

It was time to get the girl up. He went over to the bed and disconnected the rope that connected the back of her collar to the headboard. Taking hold of the hair at the back of her head, he pulled her to her feet and walked her into the bathroom. He sat her on the pot and watched her pee. When she was done, he wiped her and brought her back into the kitchen. After removing her gag, he tapped a spot on the floor with his toe and the girl dutifully sank to her knees and put her forehead on it.

The coffee was boiling so he turned it down. He flipped the bacon and pieces of steak. When they were cooked enough, he dumped them out a plate. He cracked six eggs into a bowl, poured in a touch of milk and scrambled the mixture up. He then emptied the bowl into the greasy pan and stirred the eggs while they cooked. It only took a minute or so. He dumped the lion's share of the eggs onto a plate and the rest into the bowl he had been using for the girl's meals. He put most of the bacon and steak on his plate and then crinkled the rest of the bacon and a few small pieces of steak into the bowl for the girl.

Last night she had balked when he had not given her any steak. She had paid the price for it. This morning he was feeling magnanimous; she had fucked him like a tiger the day before and even this morning, after all. She deserved a little reward.

He placed the girl's bowl on the floor in front of her. He decided that if she moved without permission he would punish her, but she didn't move a muscle. Good again. That augured well for their trip together today. She needed to obey his orders to the letter. Otherwise, he would dump her the first place he could find.

He turned off the coffee and, when it had settled a little, poured himself a steaming cup. He dripped a little milk in it and put it on the table next to his plate. He sat down and then snapped his fingers twice. The girl looked up. "Eat," he told her. Obediently, she shuffled forward on her knees and buried her face in the bowl.

The steak and eggs went down just fine. The coffee was almost perfect. The sight of the girl, her hands bound up behind her, nibbling away at the contents of the bowl, raising her cropped, red head slightly to chew each mouthful, was delightful. Her breasts wobbled enticingly as she moved. She kept on casting him quick, unhappy, sideways glances and then looking away.

She was done a little before him, and she raised her torso and sat back on her haunches. He got up and poured about a cup of milk into her bowl and signaled her to lap it up. He didn't want her to dehydrate as they were crossing the desert, but he didn't want to give her too much because he didn't want her having to pee too often on their trip.

He finished just as she was licking up the last of the milk. She looked up at him. Her mouth was surrounded by grease from the eggs. It didn't matter. He was going to give her a quick shower anyway.

He patted the spot in front of her with his foot and she bent over obediently and put her head to the rug. He washed up the dishes quickly, dried them and put them away. He scoured the frying pan, dried it and put it back in the dish cabinet. He wanted to leave the place spotless.

Yanking on her hair again, he brought her to her feet and led her into the bathroom. He had her stand there while he disconnected her wrists from her back. He took hold of her arms and lowered them slowly so that she wouldn't pull a muscle after having them bent back all night. She groaned a little from the pain, but he could tell that she was relieved to be freed from the harsh tie. He had created a little harness across her back and chest with a rope last night and now he removed it. Then he unfastened the belt that held the thick plastic prong in her rear and slowly slid it out. He turned on the shower, waited for the water to warm up and told her to get in. He didn't bother taking off her leather collar and cuffs. As long as they didn't get too wet, it wouldn't harm them. Besides, if they shrunk a little that would be okay. It would make them tighter and harder for her to slip out of them. He handed her the bar of soap. "Make it quick," he told her.

Carly sighed as the refreshing water cascaded onto her. It felt so strange to have her wrists free. She lathered her body with the soap and brushed it all over. It didn't matter that the man was watching. She had gotten over her loss of privacy from him long ago. The idea of being clean, too, was more than compensation for having him watch every little move that she made. She felt a little squeamish as she washed her breasts and her pudenda, but only a little.

Although she was enjoying the shower, her psyche felt dulled. Today they were going on the road and only God knew what was in store for her. She was reassured a little from the fact that he had let her eat a full meal and was allowing her to wash. He probably wouldn't have done either if he intended to kill her today. Or at least not until they got to wherever they were going.

She had figured out that he was probably trying to get to Mexico. But how he was going to get over the border she didn't know. One thing was for sure, he wouldn't cross it with her in the car. It was too risky, regardless of how much he liked to fuck her. That meant that he would dispose of her first. It was too much to hope that he might leave her somewhere all tied up where someone might find her. She would be able to tell the police where he had gone. No, it was much more likely that sometime before he would drive down some lonesome road, dig a grave for her in some desolate place and put a bullet into the back of her head, just like he had almost done the day before yesterday. It might take years for them to find her body, if ever.

She thought of her poor mother and Randy, her boyfriend, not having any closure to her death, not knowing for sure that she was dead, hoping against hope that somewhere she was still alive. It made her sad to think about it, sadder than she already was.

When she finished washing herself, she handed the soap back to the man. He exchanged it for the shampoo and she washed her now short, burnt orange hair quickly. When she had finished that, he turned off the water and had her step out of the tub. He dried her body quickly, brushed her hair, as much as it needed it, and made her brush her teeth. Then, to her surprise, he told her to get back in the tub. When he ordered her to lie down in it, she knew what he was going to do. He fastened her hands behind her back and her ankles together. She knew that he had to go and dig out their car and realized that she would have to lie there hogtied until he was ready to go. She suppressed a sob when she felt her ankles raised and affixed to her wrists.

Jack went back into the room and came back with the gag, blindfold and four pieces of rope. He pulled the girl's head back and mashed the gag into her mouth. She issued a little muffled squeal as he tightened it firmly behind her head and a little sob when he blinded her. He tied her elbows and knees together tightly and then tied ropes around her wrists and ankles, making double sure that she would not slip her bonds.

He dressed quickly. He was met with a blast of cold air when he opened the door to the outside. The snow was piled in places up to 3 feet deep and the car was buried. No plow had come yet for the parking lot and he began to get nervous that it wouldn't be there for a long while.

When he trudged over to the car, he saw that the old lady that ran the place and her son were out shoveling snow. The lady waived at him and said something to her son. He put down his shovel and ran into the house. Jack was brushing snow off the car with his bare hands so he could get to the little shovel he had in the trunk when he came back out. He picked up two shovels and waded through the snow over to Jack's car. He was a big fellow, over 6 feet with broad shoulders. He was wearing a heavy parka, a red and white knit cap with the Razorback's logo on it and heavy boots. He looked to Jack to be about 30 or so. He had the kind of clean cut look that usually made Jack sick to his stomach. His face was ruddy from his exertions.

"Hiya," he said as he got close. "My ma said to get ya some gloves and give ya a hand," he said warmly. He handed a pair of heavy ski gloves and a blue and gold knitted cap topped with a snow ball and tassels on to Jack.

"Hell of a storm, weren't it?" he said while Jack put on the gloves and hat.

Jack murmured a confirmation. He didn't want the kid to get too good a look at him, but he guessed he didn't have much choice now.

"Heard yer headed to Houston," the man said as he started to shovel out the snow around the car's tires.

"Yeah," Jack replied brusquely. "You don't have to do this," he said to him.

"Ahh, don't worry about it," he answered. "Just part of the hospitality. Ma's like that. Don't know why she keeps this place. It's a lot of work. I'm on the road a lot and then it's just her and my wife and the kids. I keep telling her that she should sell the place, but she won't listen."

"Yeah," Jack replied morosely. He really wanted to tell the guy to fuck off, but he didn't want to be remembered or cause a fuss. He had put the Glock in the front pocket of the cargo pants in case anything happened. He sure hoped he didn't have to use it.

The guy kept up talking the whole time they worked on the car. They cleared about 6' all around it. "The plow'll be here right soon," the guy said. "Charlie kind of works his way up the road. Usually he's here by now, but there's so much snow it's taking him a lot longer than usual. The highway's been plowed. The road's a little icy so you'll have to be careful going down the mountain. I hope you're not in a rush or anything. If you and your wife haven't had breakfast yet, my ma'll be glad to whip you something up."

"No thanks," Jack answered dully. "We've had breakfast."

"Okay then. She makes right fine flapjacks though. You'll be missing out."

"No, thanks anyway," Jack repeated. "We want to get on the road as soon as we can."

"Suit yourself," the man replied.

When the car was finished and they had shoveled the path to the cabin, Jack shook the guy's hand and thanked him, handing him back the hat, gloves and shovel. "Tell your ma that we enjoyed the venison stew. It was real good," Jack heard himself say. He knew he should say as little as possible to the guy, but it just came out. But then again, not thanking the woman would be more notable than thanking her so maybe it was for the best. "I'll leave the dish on the table when we leave," he added.

"Sure thing," the man said. "And say hello to your missus," he added.

"Will do," Jack answered.

He walked back to the cabin and, after knocking the snow off his boots and the bottom of his pants, went in. He checked the bathroom first thing. The girl was right where he had left her. He took a moment to enjoy the sight of her all scrunched up and helpless. He hadn't realized how much he had missed having control over a desirable female body. In prison, you tended to block from your mind the things you could not have. To do otherwise was the path of madness.

Back in the day, he had had dozens of pretty women

pass through his hands and he was glad to be able to say that there was not one who did not rue the day she met him. Some more than others, of course. He had passed most of them on to dismal fates, whoring them out in one of the club's knocking shops or selling them off to some pimp from Minneapolis or Milwaukie or even Chicago, or to one of the Latino gangs who ran girls all over the country and beyond. But some had gotten passed off to other club members as a reward for loyalty or turning a nice profit on some enterprise. Depending on the guy, some of those girls ended up with a pretty good deal.

When they had all gotten busted and locked up with no bail, the local rival gang had swept all their girlfriends up one night and sold them en masse to an operator out of Kansas City.

The girl was squirming, hoping, no doubt that he would release her. She was issuing muted whines from behind her gag. He hated to reward behavior like that, but he had to get her out and get her dressed so they could be ready to go. He decided that he would teach her a lesson first. He went out into the main room and returned with the switch he had cut from a branch the other day. The girl was still making little mewing sounds. He looked for the most available target. Her feet were in the air exposed and vulnerable. This would hurt like hell.

He reared the switch back and brought it down fiercely across the soles of her feet. She stiffened and screeched at the top of her lungs. He struck them two more times hard, creating thin lines of angry red across the bottoms of her feet. She screeched wretchedly at each one and began to sob.

"If you don't shut up," he told her harshly, "I'll give you three more."

She heard him. She took a deep breath. Her wails

subsided down to a little hissing sound, like air escaping from a balloon. She exhaled and took another deep breath, and then, holding her breath, silenced herself. Her body was shaking and her bound hands were closed into little tight fists. He waited about 30 seconds just to make sure she would obey him. She released her breath and began to breathe almost normally. There was still a light, piteous tone coming out of her mouth, but it was low enough that he let it go. The point had been made.

He brought the switch back into the other room. When he returned, the girl was silent and still. Now, that was better.

He decided to pack the car before he untied her, so he closed the door to the bathroom again and began the process of carrying out all their shit. He made four or five peanut butter sandwiches and stored them in easy reach from the driver's seat. There were still some munchies left and some soda and he put them there as well. He tossed out all the rest of the leftover food, cleaning out the refrigerator. The Jim Beam bottle was empty and he made a promise to himself to get another before the day was out. When he was satisfied he had done all he could, except for the clothes the girl would wear, he went back into the bathroom to free her.

She was as motionless and silent as a statue. He loosened her bonds, all except the joinder of her wrist bracelets, took hold of her hair and guided her up to her feet. Holding onto her upper arm, he helped her step out of the tub. She was shaking. He could feel the tremor in her muscle. That was okay. He needed her fear of him to be rabid if things were going to work out today. Her beating had served as a little refresher of what cruelty he was capable of.

Once he had her back in the main room, he had her

step into the short denim skirt she had been wearing the other day and, when it was around her hips, zippered it up. He released her arms and had her put on one of the t-shirts he had lifted from the army-navy store back in Wisconsin. It was lavender with yellow flowers across the front and was cut low so that her pleasing cleavage was well displayed. Taking one of the longer lengths of ropes, he wound it around her waist several times and made a cinch knot on both sides near her hips. He left enough of the ends of the rope there at the knots so that he was able to fasten her wrists in place. He triple knotted them to make sure they did not become loose. He brought over her sandals and strapped them onto her feet. Lastly, he removed her blindfold and gag.

She was ready to go. He went over to the window and confirmed that the plow had not yet arrived. He looked at the clock. It was just past 7:30. He realized that there was nothing he could do about it but wait and so he poured himself another cup of coffee and cleaned the pot. Before sitting down in his chair, he took the front of the girl's skirt and tucked it into the rope around her waist and made her spread her legs. Then he raised the hem of her tight fitting t-shirt until it was up over her breasts. He sat down in the chair and lit a smoke.

He watched her silently as he waited. All of her good parts were showing. Her hands turned and twisted slightly as she gingerly tested the ropes around her waist. On her face was an appropriately dismal expression and her eyes were pointed down so that she would not have to look him in the face. She was still shaking a little bit and it made her breasts shimmer. Her hairless pussy was stark and inviting. He was going to miss her, that was for sure.

Carly was trying desperately to control the tremoring of her body. She didn't want to show the man fear, but she couldn't help it. She was hyperconscious of her exposed breasts and sex. What she had become inured to when she was nude seemed humiliating and shameful when she was dressed. Other than the sounds he made as he took sips of his coffee or exhaled the cigarette smoke, the room was absolutely silent. She tried to keep his massive form out of her vision, but it was impossible to ignore him, just as it was impossible to avoid his fiery eyes as they slowly scanned her revealed sexual flesh.

The waiting for something to happen, for the next stage of her ordeal to begin was excruciating. She almost wished that he would do something to her to break the horrid tension she was feeling. She had watched him put the gag and blindfold away in the sole paper bag he had left to take out at the last minute. She yearned for him to reinstall them, as horrid as they were. She wanted to be as isolated from the man as she could. Every time her eyes concentrated on him, and they kept fitting back onto him, she couldn't help it, her stomach would turn sour and her heart beat just a little harder. It was like he had devised a new, hideous torture for her.

In a minute, ten, fifteen, maybe a half hour, they were going to leave the cabin. Her body ran cold as she thought of what awaited her out there. But the waiting seemed worse than the reality could ever be. She yearned to hear the sound of steel scraping the macadam signifying the arrival of the plow. "Please! Please! Please!" she thought. "Just get it over with! Please!"

She realized that this was just one more way the man was driving home to her her status as his slave. She was not permitted to do anything that would expose any human aspect to him. She was just a thing. Things don't whine and complain. Even a dog had that right, but she didn't. She realized that beyond the pleasure it brought the man to humiliate her, it was also so that it would be easier to kill her when the time came. It would be as easy as turning off a light. A fierce chill went through her and she suppressed a sob.

From time to time, Jack peered out the window between the closed slats of the blinds. The damn plow was taking its own sweet time in getting there. It was 3 minutes to 8. He had been sitting there, waiting, for about a half an hour. Watching the girl was amusing, but he was as edgy as a rattlesnake and he wanted to get going. He had finished his coffee long ago and his 3rd cigarette.

He looked back at the girl. His cock gave a little twinge at the sight of her bare, exposed pussy. Well, if he had to wait, he might as well spend it pleasurably, he thought.

He stood up from the table. The girl flinched. He took her by the hair at the back of her head and brought her over to the table until the front of her thighs were up against it. He pushed her head down until her bare breasts were squashed under her onto the table. Then he told her to spread her legs. He lifted the back of her skirt.

Carly felt the man's devilish hand stroke her sex. It made her shudder. He was such a hard, cruel man, but his touch was so light that it almost felt like a butterfly was beating its wings against her intimate flesh as his fingers flitted over her exposed labial lips. Her mind filled with distress even as the wry warning that her mother use to give her all the time slipped through her mind: be careful what you wish for.

She had been wishing for something to break the awful terror of her waiting. The seconds and minutes had been dragging on so slow that she felt like she had been standing before the man so brazenly displayed for an eternity. And it had been an eternity spent subsumed in a fear so intense that it had made bile rise to her throat. It was like when she was a child and waiting for the licking that her father had promised her, only much, much worse.

Time and space were distorted. A vibrating intensity went through everything. Her stomach seemed bottomless and empty. She had to resist with all her being the impulse to throw herself to the floor and beg the man for mercy, an event that would have only precipitated the thing that she feared the most, the initiation of his angry violence upon her.

It seemed impossible that she should be there, bound, helpless, utterly powerless, awaiting her doom. It had been like when he was going to shoot her the other day. What was happening seemed incredible, like something that was happening to someone else and yet her sense of the reality of everything around her was all too vivid.

She had tried to close her eyes, to block him out, but he had ordered her curtly to reopen them. If she were to have darkness it would be when it suited him, not her. She didn't know where to put them. Everywhere she looked was some reminder of something dreadful, the chair on which he had bound her for so long yesterday, blind and deaf, tied grotesquely and on which he had beaten her, the bed on which he had fucked her so many times, the pipe to which he had tied her, the floor on which she had been forced to place her head obsequiously as a supplicant to a god.

There was the door through which she desired so fiercely to flee. There was the window which looked out on a world that was indifferent to her fate. There, in the corner was the switch he had used to whip her and in the crumpled supermarket bag on the floor near the door were the gag and blindfold and chains and ropes with which he had tormented her body.

And then there was him. Whenever her eyes nervously slipped over him, her heart would fill with dread as she saw him so patiently, so frankly, appraising her intimate features like a beast examining its meat. She would have done anything to escape his evil gaze.

But now that she was pressed down, bent over against the table, its lip pressed hard against her thighs, she immediately began to rue her wish for something to break the tension between them, for now she would once again, she knew it as much as she knew anything, abandon herself to the shameful depravity that he would force upon her.

Jack took a finger and drifted it along the girl's labial divide. She responded with a deep intake of breath and the weakening of her knees. He drew it up and down, up and down, just touching her flesh ever so lightly. He teased the nubbin at the top of her sex by flicking the end of his finger across it gently. Her crevasse moistened obediently. He stroked her pudenda lightly several times and then slipped two fingers along her crevasse, pushing them more deeply between her outer lips again and again until he could ease them into her soft, oozing hole. When he plunged them to their depth, the girl's torso squirmed and she moaned.

In a few swift movements he slipped his rigid member from his pants and began to stroke her pussy with it, up and down, up and down until it had become slippery with her fluids. Then he probed her sex until the head sat just inside the entrance to her cavern and slowly, slowly, slowly, slowly, sunk it in.

"Ohhhhhhhhhhhh!" Carly moaned softly as she felt his thick rod traverse her inner self. The slow, inching along of the man's member was excruciating, prolonging her dreadful unhappiness at being penetrated once more. "Oh, please don't do this! Please! Please! Please! Please!" she prayed unhappily. She said nothing of course, uttered not one word or sound of protest, moved nary a muscle in refusal. She knew that nothing short of a meteor crashing through the roof of the little cabin would deter the man from his intent.

He moved back and forth ever so slowly. It was like he was not really fucking her as much as occupying her to pass the time. He kept one hand firmly on the middle of her back, pressing her torso down hard, while the other one drifted lazily up and down her thighs, over her buttocks, along the small of her back. Her skin celebrated everywhere it went in crass rebellion to her wants. And the cock kept moving, slowly, slowly, slowly, emphasizing each second of its occupation.

Her velvety tube welcomed him and her lusts were growing. She tried to fight it, but her mind soon sunk into a trance-like state. The whole universe was standing still except for the hot, steely presence inside her. She moaned again. And again. Her hands lay limp at her sides, affixed to her hips. She could feel the slackness of her face. Her eyes were closed, her breath drawn out and deep.

Her body quivered as her orgasm approached. Some part deep down inside her protested, but the rest of her opened up to it, needed it, wanted it. When it came, her mind went into a fugue and her physical self celebrated with a languorous joy. Her pussy gave her four, five, six and more pulses of pleasure, one flowing into the next as it issued firm, leisurely throbs and contractions around the man's meat.

She entered a torporous phase. Her body was limp. Her toes were touching the floor, but gave her no support.

It felt like she was going to melt right there on the table, a delivery into oblivion she would have welcomed.

Jack was reveling in the soft hotness around him. His cock was sending him a steady flow of mellow delight. There is nothing like a pussy, he thought. He felt and sensed her orgasm. Her pussy's contractions sent currents of thrill all through him. He kept going. He could do this all day. He felt like he was at the center of the world. "This is what paradise must feel like," he thought. He was so glad that he had kept the girl. It was a moment of such incredible bliss that he knew that he would remember it forever.

The girl orgasmed again. And then again. The last time her intensity had begun to grow. And now she was beginning to squirm and groan beneath him. She was issuing little whines. He heard a rumble out there in the world. Without missing a beat, he slipped his fingers between the blinds and saw the plow beginning to push across the parking lot. It was time to get going.

He increased the pace of his motions. He wasn't going to hurry himself. He would come when he was good and ready, when his need had become so intent that he would be near exploding. He began to build himself there. His thrusts became harder and shorter. He pressed down harder on the girl's back. Her whining was becoming louder. Her hands began to wriggle at her sides. Her thighs pressed back hard on his. He could feel the train inside him building speed. It was coming faster and harder. His brain seemed to short out. His balls tightened. He was holding it back, holding it back, holding it back, and then it came.

"Arrrrrrrrgh! Arrrrrrrrrrgh! Arrrrrrrrrrrgh!" he groaned. The table was shuddering up against the wall, the girl was moaning loud in rapid, short bursts. His fluids jetted from his cock in fierce spasms. The girl's pussy was throbbing hard against him gripping him tightly. "Ohhhhhhhhhh! Yes! Yes! Yes!" he thought. "Yes!"

Carly was embroiled in a body and mind wrenching climax. All thoughts of resistance were long ago gone. All of it, everything that had happened, everything he had done to her, all seemed worth it as her very soul rejoiced. "Don't stop! Don't stop! Don't stop!" was all she could think. A river of ecstasy was flowing through her, a river that knew no bounds, had no end, no beginning. She tried to bring her thighs together to better grip the cock that was driving her raging lusts, but his thighs were in the way. She felt him tense against her, heard his almost anguished groans, felt his cock come alive inside her. Her pussy erupted in fiercely intensive jolts. They made her whole body cringe again and again as they arrived in relentless, rapid succession. "Oh! Oh! Oh! Oh! Oh! Oh!" she called out. And then a long, anguished one, "Ohhhhhhhhhhhhhhhh!"

She didn't know when she stopped coming. The man continued his motions even though she knew he was spent. Her pussy delivered a series of slowly diminishing aftershocks. When they had vanished away, she took a deep breath and her whole body softened.

A moment later, he was outside her. She heard him zip up and then felt him grasp the hair at the back of her head and lift her up from the table. She could barely stand. He stabilized her and lowered her t-shirt, covering her breasts and rolled her skirt free of the rope in the front and let it hang down.

It all happened so quick. She was in a delirious daze. He put her overcoat on her and zippered it up the front, concealing her bound hands, stuffing the empty arms into her pockets. He took the little, blue rubber ball from the paper bag and pushed it rudely into her mouth. She was free for a moment as he put on his jacket and then she felt a tug on her arm.

The door to her prison opened. She was outside. The brightness blinded her. It was a few short steps to the car. He opened her door and pressed her down into the passenger seat. He put the bag on the driver's seat and removed two of the short ropes. He spread her legs and tied off her ankles to the frame under the seat. He took another one and fastened the back of her collar to the head rest. He crossed her torso with the seat belt and clicked it locked beside her.

She had just begun to realize where she was, what was happening, and start to look around when he slipped the blindfold over her eyes. He opened the glove compartment and she heard him take something out. A second later he put a pair of glasses on her face. Sunglasses. They had to be sunglasses. "Oh my god! We're leaving! We're leaving! Oh god! Oh god! Oh god!" she thought desperately.

Utter blackness surrounded her. The car door slammed. She heard a man's voice. It was a distance away. Not the man's, someone else.

"You have a good trip now," it said happily.

Then the man's voice. "Yeah, thanks for everything."

The driver's door opened and shut. He was sitting next to her, less than a foot away. She strained at her bonds. She twisted and turned her neck. "No! No! Help me! Help me!" she thought desperately. "Can't you see? Can't you see? Help! Help!" A forlorn whine escaped her gagged mouth.

The engine roared to life. The car rolled backwards for a few moments and then forward in a wide arc, making her lean slightly towards the front passenger door. It slowed for a second or two, went over a little bump and then accelerated quickly, pressing her back in her seat, and leveling off after about 30 seconds. They were on the road.

"Oh god, please help me!" she thought as an icy feeling permeated her veins. "Please! Please!"

CHAPTER TWO

Special Agent Jason Holmes was seething with rage. He had just gotten off the phone with the Deputy Agent in Charge of the New Mexico District. The news he had gotten was not good news at all.

The two agents who had been monitoring Agent Kramer as she made her attempt to infiltrate the Rogues' New Mexico chapter had lost her. The GPS had indicated that she was in the bar until a little after 2 a.m. The sounds of the bar, the loud music, the crowd, had been coming in perfectly. At exactly 2:07, the GPS indicated that Agent Kramer was on the move. Once they had noted her departure from the bar into the parking lot, the agents had moved their vehicle into position to follow any vehicle which she was in, hoping that she would take them to the Rogues' secret safehouse which served as the hub of their human trafficking enterprise.

They watched as a motorcycle bearing a woman on the back dressed like Agent Kramer exited the parking lot and headed south. The GPS confirmed that it was her. They followed at a discrete distance. About 10 miles down Route 70, the bike took off down a narrow, dirt trail. The agents followed the bike with some trepidation. The Agent in Charge would not like it if they bottomed out one of the Bureau's cruisers. They were about 3 miles down the road, it was getting narrower and narrower and more and more rutted as they went on, when they noticed that Agent Kramer was no longer on the move. They knew that there had been no success in finding the Rogues' safehouse and their hopes rose that this was it.

There would be commendations for everyone.

They waited all night. When dawn came, they got out of the car and proceeded on foot. The GPS indicated that Agent Kramer was about two miles away. If there was a house there, they could get a good look at it and then radio in. The local Assistant US Attorney could get a search warrant and they could move in for the kill.

But as they got closer and closer, it was clear that there was no house. They couldn't figure it out. The GPS said that Agent Kramer was no more than 200 yards from where they stood. They crept up closer and closer. They were starting to get a bad feeling and began to dread that they would find Agent Kramer's lifeless body. Instead, as they came over a rise, there they were. Agent Kramer's boots. And the body mike and its wires were circled all around them. They knew they were in deep shit.

It was a little after 10 in the morning. Special Agent Holmes was in the parking lot at the Kansas City International Airport. Carly Walker's car had been found. A team of local agents were going through it meticulously, gathering stray hairs and other possible DNA evidence, dusting for prints, taking pictures. It was useless with regard to the effort to capture Blackjack Jackson, but there was some comfort in routine. Yesterday DNA evidence had come back from the sporting goods store in western Wisconsin confirming that Jackson had murdered the unfortunate sales clerk and made off with a considerable cache of weapons and cash. A motel owner had recognized his picture. He was probably the only person in all of Wisconsin who had not heard about Jackson's escape. No TV. No radio.

Another FBI team was at the motel now and they had located evidence that Jackson had almost certainly cut his hair and shaved. That was no surprise. His and presumably the girl's DNA had been all over the sheets. They had found his empty cans and other detritus and numerous rope fibers. The clerk at the all night convenience store had said that Jackson had bought rope so that was no surprise either.

Holmes had received a number of calls from the chief of the Wisconsin State Police. He hadn't returned them yet. He doubted if he would. Word had gotten out through the law enforcement grapevine that Jackson had not died in the conflagration at the Wausau clubhouse and Holmes wanted that asshole to squirm for a long time until he decided to release it officially. The chief would have to endure a firestorm of his own. Well, that's what you get.

Holmes had been thinking positive for the first time since the whole thing began. He now had Jackson's trail, at least as far as Kansas City. It meant that his hunch was probably right when he guessed that the outlaw would head for New Mexico. But the news of Agent Kramer's disappearance was a real blow. She had been a protégé of his. He had sent her down there to see if she could get wind of any plans to help Jackson. And now the Rogues had her. What they would do to her was uncertain, but it surely wouldn't be nice.

Already a flood of agents was pouring into New Mexico from all over the country to put out a dragnet for Agent Holmes. She was the first priority now. That girl Carly was probably already dead or soon to be. Things like this had a way of getting out and as soon as the news of Agent Kramer's kidnapping became news, Jackson would know that he would have to pass through a virtual sea of FBI agents to get to Mexico. Having the girl with him would be a risk too big to take.

They had raided Ike's Bar first thing. All they found

there were some buttons from her blouse on the floor. They had picked up a few of the well-known Rogues and their girlfriends for questioning but none of them were giving any statements. Ike and his sidekick, Mouse, as he was known, had disappeared. Every cop in New Mexico was pulling in their informants. But they too would get nowhere.

The problem was that Blackjack Jackson was taking on the aura of a cult hero. Already there had sprung up several Blackjack web sites. The Internet was abuzz with him. A guy in Oakland had been picked up for selling Blackjack t-shirts, but they had to let him go. And when word got out that he was still alive and on the loose, Blackjack Jackson would go viral.

"Fuck!" Holmes exclaimed when he clicked off of his Blackberry. "Fuck! Fuck! Fuck! Fuck!" He scanned the parking lot. There had to be 3 thousand cars there. Somewhere out in the world was a guy, or a gal, who was going to come back to Kansas City and find his or her car missing. Until then, they wouldn't know what kind of car Jackson was driving. The one good thing though was that there were only 3 or 4 good routes to New Mexico from the Kansas City area. Of course, Holmes' hunch about New Mexico could be wrong, but the only good thing about Agent Kramer's disappearance was that it tended to confirm it. Maybe the Rogues would want to do a deal, Jackson for Agent Holmes. It was tempting to think about, but the upper echelons of the Agency would never go for it.

Just then a weary traveler carrying a suitcase and a briefcase came stumbling up to them.

"Are you guys cops?" he asked.

"Yeah," Holmes replied.

He put down his load wearily. "I think somebody stole

my car," he said.

* * * * * * * * * * * * * *

The building that the local Rogues used for their safehouse, some 65 miles southwest of Albuquerque, was an old mansion that had once served as the *hacienda* for a bustling cattle ranch. Years ago there had been a broad, spring fed, sweetwater creek that ran lazily through the slightly undulating flatlands and emptied into a shallow but broad lake. There had been just enough rain to maintain the scrub on which the cattle fed. The ranch had hosted 20 or so *rancheros* every spring to oversee the calving and the branding. There had been a large bunkhouse, a chow hall, a complete stable with a large corral for the many horses necessary for the running of the ranch and a forge for the blacksmith.

In the winter of 1885, a category 3 earthquake had hit the area early one morning. It had shaken the *hacienda* to its foundation. The cattle had stampeded. Part of the stable had collapsed. But more importantly for the survival of the ranch, the earthquake had caused the flow from the spring to shift underground. By the end of the day, the creek was completely dry. The water in the lake lasted until early spring. The cattle were all sold off and the ranch abandoned.

The out buildings had gone quickly, falling into rapid disrepair until they eventually fell of their own accord. The *hacienda,* two stories high, a magnificent building constructed to the exacting specifications of the baronial owner, had been made of sterner stuff.

In 1919, with the coming of prohibition, an enterprising local gangster had converted the place into a speakeasy and a whorehouse. A drill rig had been brought in and they were able to dig deep and tap into the groundwater some 200' down. A generator was rigged for electricity. The place was about 10 miles out from the nearest paved road, what became known as Route 85, today Interstate 25, so a primitive bulldozer was brought in to scrape out an adequate dirt pathway so that the local *hoi polloi* could have easy motor vehicle access to the place. The county sheriff had been paid off, the county aldermen all got a share of the profits and occasional gratis use of the whores. There was live music and dancing and gambling with a large, gaudy roulette wheel and a craps table. The place changed hands several times with local gangs vying for control of it. It was a veritable gold mine.

When prohibition ended, the place died out quick. Operations were moved to the nearest crossroads, a small town called Belen, and the *hacienda* again fell into disuse. In 1948, the Belen operation was permanently shut down due to the accession of a reform ticket which ousted the then current stock of corrupt aldermen and the sheriff.

In 1971, Deke Peterson, the then president of the Rogues' Alamogordo chapter, rediscovered the place while out one afternoon on his Harley. The gang started using it about a year later as a transshipment point for loads of Mexican weed brought up from Juarez. In the nineties, when cocaine got big, they used it for that too. A short airstrip was added. And then, when the big money started accumulating on the other side of the border with the various Mexican gangs, and demand grew for the pale skin of young, beautiful *gringas* as trophies of success, the place became the central gathering point for the various strays and runaways that came into the Rogues' hands as well as such other desirable females that fell into their clutches.

Good looking, youthful, brown skinned girls were shipped the other way to populate brutal, gang run brothels in Los Cruces and Albuquerque and places north, east and west.

The existence of the place was well known, in theory at least. Members of the club came into specific knowledge of it only on a need to know basis. No law enforcement agency had been able to discover it. It served as one of the percs of higher office in the club and a brace of girls were usually kept out there for convenient use. There was little concern that the girls might reveal the location of the hideaway to anyone. They were all brought out there blindfolded, bound and gagged and when the club officers became tired of them, or more appealing replacements found, they were sold off to one of the several Mexican gangs they dealt with and never heard from again.

On the morning that Special Agent Holmes was celebrating the discovery of the identity of the car that Blackjack Jackson was now driving, Agent Linda Kramer was ruing the chance she had taken in infiltrating the well-known Rogues hangout the night before. Her wrists bore tight leather bracelets and were hooked behind her back. Her ankles, bearing similar confinements, were locked together and secured to her wrists by an 18" long chain. A thick leather gag filled her mouth and she was in complete darkness. On all sides of her were the steel bars to a 4' high, 3'x 3' cage. And, she was naked.

It had been quite a while since the men had stuffed her into it. Enough hours so that the need to urinate had become, if not pressing, a more than conscious need. She had gotten a mere glimpse of her neighbors, two frightened, naked young girls bound much like she was. Once she had been secured, the men left and put out the light. After that, the only sign of the other girls' presence was their occasional sob or groan of unhappiness.

Agent Kramer knew that she was miles and miles from nowhere. She had lost her GPS transponder when they had removed her boots. She was deep in the basement of the building they had brought her to. The only sounds she could make were muted, dull moans or groans, and she knew that there was no one to hear them but her unfortunate companions.

She had tried pulling and twisting at her bonds for a long time, well beyond the point where she had confirmed to herself that they were inescapable. It was a part of her training. If captured, continue attempting all available means of escape except when under direct supervision or threatened with immediate, disabling violence, or where the safety of a civilian hostage might be at stake. But eventually she became convinced not only that her efforts would be unavailing but also that continued struggle would convert her dark feelings of fear to ones of unbridled, panicked terror. She needed her sanity. She needed to be able to think straight. Somehow, she would be saved, or she would escape. She had to keep that faith at all times. That was survival lesson number 2.

But that was in books. This was not a training exercise. The men who had kidnapped her had dark designs for her. They could never let her go. That was clear. Her only hope was escape. But was it realistic to think that she would be able to mount an escape from ruthless men who had made a science of making women their helpless prisoners? Not one woman had ever come forward with the tale of her kidnapping by the Rogues. Not one. Which meant that the women who did manage to somehow get free spent the rest of their lives in abject fear of retribution from them or the men to whom they had been sold. Or, none ever escaped.

A coldness crept over her. "Don't give up hope! Don't give up hope!" she said to herself again and again. But the chains that held her bound were so implacable, the probability that the men would do her grievous harm so high, that the repetition of those words seemed but a hollow gesture.

She had never been so frightened in her life.

Last night had been a harrowing, hellacious, degrading ordeal and she cowered now, in shame, for what the men made her do.

She had come out of her stupor just as they were putting the gag in her mouth. It took her a second to figure out what had happened, but only a second. By the time though that she began to twist and turn her already bound body, shrieking into her gag, an effort that produced only what sounded like a desperate whine, it was too late. One man held her shoulders down while the other took hold of her legs and pushed them back until they touched her bound hands. A moment later and they were affixed together.

There was no chance at all at resistance as they picked her up and dumped her unceremoniously in the tool box. When the lid slammed closed, she was in absolute darkness. She tried to keep making noise in case someone might hear her, but it was clear that none of her raging howls for help, muffled as they were, would escape her little prison.

The truck bounced a little as it rode on the unpaved rocks and dirt in the backyard of the tavern. When the ride smoothed out, she knew she was in the parking lot proper. She sensed the truck making a right, turning north. She knew that the two men from the local agency who were monitoring her, her backup, were sitting in their car just a few hundred feet up the road. Her screaming got louder as she approximated the truck passing them. She banged her head on the side of the steel box as hard as she could until it hurt. She called out in her mind, "I'm here! I'm here!"

It was then that she realized that she had lost her boots. As far as the agents would know, she was still in the bar. And that was when she began to get frightened. She was on her own.

The ride took a long time. She kept squirming and twisting at her bonds, but to no avail. Her head was woozy from the booze she had consumed and the blow to her chin. Her arms and legs felt rubbery. After a while, she gave up and lay there still and quiet.

She knew that they were probably heading for the safehouse. She had already found out more about it than dozens of other officers over many years. It was north of the bar they had just come from. She tried to keep track of the turns they made and how long it took them to get to each one. They had made a left after about forty minutes or so of driving. Then they had driven more or less west for about an hour. Then the truck went through some twists and turns and she lost track of their direction. About a half hour after that, the truck left the road and started down a bumpy trail.

The truck had slowed and they travelled on the uneven road for a long time. It made several curves. And then the truck came to a halt. She heard the engine turn off. Her stomach twisted and her body ran cold. They were there.

She heard the gate to the flatbed fall and felt the truck dip a little as the men hopped up onto it. She heard the lock being freed above her. Right now was when she should have been coiled, ready to spring at her captors the moment the lid was lifted. She remembered that from one of her lectures. It wasn't going to happen though because she had never accomplished the first step, freeing herself from her bonds.

The lid popped open and she heard one of the men's voices. "Come on, baby. Time to come out and play."

The other fellow laughed. "Yeah, fun time's about to begin. We're going to get to know you real good before the night's out."

He reached down and took hold of her long, blond hair to pull her up so they could get a hold on her. It came off in his hand.

"Whoa!" he blurted out. "What's this?"

"That's part of her disguise," the other man said. "She was supposed to be under cover. That's a hair extension."

"Deceitful bitch, ain't she?"

"Don't worry," the second one said. "All will be revealed." They both laughed again.

The first man snuck his hand down in the box and this time took hold of her real hair, which was blond all right, but went down only to the middle of her neck, a businesslike cut for an up and coming professional. There was plenty enough to grab.

She shrieked as he yanked on her blond growth, arching her body up. The other man reached in and took hold of her arms. He held her there while the first man scooted around and took hold of her bent knees. The men both 'ooomphed!' as they took her out. They dropped her on the flatbed. She groaned as she landed. Her breasts were naked from her torn shirt and they scraped on the dusty, rough steel.

Without delay, they disconnected her ankles from her wrists. Before she could start to squirm and writhe, they took hold of her under the arms and dragged her down the length of the flatbed. At the end, they left her torso part hanging off of the lowered gate as they jumped down. They dragged her off of the gate as they walked away. Her bare feet slid off and struck the ground hard, painfully stubbing her toes and sending a shudder up her body. She groaned.

The men paid her no mind. She had no time to look around to get a fix on where they had taken her. It was too dark anyway to see much anyway. They dragged her up a set of wooden steps and then across a porch. They stopped while one of the men opened the door. They dragged her into the building.

The men's boots echoed off of the bare walls as they took her through the darkened, empty foyer. To the left, a light emanated from the next room and they dragged her into it.

It was the old gambling room from the casino days. All of the gambling equipment was out, and the old furniture, but the crystal chandelier had been left behind and it lit up the room nicely. The gang had brought in a clutch of old furniture, a few couches and easy chairs, some coffee tables, a couple of floor lamps. The walls were a faded, light green. They were covered haphazardly with gang slogans and other graffiti as well as a number of old movie and concert posters. Some were ones you might expect, Easy Rider, Brando in The Wild One, some Grateful Dead posters, one of Janice and a blowup of a James Gang cover. There was also a poster of Bogart from Petrified Forest where he played escaped convict Duke Mantee, and an obscure Dennis Hopper biker movie called The Wild Angels.

Along the far wall were four cages, much like the ones down in the old wine cellar where Linda now reposed. Three of the cages were occupied by dour looking, naked, attractive young women, a blond and two with long black hair. Three of the easy chairs were occupied by gang members, rough looking boys dressed in denims and leather. They were drinking Jack Daniels and watching a movie on a 60" plasma TV mounted on the wall. The room was hazy with cigarette smoke and a fat joint was being passed around.

Next to the cages, mounted on the wall in orderly array, on a pegboard screwed into the wall, were a series of whips of various configurations and several sets of manacles with chains. Under the peg board was a battered, old, mahogany dresser with deep, wide drawers. To the right was a broad stairway that led up to a balcony along which were a series of doors.

Linda's captors dropped her on the floor in the middle of the room. She landed with a 'thud!'

"What ya got there Chaz?" one of the men asked. "A new recruit? She looks kinda old."

Chaz stood about 6'2", had long black hair gathered in a ponytail. He had a hard face and bear claw like hands. "Nah," he answered. "She's a cop who Ike caught sniffing around his bar tonight. Since she wanted to find out all about us, Ike thought it would be a good idea to bring her here for a little chat."

All the men in the room laughed.

Linda raised herself to her knees. She looked carefully around the room. Two of the men she recognized from pictures Agent Holmes had shown her. The others were new to her. As she had been taught, she burned their faces into her memory. A second later, she remembered that her shirt had been ripped open and her bare breasts were brazenly displayed.

"Nice tits," one of the men said.

The man who had helped Chaz drag her in, Billy

Boots, as he was called, raised his booted foot and pushed Linda back to the floor. "What you looking at, bitch," he snarled. Billy was a little small to be a biker, but his meanness made up for a lot.

One of the men who had been seated got up from his chair. He was holding the joint they had been passing around and he took a nice hit. He had stringy, black shoulder length hair and a droopy black moustache. He was wearing a black leather vest over a denim shirt and tight blue jeans with brown leather tassels sewn on up and down the outside of each leg. His name was Rocker. When he exhaled, he wheezed, "What are you guys waiting for? Let's string her up and see what she's got."

Linda panicked and began to try and crawl away, but Chaz took hold of her bound ankles and dragged her over to the side of the room. A chain dangled there from the ceiling and ran through a pulley to the near wall. Boots went over to the wall and lowered the chain. Chaz took hold of the end and connected it to the bracelets that confined Linda's ankles. Linda, frantic, tried to kick herself away, but a second later she felt her ankles being pulled skyward. She squealed an unavailing protest. Boots was yanking at the chain and her body rose in spurts. First, her legs were off the floor, then she was resting on her shoulders, then her head swung free. One more yank and her head was a good 2' in the air.

The man gathered around her. Boots stepped forward and took hold of her fat, fear stiffened nipples and twisted them. Linda groaned from the pain. The men all laughed.

"That's not the way to welcome a guest," the one they called Rocker protested. "Ya got to treat 'em nice. Here, let me show you how."

He pushed Billy Boots aside and crouched down so that his mouth was level with Linda's breasts. Her loose shirt had fallen away to her sides due to her upside down position and her melon sized breasts were swung out from her chest enticingly. Her nipples were plump and sat centered upon silver dollar wide, smooth, burgundy colored areolas. Rocker turned his head and spoke to his mates. "Ya got to say hello nice and friendly like. Watch and learn motherfuckers."

He moved his head to her right breast. "Hello there little tittie," he said. "Nice of you to join us. How's about a little kiss?" His companions expressed their mirth at this.

He subsumed Linda's nipple into his mouth and began to suckle it. His hand was grasped around her breast firmly, his other hand around her back. Linda squealed and writhed, but he held on tight. His mouth was hot and her nipple started to send an unwelcome tingle to her. "Ouuuuuuuuuuuuuuuu!" she shouted through her gag. "Ooooooouuuuuuu!"

This gave the men a good chuckle. "She likes it," one of them said.

Rocker drew his head back and Linda's nipple popped out of his mouth. Rocker looked at it. "Are you going to introduce me to your friend?" he asked. He waited a second and tilted his ear towards it. "What's that you say?.....Oh, okay."

Grinning, he moved to Linda's other breast. "Hello, left tittie," he said facetiously. "I've met your sister and she's delicious. Do you taste just as good?" He put his ear to it. "Oh, thank you," he said politely to the imaginary voice emanating from her nipple. "I don't mind if I do."

He placed his lips over Linda's left breast and took in her plump teat. Linda felt the tug of his suction. His hand held her breast, squeezing it hard. "Nnnnnnnnn! Nnnnnnnnn!" she yelled, but Rocker just kept right on suckling. Linda hated it, but the feel of his hot, wet mouth on her teat sent a shiver of pleasure through her.

He let the nipple pop out and rose. He turned to the others. "Now that's how you say hello to a lady," he said, grinning.

All the men were amused except Boots. "Fuck that," he growled. "I hate cops and I don't care if it's got tits and a cunt, it's still a pig."

Chaz put his arm around his shoulders. "Take it easy, cuz," he said. "I'm sure that when Ike gets here he'll let you have a little piece of her."

There was assent from the others.

"Let's see her pussy," one of the men suggested. Chaz nodded agreement. He unbuckled the belt at the front of Linda's jeans and raised the zipper. Linda squirmed and moaned, shaking her hips in protest. It didn't faze Chaz one bit.

When the zipper was fully open, he took hold of the waist of her pants and began to tug them upwards. The jeans were very tight and it was rough going. Linda's body was shaken this way and that. He finally got them over her hips and he pulled them up past her knees where he joined the belt back together tightly to keep them in place. Linda was wearing a pair of light pink bikini panties. Chaz drew his blade from his pocket and clicked it open. He quickly sliced through the gussets and pulled the fabric from her body. He stepped back so everyone could see. There was a pause as they all took time to appreciate what had lain underneath.

"Well, it's good to know she's a natural blond," one of the men said.

"That's surely a sweet sight," said another.

Linda's adult growth was light and silky, just barely shrouding her plump pussy. She trimmed it once in a while, just so that the hair didn't peek out from the sides of her underwear, and just a little at the lips so that her boyfriend could suckle her there without complaining about getting hairs in his mouth.

"Wait a minute," Rocker said. "I think it's trying to say something."

He crept back up to her and put his ear to her crotch. "What's that you say? What? You'll have to speak louder." He paused as if listening. "Oh, okay," he said after a few seconds. He turned to the others. "It wants me to say hello," he told them. There was more laughter.

He leaned forward, circled his arms around Linda's thighs and pulled them open a few inches. He placed his mouth near the top of Linda's crux and stuck out his tongue. He flicked it a few times over the little nubbin at the top and then insinuated it inside her labia as far as he could reach, washing it up and down.

"Mmmmmmpf! Mmmmmmmmpf!" Linda protested. She swung her head to try and bang the man in the testicles, where she had been taught was the most vulnerable spot of any male assailant, but was only able to strike him in his knees, which he ignored. The tongue was agitating her private flesh in a way that did not please her at all. She tried to squeeze her thighs back together, but Rocker was too strong and had too good a grip.

"Mmmmm-umm-ummmm!" Rocker hummed as he supped at Linda's divide. He raised his head and stepped back. His finger replaced his tongue and he teased the now stiffened love bud and then squished the digit between her labial lips.

"You dirty whore!" he exclaimed. "You're all wet!" The other men were amused. Linda was mortified.

"Hey Rocker," one of the men said, "I'll bet you a hundred bucks you can't make her come."

Two of the other men announced their participation in the challenge.

"You're on," Rocker replied to Linda's dismay.

He leaned down and took hold of the upside down girl's breasts. "Let's start at the beginning," he proposed. He carefully massaged and stroked Linda's orbs. He tweaked her nipples, he ran his hand over her belly. He took her teats in his mouth again, one after the other, this time suckling them gently and swirling his tongue over them. Linda tried to squirm her body from his grasp, but he always kept one firm hand on her naked back to steady her, her shirt having slid down by the force of gravity.

He slowly rose, running his hands up along the woman's torso, rubbing them lightly over her hips, up her thighs and back down again. Linda was twisting and issuing unhappy grunts, but the sensations were beginning to get to her. That and the fact of being displayed so brazenly before a group of testosterone loaded men.

This time, when Rocker approached Linda's slice with his tongue, he started by flitting it lightly over her stiffened love bud. He had spread her thighs again, this time a little wider and he held them apart with one hand while he slipped the fingers of the other in from behind her and began to stroke her divide.

A couple of the men had lit smokes and one had gone over to the refrigerator and gotten a few long necks. Linda could hear them as they were popped open. It just added to her chagrin at being used as an amusement for these hardened criminals, reprobates, scum of the earth.

She could feel Rocker's fingers slip sliding along her crevasse. She knew that what the man had said earlier was true. She had lubricated. And his skilled application of tongue and fingers was making her pussy hot.

"I can't do this! I can't do this! I can't do this!" she

kept repeating to herself. She grunted a groan of unhappiness and anger. She tried to force her thighs together. She twisted and turned her body. She banged her head on the man's legs. But the glow he had initiated in her loins was getting stronger and stronger.

She tried to put the man's actions out of her mind. She tried to think of what scum these bastards were. She tried to think of some way that she was going to free herself of her predicament. She closed her eyes tightly and gritted her teeth. She gripped her hands into fists. She shook her thighs and hips. She grunted and groaned her resistance. But the man kept up his skillful work. His tongue was like a salamander that had covered her sex and was squirming and squiggling inside and outside of it.

The man's hand shifted, pressing his fingers deeper into her crevasse. They found her now slippery and dilated tunnel and slid themselves in.

That was when she snapped. He kept plunging his two thick fingers in and out of her canal while his tongue and lips worked her clit. "Arrrrrrrrrr! Arrrrrrrrrrr!" she protested, but it did no good. The feelings kept rising and rising. "Arrrrrrrrr! Arrrrrrrrrr!" she protested again. "Arrrrrrrrr! Arrrrrrrrrr! Arrrrrrrrrrrr!" she raged.

Suddenly, a warm, tingly feeling spread over her loins. "No! No! No!" she thought madly. One of the men spoke.

"Looks like she's getting ready," he said.

And she was. Her thighs now were shuddering. Her breath was coming deep. She was biting down on her gag. Redness had broken out all over her chest and her breasts had become hard and were pulsing. The man accelerated his actions. His fingers began plunging in and out rapidly. His tongue stroked her clit hard again and again at an infuriating pace. He sucked hard at it while flicking it with his tongue. It felt like all of her being was being drawn to her pussy. It became the center of her universe. "Nnnnnnnnnn! Nnnnnnnnnn!" she protested desperately.

And then it hit her. Her thighs began to shake and her body began to jerk. Her pussy erupted into a series of hard, harsh contractions that made her grunt with pleasure. "Ugh! Ugh! Ugh! Ugh! Ugh!" and then, "Ugggg-gggggggh! Uggggggggggggh!"

The men exploded with merriment. "That a boy, Rocker!" one exclaimed.

"Go get her boy!" another called out.

"Oooooooooouuuuuuuueeeeee!" yodeled another.

After what seemed the longest time, Linda felt her pussy's convulsions slowing, grateful that her ordeal was at an end. But Rocker had other ideas. He slowed his efforts just long enough to lap his broadened tongue over her plush sex several times and then went back to work.

"Please stop! Please! Please!" the unhappy woman called out in her mind. It was not to be. Her lusts began to rise again rapidly. Her loins swelled with need. It wasn't long when her pussy erupted again. "Arrrrrgh! Arrrrrrgh! Arrrrrrrrgh!" she grunted as the ecstasy producing contractions began anew. "Arrrrrrrgh!"

Finally the man relented. He gave her clit one last prolonged kiss and stepped back, giving her naked ass a fierce slap. "Now that's a hot bitch!" he exclaimed. He turned to his buddies. "Okay, motherfuckers, pay up!"

Three crisp hundred dollar bills exchanged hands. One of the men handed Rocker a Lone Star longneck. He wiped his face with the sleeve of his shirt and took a long drink. "Ahhhhhhhhhhhhh!" he sighed. "Pussy and beer, now that's a combo!"

The one they called Stitch, an older fellow with speckles of gray in his short, jet black hair, who was sort of the custodian of their little playhouse, spoke up.

"Okay boys," he said. "You've had your fun. Let's leave the rest to Ike and Mouse when they get here."

Everybody was laid back at the safe house. No one gave him an argument, not even Billy Boots who was itching to make the bitch yelp with pain. Nobody wanted to fuck with Ike neither. And besides, there was other pussy just sitting around waiting for something to do.

The group dissipated, and the men headed over to the chairs and sofas. Each of them that passed by Linda gave her bare ass a little swat as if for good luck. Boots was last and he gave Linda's rear cheek a hard, solid slap that made her cringe with pain.

Linda watched from upside down as the men resumed their drinking and watching their movie. One of the men, Chaz, went over to the cages which held the unhappy looking young women and perused them for a moment. The girls were ungagged. Their hands were confined by short chains to rings in the leather collars that they all wore. An 18" long chain connected the bracelets on their ankles. Chaz took his time examining them. They all looked at him dourly, knowing full well that his interest in them was not academic.

He spoke to the blond girl, who occupied the cage on the right end. "What's your name, girl?" he asked her.

"Camille, sir," the girl answered in a wavering voice, looking up at the mountain of a man before her.

"What say you and me get better acquainted, Camille," he said more than asked.

The girl had no answer for him.

Chaz turned to Stich. "Let me have the key."

"You can use her," Stich replied as he handed him the key to the padlock holding the cage door closed, "but don't mark her up. Esteban Morales is coming the day after tomorrow and Ike wants to unload her. And the others too. He's expecting a load in a couple of days so we can get a fresh batch. These three are getting a little long in the tooth, if you know what I mean."

"No problem," Chaz replied.

He stepped back to the cage and unlocked the padlock, swinging the cage door open. The girl drew her body back. Linda noticed that her expression had gone from dour to outright unhappy. Undoubtedly what the older guy had said had been news to her. Whatever the callous men had done to her, she could be sure that any change in her future would be worse. It would be another step deeper into captivity, another step away from wherever she had come from.

Linda roiled in anger at what these outlaws were going to do to the poor girl, what they had done to probably hundreds over the years. She pulled at her bound hands futilely. If only she could get free. Somehow she would get away. Maybe she could get help in time to save poor Camille and her two companions. But she had to get free first. "Damn! Damn! Damn!" she castigated herself.

"Come on," Chaz ordered the girl in a deep, harsh voice, "get outta there. And don't get smart. I know plenty of ways to make it hurt without leaving any marks. Just give me a reason to and I will."

Camille had broken into silent tears. She shuffled herself out of the cage on her knees. Her blond hair was almost yellow and hung down to the middle of her back. She was thin but curvaceous. Her breasts were solid and pert. Apparently the men had not been so cautious in her care before now because she bore the faded remnants of a whipping on her breasts and thighs.

As she cleared the cage, Chaz took hold of the hair at the back of her head and lifted her to her feet. She gave out a little squeal of pain.

"Shut the fuck up," Chaz told her. She nodded back. Her face had devolved into an expression of her misery.

"Use the bedroom at the end to the right," Stitch told Chaz. "And don't forget to keep her chained to the bed. I don't want her running off if you pass out after you fuck her."

Chaz laughed. "It won't be me who'll be passing out. I'm going to fuck the living shit out of this little honey."

"Yeah, yeah," Stitch answered. "Just do what I say."

Chaz smiled. "Sure, Stich. Just like you say," he replied. "Come on, Camille," he said to the girl, shaking her head harshly. "Let's go fuck."

He pushed the unhappy girl in front of him. She could only take small steps due to the chain between her ankles. The man was taking long strides and she had to double time her feet like a hurrying geisha in order not to trip and fall to the floor. He led her to the staircase and up where the girl had to take little mini steps to navigate the risers. Linda's heart went out to girl. She was about 5'6" tall, and the big man towered over her. When they reached the balcony, he turned her to the right. Linda watched as he led her to the door on the end. He unlocked it and pushed her rudely in. He stepped in and slammed the door behind him.

There was nothing for Linda to do but keep wary eyes on the men and the stupid movie they were watching. It had a lot of car chases and shoot outs. Linda didn't recognize any of the actors. The men kept smoking and drinking long necks and taking swigs from the Jack Daniels bottle. They exchanged appreciative commentary on the movie action, cheering whenever the activities became particularly violent and hooting when one of the many big breasted, barely dressed babes were slapped around or otherwise discomfited.

At one point, Rocker took one of the black haired girls out of a cage and had her suckle his prick while he leaned back on one of the sofas and smoked another joint. Another man, the one they called Jawbone because of his prominent chin, stripped down and had the third girl come out of her cage. He fucked her right there on a leather divan, her knees bent back and almost touching her shoulders, while the young girl groaned and sobbed. When he was done, Stich fucked her next, not bothering to disrobe, but just lowering his fly and fucking her as he was.

In the meantime, Rocker finally got off and Billy Boots, after slapping the girl back and forth a few times for issuing a whine of unhappiness, bent her over the side of one of the couches and took her rear entrance, making her screech and howl in complaint.

When Stich was done, he reconnected the ankles of the girl he had been using, freed her hands from her collar and told her to go to the kitchen and warm up some food. She shuffled off obediently, if unhappily. At first, Linda wondered how the men could let the girl go off on her own like that, but then she guessed that all the other doors and windows except the front had been boarded up or hammered shut.

When she came back about 20 minutes later, Boots' sobbing victim had been restored to relative safety in her cage. The first girl, who answered to the name of Maureen, had large, round breasts with dark, wide areolas, wide hips and a simple, childlike face. She looked about 19 or 20 at most, had pale, almost pasty skin and had straight, jet black hair that ran down her back to just above her waist. She was carrying a tray with a large bowl of what looked like stew with several smaller bowls and a series of spoons and napkins. She brought the tray to

Stich first and he spooned himself out a bowlful. She then presented the tray in turn to Rocker, Jawbone and Billy Boots. Boots passed, but Rocker and Jawbone filled bowls to the brim and placed them on their lap.

When she was done serving the men, the girl stood in the middle of the room, her brimming eyes downcast, holding the tray in front of her, awaiting further instructions. Stich looked up at her when he was finished eating and asked her if she and the other girl, who he called Julie, had eaten.

"No, sir," Maureen answered timidly. Her inner thighs were shiny from the cum leaking from her shaven crevasse.

He filled his bowl and Rocker's, who had finished his as well, and placed them on the floor. He released Julie from her cage, refastened Maureen's wrists to the chain that led from her collar and told them to eat up and be quick about it. The girls knelt in place, shaking their heads until their long black hair was behind them, then leaned over and began to eat. Stich filled two more bowls with beer and placed them beside the others so they could drink.

When they were done, he told them both to pee in the larger bowl and then, after they squatted and performed, to the amusement of the men, ordered Maureen back to the kitchen to clean everything up. Julie went back in her cage.

Once Maureen came back and was restored to her confinement, things settled down a bit. The movie ended and another one came on. It was a slasher movie and Linda watched with horror as the pretty young girls in the picture were slaughtered viciously, one by one, by a man with a ski mask over his face. All the while, Linda could not help being self conscious about her state of virtual nakedness. The men looked over at her once in a while, as if reminding themselves that she was still there. Every time their eyes cast over her, a wave of humiliation passed through her. At one point, Billy Boots came over, he seemed pretty drunk, and started slapping her breasts harshly, back and forth, calling her a cunt and a pig and promising harsh treatment to come, making Linda squeal and cringe, until Stich told him to cut it out.

They were about halfway through the second movie when Linda heard the unmistakable sound of motorcycles pulling up outside. She shuddered with fear. The engines turned off and a few moments later she heard the front door open and close and then the step of heavy boots on the foyer floor. Her back was to the entrance of the room and she twisted her body so she could see who was coming in.

It was Ike and his major domo, Mouse. The boys all greeted them. Ike and Mouse murmured gruff replies and then went over to the refrigerator and got themselves some beers. They popped them open, took long drinks and then sauntered over to where Linda hung helplessly. They just stood there, perusing her, while they drank. Linda felt her stomach go sour with fear and she had to suppress the whines of unhappiness that kept trying to emerge from her gag. The men had been waiting for their leader so that the fun could begin. Well, here he was.

Ike was a fearsome looking dude. His wildly bearded face looked like it had a permanent scowl. His chest was broad and muscled. His hands looked as big as bear's paws. He stood there arrogant and powerful and his mien bespoke a ruthlessness and cruelty that made Linda shiver. She could tell that visions of the horrific acts he was going to perpetrate upon her were circling around in his brain.

Mouse, as described heretofore, had a pointed face with a snout-like nose. He was balding in front and his scraggly brown hair hung down to his shoulders from the circlet around his bald spot. He stood about shoulder high to Ike who was about 6'4". Although Mouse was a little over 5'10", since he was always standing near or next to Ike everybody thought of him as a runt. He was as loyal to Ike as an apostle and always carried out his orders swiftly and surely, whether it was arranging a hit on some transgressor, keeping gang members in line or making sure that Ike got his cut of every licit or illicit enterprise that gang members engaged in.

Ike gave Mouse a look. He didn't have to speak his order. Mouse knew what to do right away. He flipped open his pig sticker, stepped forward, and began to cut away the remnants of Linda's attire.

While Mouse was tearing through Linda's jeans, cutting up each leg so that they could be removed without freeing her ankles, Ike moved over to the rack of whips on the wall. He chose a long, leather encased, steel switch with a polished wooden handle. When he came back, Mouse was pulling the remnants of Linda's jeans from her body. Ike waited until Mouse had cut away her torn rhinestone studded, denim shirt before speaking.

"Go through her pants. See if there's anything inside them that says who she is," he told his minion.

Mouse picked up the quartered jeans and went through the pockets. He produced a small wad of cash and a plastic i.d. He looked at it cursorily and then handed them both to Ike.

Ike put the cash in his pocket and then took a look at the i.d. After a moment or two, he tossed it aside. He stepped up in front of the dangling girl.

"Well, little FBI girl, first, we're going to have a little

lesson in obedience," he told the wide eyed, panicking young woman. "It's always best that we get right to the heart of things. Then, when I start asking some questions, it will be clear what the consequence of not answering will be."

Linda couldn't help issuing a whine. She had been eyeing the switch fearfully. It was about 3' long, but looked like a toy in Ike's supersized paw. Right then she decided to tell them anything they wanted to know. It was too bad that she was gagged. But it wouldn't have made any difference in the end. All the girls got a whipping when they arrived and there was no reason to treat this one any different.

The men had gotten up from their chairs and made a little semi-circle around Linda, Ike in the middle. Ike spun the handle of the switch around in his hand a few times to get the feel of it and then reared back. Linda's whole body cringed and she jammed her eyes tight. She heard the whirr of the instrument as it cut the air.

It made a slapping sound as it struck her across her naked, joined thighs several inches below her knees. Linda's eyes sprung open, her body jerked wildly and she screeched into her gag. Ike counted to 5 slowly and then he delivered another vicious blow a few inches below the other. Linda's body contorted again and her tormented voice emerged from behind the wedge of leather implanted firmly in her mouth.

"Eeeeeeeeeeeeeeee!" she called out. "Eeeeeeeeeeeeeeee!" Tears were already pouring down from her eyes into her hair. She saw Ike's hand rearing back again and she bit down hard on the wad of leather between her lips. This blow landed a few inches down from the second, at what would have been the tops of her pale white thighs if she hadn't been upside down. It left, like the others, an angry red line amidst the field of white. Linda screeched again although she had promised herself that she wouldn't this time. She knew was tougher than this, but the hopelessness of her situation, the callousness with which the men had treated the other women, Ike's fierce demeanor, the leering eyes of the other men, all combined to undermine her resolution. In spite of herself, she started to beg for forbearance.

"...eeeeeeeeease ...op! ...eeeeeeeeease ...op! ...eeeee-eeeease!" she tried to yell through her gag. Her pleas only served to give the men amusement.

The next blow struck her across the belly. Ike worked his way slowly down to her breasts. Linda screamed and contorted her body in an attempt to avoid the blows, but Ike merely awaited his opportunity and struck her breasts again and again.

When he stepped behind her, Linda started to sob. Before proceeding further, Mouse loosened her hands from behind her back and, with the help of Jawbone, since Linda struggled mightily to avoid it, joined them in front of her exposing her long, naked, graceful back to depredation. Each blow, from the back of her shins to her plump rear orbs, up her back to her shoulders, one after the other in a demonically slow pace, delivered an intolerable line of fiery pain. She screeched and moaned and sobbed and called out muffled, half formed pleas for forbearance. The men around her were all silent, mesmerized by the display of unmerciful violence. The girls in the cages cringed and sobbed as they recalled their own turns at Ike's mercy. Linda's howls filled the room, mingled with the screams of the tormented, beautiful young woman in the movie.

When Ike was done, Linda was sobbing uncontrollably. Billy Boots opportuned Ike for a turn and when he received his leader's nod, went to the peg board and selected a multi tasseled flogger. Linda saw him approach with the instrument in his hand and screeched and sobbed and begged to be spared further abuse, futilely attempting to communicate her willingness to reveal everything she knew about anything the men wanted to know.

Billy displayed a maniacal grin as he released the first blow of the flogger across Linda's breasts. She attempted to ward off the second with her bound hands, but at Billy's request Jawbones knelt down and pulled Linda's disobedient hands down, away from her torso to prevent interference with Billy's pleasures.

He worked the flogger up and down her front. His face was contorted into a masque of anger and spittle emerged from his tightly compressed lips. One could extrapolate from his mien the expletives rattling around his brain each time he married the harsh, hardened, leather strands to Linda's body. "Cunt!" "Pig" "Bitch! "Whore!" "Scumbucket!" and so on. Where the whip landed emerged bright splotches of red on her skin.

Linda cried and moaned and twisted her body. When he was done with the front, he went to her back, tracing the path that Ike had followed until he was down to her shoulders while Linda screamed and sobbed. When he was done, and a scrim of redness had been produced from her shins to her shoulders, he moved towards her front again to resume his assault on her breasts, but Ike caught his arm and told him firmly that that was enough. Fire erupted in Billy's eyes, but he obeyed his superior nonetheless, knowing full well that Linda's night of torment was not yet finished. He would make sure he got another turn with her.

Linda did not resist as her arms were refastened behind her back. She was moaning disconsolately. Her body swung slowly back and forth. A river of tears had flowed into her golden blond hair. Someone handed Ike the bottle of Jack and he took a nice swig.

"Wow, that was beautiful," Rocker gushed.

"That's the way to do it," Jawbone proffered.

Stitch just nodded his head in agreement.

Mouse had handed back Ike his beer and he finished it off. He handed the empty back and Mouse dropped the dead soldier into the large, green, plastic garbage can already half full with empties. It made a tinkling sound as it landed.

Mouse crouched down, unbuckled Linda's gag from behind her head and pulled the plug from her mouth. Linda's lips formed into a grotesque grimace. She looked up at her captors piteously. FBI training at Quantico had never prepared her for this. Two years out of the academy, she had been taken under Special Agent Holmes' wing. She had been the 2nd ranked graduate from her class. She was on her way to the top. She had volunteered for this dangerous duty at his urging and so her star could continue its ascendancy. She had thought she knew the risks. Her instructions were to make contact with the Alamogordo Rogues' leadership. For one golden moment earlier that night, she had thought she was within reach of her goal.

She had recognized Ike right away from the pictures Holmes had shown her. When the man who she knew now as Chaz had proposed that he introduce her, her heart had thumped with excitement. She was envisioning the headlines, "Special Agent Linda Kramer Smashes Decades Old Slavery Ring." There would be awards ceremonies, promotion and star status as she testified against them at their inevitable trial. She had reached out her hand to shake his, calculating her next move. She was willing to do whatever it took, even if it meant fucking the burly monster. So much was at stake.

And then, so fast that her eyes barely perceived it, his fist had lashed out. She remembered only the flow of pain from her jaw upwards. The lights had gone out. The next thing she knew, one of the men was stuffing a mass of leather into her mouth. Her wrists and ankles had been confined. She barely had time to struggle before they had dumped her into the tool box.

And now, her worst nightmares had come true. She had suffered a torment that had been previously unimaginable. There was undoubtedly more to come. She knew her duty. She should give the men no information that could be helpful to them in protecting their nefarious schemes. She should suffer death before dishonor. But she knew that she would answer the cruel men's questions even before they asked them.

Ike crouched down before her. He tapped her cheek with his meaty hand. Not lightly. It was not an affectionate gesture. She could feel her cheek glowing red where he struck her. A river of cold flowed through her veins. "Oh, god! Oh, god! Oh, god!" she thought unhappily.

"Okay now, little Miss FBI girl, it's time to have a little chat," Ike told her. "What were you doing in my bar tonight?"

He didn't have to ask any more questions. Linda gave him the whole thing. They knew that Blackjack Jackson was headed this way. They knew that the Alamogordo Rogues would help him cross the border to freedom. They knew that it was a chance to break the gang wide open. They knew there was a safehouse somewhere and it was her job to try and find it. She was told to do whatever it took.

"Well, little miss FBI girl," Ike told her, "you found it. Or, rather, it found you. I guess you know by now that you'll never get the chance to tell anyone about it. The only question is whether we bury you somewhere way out there in the desert or find another use for you. One of our Mexican friends is coming in a day or so. He hates the FBI with a passion. I think he might like playing with you for a little while. Your boys rolled up one of his networks a little while ago and he would probably enjoy some payback. So, if you're a good little girl, we'll keep you alive until he gets here just to see. Otherwise I'll let Billy Boots here take you down to the cellar and have some fun with you. We'll get it all on tape and send it back to your FBI friends. So what do you say? Ready to have a little fun?"

Linda knew what fun meant. She had seen some of it a little while ago. Part of her wanted to resist these despicable, cruel men. But most of her was so filled up with fear that her ability to resist them was at nil. She drew her lips into a grimace and nodded dolefully.

Ike nodded to Mouse and he went to the wall and released the chain that was holding her aloft. Her body crashed to the floor. She issued a moan of pain. Mouse took hold of her hair and pulled her to a kneeling position. Ike had gone over to the dresser under the rack of whips. He opened it and took out a quart sized glass jar and a pair of pliers. He stepped back to where Linda knelt. The men were circled around her. She looked at the jar with shock and horror. It was half full with teeth. Ike shook it for her and the teeth rattled around noisily.

"You see," Ike said to her, "it's not unusual for some of the broads who come through here to believe that sucking cock against their will is a fate worse than death. It doesn't happen too often, but enough so that we've been able to assemble a fine collection of teeth. We start from the back, a molar or two wrenched right from their gums. We save the fronts for last since most guys don't want a blow job from a broad with flapping gums. But I have to admit that once or twice we had to go all the way." He shook the jar again. "So, what do you say? You'll probably do it anyway once we rip out one or two, so what's the sense of making us go to all that trouble? Are you going to cooperate or not?"

There's something grotesque looking about teeth after they've been torn from their natural habitat. The roots seem unnaturally long and usually carry a trace or two of blood, not at all the bright, shiny things that grace a pretty smile.

Linda shuddered with fear. She knew that Ike wasn't bluffing. He had no reason to. She looked about at the men surrounding her. She counted up the blowjobs: six, including Ike. And one more if that guy who went upstairs came back. Six or seven blowjobs against gut wrenching agony. She knew they wouldn't stop until they were all out. And then she'd be a useless hag to them. The Mexican gang lord, she knew Estaban Morales' reputation well, wouldn't buy her if she had no teeth. She would end up buried amidst the almost limitless expanse of sand out there somewhere. And if the FBI and state and local law enforcement hadn't been able to find the safehouse after all these years, they would never find her grave.

She knew she should refuse. She knew she would never be the same afterwards. But she also knew that as soon as the first tooth had been cruelly extracted from her mouth she would be begging to do it. Tears were streaming down her face. Her hands writhed in their bonds. Her stomach had contracted into a knot and was turning somersaults. Her body was sweating all over. Her mouth was dry. She felt herself starting to shake. Her mouth turned into a dismal frown, she nodded, "Yes."

Mouse took the jar and the pliers from Ike's hands. Ike lowered the fly to his metal studded jeans. He drew out his cock. "I'm first," he said.

Linda cried and whined all during that first blowjob. The man's meat was thick and long. It filled her mouth to capacity. It was hot and salty and hard. He had hold of the hair on the back of her head and guided her up and down his pole, castigating her from time to time for lack of enthusiasm. He pulled her off once and gave her face a mighty slap to encourage her to better effort. She kept her lips held tightly against his shaft. She suckled the meat almost tenderly, if not at first, certainly after Ike's fierce remonstrance. She swirled her tongue around it. She did everything she could think of, all the things her boyfriend, a person she was not likely ever to see again, had taught her.

Ike took his time in coming to fruition. He had gotten a blowjob from one of the barmaids after he had closed his joint earlier, so the edge was off somewhat. Linda's jaw began to get tired. It seemed like the man would go on forever.

And then his hips began their motion. She heard him release a long, impassioned sigh. The other men began to call encouragement. Just before it happened she had a premonition of his cock throbbing and jerking in her mouth, his white sauce filling it and running down her throat. Her body went queasy at the thought.

And then it happened. His meat began to spasm. His thrusts into her mouth, timed perfectly by his control of her head, became quicker and more urgent. He groaned loudly. She felt the hot discharge filling her mouth. She tasted its salty, semi-bitter flavor. She felt her stomach flip over and she thought she was going to wretch, an action that would surely produce more pain and corporal discipline. She whined and sobbed, but she swallowed it all.

Next was Mouse. He was quicker. Then Stitch, who took his time.

By the time she got to Rocker, the men had resumed watching the movie, smoking and drinking, and she had been dragged over to the couches where Rocker leaned back and enjoyed it, like he had with the black haired girl, Julie, making her take her time, slowing her down time and again when he got close, and then, like the others, filling her mouth with his salty cream.

Jawbone followed suit with Rocker, but he was not as patient and she was done with him quickly.

She shuddered when it was Billy Boots' turn, with good reason. He pushed her to the floor onto her back, placed his knees on either side of her head and plunged his cock between her widespread, unhappy lips. She gagged as he thrust into her throat, her body writhing and twisting in protest. He held it there until she began to choke and cough and groan. He thrust it in again and again, each time waiting a little longer, until she thought she was going to faint. Finally, in cruel, hard thrusts that bruised her lips, he called out and groaned, his hands holding her hair tightly to the point of pain as he came.

The miniature biker locked her ankles together again and reinstalled her gag, affixing it so tightly behind her head that it pressed up against her gums and made her grimace.

They left her lying on the floor for a long while. She kept her eyes closed and her head turned away from the men, stewing in self-pity and remorse.

Deep down in the basement of the *hacienda*, Linda

remembered bitterly what came next. After the movie was over, an event punctuated by the screams of the last beautiful young woman to meet her fate, Ike got up and pulled her to her feet by her hair. He loosened her ankles and affixed a 12" long chain to them. She moaned and sobbed as he took her up the stairs. She waited unhappily on the mattress of the bed in the room he took her to while he undressed, revealing his muscular, scarred body. She promised herself that she would not react when he bound her wrists to a chain that led from the headboard and he freed her ankles. But she screamed and groaned with passion as he fucked her brutally fore and aft.

Now, in the darkness, in her cage, she wondered unhappily what was wrong with her. She rued her roaring, body wrenching orgasms. She dreaded when they would come and get her again. She heard a loud whine and a sob and realized that it was her. She closed her eyes and prayed to God for help.

CHAPTER THREE

The day's journey had been uneventful. Jack stopped for gas early on to top off the tank. He left Carly as she was, after warning her of the consequences of making trouble, while he paid the cashier and filled the car with gas. He took Route 264 west out of Cave Springs and then dropped down to 412 just before Siloam Springs near the Oklahoma border. His plan was to follow Rte. 69 to Dallas and then hop on 380 and take it to Roswell, New Mexico where it hit up with Route 70. Then it would be Route 70 all the way to that little bar just outside of Tularosa.

He had forgotten it was Sunday until he passed a couple churches with parking lots chock full of cars. It made the driving much easier since all of the business traffic was off the road. It was slow going coming down the mountains in Arkansas, but as soon as he hit Oklahoma, the road was flat and clear.

At about 11, he drove down a dirt road off of 69 so that he and the girl could piss, and then back on the road again. He gassed up just outside Dallas where he bought a map of Texas. At about 2:30, he pulled off the road again so they could relieve themselves. He took a 15 minute break to eat a couple of the peanut butter sandwiches and drink some soda. He didn't give anything to the girl. Whether she ate or not was of supreme indifference to him. He only had so many sandwiches and if he ended up dumping her anything he gave her would have gone to waste.

It got warmer the further west they went. He

eventually took off his overcoat and the girl's too. He didn't care if she got hot or not, but it would look stupid with her all dressed up in a winter jacket and him in a t-shirt.

He was glad that he had brought her on this leg of the trip. It broke the monotony to rub her spread open thighs while he drove or play with her pussy or tits. He got her all worked up a number of times and let her come twice. She moaned and contorted and twisted in her bonds as she came, to his amusement.

So far, so good. About 5, they pulled into a little gas station just south of Lubbock. He gassed the car up again. He broke down and gave the girl some soda to drink which she gurgled down enthusiastically. He had just gotten back in the car and turned on the ignition when he heard it on the radio.

A reporter was speaking:

> "...the FBI has issued no comment, but Radio 98 has learned that the reports of fugitive Jack 'Blackjack' Jackson's death in a fire at the Rogues motorcycle gang head-quarters in Wausau, Wisconsin have been proven false. An un-named source in the Wisconsin State Police has informed us that there has been confirmation that Jackson is a suspect in a murder and robbery of a sporting goods store two days ago in the small town of Nellsville, Wisconsin, some 75 miles west of Wausau.
>
> Authorities believe that Jackson

and his 22 year old hostage Carly
Walker are heading south towards
the Mexico border. There has been
confirmation that he is responsible
for the theft of a metallic blue, '94
Mercury Grand Marquis with
Kansas plates from the parking lot
of the Kansas City International
Airport. Authorities are concentrating their search in Texas and in
New Mexico. A copy of his FBI
wanted poster with his suspected
new, altered appearance and a
picture of Carly Walker can be
found on our website, 98allcountry-
radio.com. Jackson is known to be
armed and is extremely dangerous.
Authorities are unsure of whether
he still has possession of his
hostage or whether she is still alive.
Any member of the public who
believes they have sighted Jackson
should refrain from confronting
him and call 1-800-98-radio.
That's 1-800-98-radio. Keep tuned
to this station for further bulletins
as they arrive."

Jack didn't react right away. He calmly eased their car
back out onto the road and continued their journey west.
He was steaming inside. He flipped off the radio and then
decided better of it and flipped it back on.

The broadcast was a kind of good news/bad news kind
of thing. It was bad news that the FBI knew what car he

was driving and where he was headed. It was good news that that knowledge had somehow leaked to the press. Forewarned is forearmed.

It would be getting dark in about two hours. He pulled out his Texas map and looked for a likely, lonely spot to turn off the road. He saw a place called Mound Lake just north of 380 about 10 or 15 miles west of them and he headed for it. He turned off of 380 onto a two lane secondary road, drove about 3 more miles and followed the signs. He found a road that circled the lake and drove along it north until he found a dirt trail that led off of it. He turned down it and drove right up to a ridge that overlooked the lake. He made sure that the car was not visible to anyone using the lake and turned off the engine.

Carly had heard the broadcast too. She realized immediately that she had become a distinct liability.

During the long ride, Carly had been unable to see any of the countryside they were travelling through. All she saw was a blackness that matched her deep despair. She could hardly move any part of her body. Her hands could clasp and unclasp. She could move her head to some degree. Her toes could wiggle. But that was all. Her legs were splayed wide. She realized why when she felt his hand on her thigh. At first, she had abhorred the ready availability of her tender, sensitive skin. But as the miles went on, miles filled with an utter lack of any stimulation of any kind, other than the twangy country radio stations he kept finding, the touch of his hand was a perverse sort of welcome diversion.

When he slipped his hand over her pussy she realized why the seat had been set to lean backwards. It made her pussy lips readily available. As had been happening, the moment he touched her there, her lusts began to rise. He toyed and fingered her there for a long time, starting and stopping, measuring her excitement by her squirming and her moans, his light fingers delivering just the right amount of varying sensations to make her pussy yearn for completion. When he got her near the top, he would stop. She would issue an irrepressible groan and he would laugh and pat her on the thigh. Ten or fifteen minutes later, he would begin again.

Twice he had let her come. She groaned with pleasure and her body shuddered with each mighty contraction. And afterwards, she was ashamed of how easily he manipulated her, how desperate she had been for release. She would cry silently, knowing that he couldn't see her tears and would have no pretext to punish her.

But most of the time had been spent in terrible isolation. Hour after hour after hour. It was like those times the day before he had left her in total isolation, almost as if that time was a dry run for this trip. All she could do was think dreadful thoughts. Several times she started crying out of the blue and had to control herself lest she break out into heartfelt sobs, an event that she knew would not go unpunished.

The fact that they were travelling in broad daylight made it seem all the worse. The world was out there. She couldn't see it, but it could see her. She knew that people had to notice her sitting so seemingly peaceably in the front passenger seat. When he stopped for gas, she could hear other people around, men and women, even kids. She wanted to cry out to them, beg them for help. But she knew that she daren't make a single sound to attract attention. He had as much as told her each time he left the car to pay and pump the gas. But she kept alive the hope that someone would notice the blindfold under her sunglasses, the bit of blue from the ball stuck in her mouth, the helpless way she turned her head back and forth. Maybe recognize him and call the police.

The thought kept going through her mind that this was her last day on earth. She yearned to see the sun, the faces of other people, to feel a part of the world for one last time. He was going to snuff her out like an unwanted pet. Her mind was filled with the dark thoughts of nothingness. It was no wonder that she welcomed the distraction of his hand on her flesh, took pleasure in the stroking of her cunt, yearned to be brought over the waterfall of passion, to feel the blood rushing through her, to feel her heart pumping wildly, to feel the thrill of her sexual organ in celebration.

When they stopped for bathroom breaks, she stretched her legs as well as she could, enjoying the brief release from her harsh confinements. When he tied her back into her seat, she would have to control herself to prevent herself from breaking out into miserable sobs. And each time they pulled down a bumpy country road or trail, she would fill with panic that now was the time, that he had finally decided to get rid of her. It was with great relief to find that he had stopped merely so that he and she could piss.

But this time, this was different. She had heard the news broadcast too. It was like the FBI had read his mind. She felt a surge of gratitude that they were still looking for him, for her, that they hadn't given up. But she knew, at the same time, that anything that increased the likelihood of a confrontation with the authorities was a danger to the man. And her sitting with him in this car was one of those things.

She hadn't known that he had killed a store clerk back where they stopped the first night. She had been locked in the bathroom in the tub at the time. She confessed to herself that she knew that he had done something awful when he came back with the guns and the clothes and the money. If she had given it much thought, she would have realized that he couldn't leave any witnesses to his depredations. She had been too wrapped up in the thoughts of her own survival to think about it. She felt bad about it now.

She wondered who the clerk was, whether he had any family, any children. Someone would mourn for him, that was for sure. The radio hadn't said whether it was a man or a woman, but she assumed it was a man since if it was a woman the news people would have made a bigger thing of it. Despite her anger at God for letting her become the prisoner of this animal, she said a little prayer for the clerk's soul.

But her thoughts of the man's fate soon passed. As soon as they turned off the highway, her blood ran cold. Then, when the car made a couple of twisty turns, she knew for sure that he wasn't just stopping for gas or something. When the car started to bump and rock, she knew that they were on a dirt road and that the man was seeking an isolated spot where no one would see them. She started to cry.

Jack turned off the engine to the car and leaned back in the seat. He lit a cigarette. He could hear the girl sniffling. Well, she had good reason to be afraid. He knew she had heard the broadcast. It didn't take a rocket engineer to figure out that there was a problem and she was it. He looked about. There was nothing all around except for a nice stand of cottonwood trees just starting to bloom. The ground was covered with green prairie grass about 6 or 7 inches high. It had rained recently and the ground looked soft and would be good for digging. It was a beautiful place, kind of like a glade.

He had promised himself that if he had to do it he

would find someplace nice where he could think of her sleeping until eternity. Somehow that made the thought of ending her life just a little easier to take. In years to come he would think on it and realize that he had done right for her after all the pleasure she had given him. It was a shame though. She had almost made it all the way. But it was as good a spot as any.

He tossed the cigarette out of the window and got out of the car. He slammed the door shut and walked around to the passenger side. When he opened the door, the girl jumped as if startled. He untied her feet and her neck from the head rest, unclasped her seat belt and pulled her from the car. He led her to a spot about 15' away and told her to kneel and then put her forehead to the ground. She complied meekly.

Her posture lifted the rear of her short denim skirt up to the top of the back of her thighs. He couldn't resist crouching down and flipping up the skirt to get a view of her naked ass and the fleshy slit between her thighs. He rubbed his hand over her soft rear cheeks. She was a good one all right, he thought. About the best he ever had, and that said a lot. He delved his hand lower, slipping his fingers over her love lips. There was just a slight stubble and he remembered that he had forgotten to shave her there earlier today. Well, it didn't matter now.

He knew that he should get on with it before he lost his resolve, but the feel of her hot flesh was so delicious that he couldn't stop caressing it. The girl shuddered and it made him think of the passion with which she had fucked him. It made his cock stir. He slipped a finger between her labial divide and felt that she had lubricated.

He looked around again. Nobody to be seen for miles. He had about an hour and a half until dark. There was time enough for one last fuck. There would still be a residue of light with which to dig her grave. He would shoot her first though. He had promised himself that. He would make it quick and painless. She wouldn't even have to get up from where she was kneeling now. The gun was in his pants pocket. As soon as he was finished, he would slip from her pussy, draw the gun out of his pocket and then, 'pop!'

He sank to his knees and maneuvered himself into position to fuck her. He reached between her legs and made her spread them wider. He lowered his fly and fished out his already stiffened cock. He crept closer to her on his knees and then ran the head of his cock along the soft line between her labia. Her pussy was hot.

Just before he pierced her, his pants rubbed against her skin. He realized at once that it would be a better, fuller, richer experience if he could lay the front of his naked thighs against her flesh when he sank within her. He sat back and quickly unbuckled his belt and untied his boots. He kicked them off of his feet and then pulled his pants and shorts free. To make it complete, he drew off his t-shirt.

When he turned back to the girl, he realized that what he wanted was the girl naked too. If this was the last time he fucked her, he wanted it to be as close to perfect as possible.

He pushed the back of her skirt up to around her hips, tucking it into the rope. He then took hold of the hair behind her head and made her kneel back. He lifted the flowery, blue t-shirt up her torso and over her head. It went down as far as her elbows and no further. His knife was hooked into the belt of his pants. He took it out and cut through the fabric, halving it. Then he pushed the remnants down to her wrists.

She was technically not completely naked, but it

would do for all practical purposes. He pushed her back down so that her forehead was on the ground and then ran his hands over her wonderfully plump rear orbs and the skin of her back. Now that was better. Much better. He took his cock in his hand, pushed it along her labial lips once or twice to pick up her slick moisture and then pressed himself forward, slowly burying his cock in her crevasse until it was fully seated. He sighed with appreciation.

When Carly felt him cut the t-shirt from her body, she knew that it was the end. His signal was clear: she would have no further use for it.

When he had made her kneel down in the grass, she had had a glimmer of hope. When he stroked her quim, so soft and tantalizing, making her lusts rise, like he had done so many times before, her hopes had risen that she had been wrong yet again and that he wanted no more than to fuck her. Even when he had rolled up her skirt and drawn her t-shirt over her head. He wanted her naked, that's all, or as close as he could get it with convenience. But when she felt the knife cut through the fabric, she knew that she had been right all along.

Her stomach turned sour and her body chilled. She bit down hard on the blue rubber ball in her mouth and sobbed. She lifted her head, turning it this way and that in a desperate attempt to take a last look at the earth around her. But all she saw was darkness.

The man was taking his time fucking her. His hands were on her hips, rubbing over them and up and down her naked back. His cock was scouring her crevasse in long, leisurely strokes. Despite her despair, his meat was having the effect on her that it always had. She tried in vain to deny it. It was so shameful to be deriving pleasure from the man who would end her days forever as soon as he was done with her. Her soft sobs began to become intermingled with soft moans and groans of passion.

And then it struck her. Why shouldn't she obtain delight from her last act on earth? Why shouldn't she enjoy the fruits of ecstasy that her body could bring to her? It was the last time. The last time. And then her torment would be over. She would be rid of the man and his evil power over her forever. There had to be something better waiting for her! There had to! Why not go out in celebration of life rather than encased in dismal shame and sorrow?

She let the feel of the man's steel like rod traversing her fevered flesh seep into every pore of her body. "Yes! Yes!" she thought. "Yes!" She squeezed her vaginal muscles as hard as she could, seeking to maximize the friction the man's cock was bringing her. "Yes! Do it slowly! Slowly! Slowly!" she urged him with her mind. "Take your time! Enjoy it! Drive me mad with lust! Make me come again and again! Do it! Do it!" she thought feverishly.

The rhythm of his strokes was sending delirious messages of pleasure to her. She felt her orgasm building. She welcomed it rabidly. "Ohhhhhhhhhhhhhh! Ohhhhhhhhhhh! Ohhhhhhhhhhhh!" she moaned through her gagged mouth. "...essssssssssss!"

It struck her hard. Her pussy clenched around the rigid tube inside her. It convulsed with delirious contraction after contraction. She groaned and pushed her hips back in an attempt to drive the pleasure giving cock deeper inside her. When her contractions began to fade, she began to rock back against the man, urging the wonderful feelings to return.

Jack was relishing the girl's passion. He felt her pussy grab him tightly again and again as she came. It was better than he had imagined, better than he remembered. It was cold even for him to be fucking a girl he was going to murder minutes later, and he knew that he would regret it, have those feelings he had about that other girl he killed return. It would haunt him all his days, but he wouldn't have missed feeling these sensations one more time for all the world.

He felt his orgasm rising and purposely slowed his thrusts. The girl had been fucking him back and he pressed his hands into her hips, bringing her motions to a halt. She moaned a moan of frustration. "Don't worry, there's more, there's more," he told her mentally. He reached down and took hold of her arms and lifted her up so that she was sitting on his cock. He pressed her back against his chest and ran his hands over her belly and breasts. "Ohhhhhhh, yes! Ohhhhhh, yes!" he thought. Her skin was smooth and hot. Her breasts were firm and resilient to his grasp.

She had tilted her head back and it laid against his shoulder. Her breathing was coming hard and strong and she moaned as he caressed her. He took hold of her rock hard nipples and twisted them slowly and firmly until she screamed with lust through her gag. The heat of her body was driving him wild. He pushed her forward again.

He placed his hands hard on her back, pinning her in place. And then he fucked her, fucked her, fucked her, as hard and as fevered as a demon. He pounded his loins into her thighs. She moaned and groaned and rocked back at him fiercely, giving as good as he gave. He felt his explosion building. He wanted it to last, but it was too late to stop. "Ahhhhhhhhhhhh! Ahhhhhhhhhh! Ahhhh-hhhhhhh!" he called out as his meat began to throb and jerk inside her fevered tunnel. It set her off and she grunted back at him, loud and raucous. Her pussy clamped down on him again and again. It was a sensation he wanted to last forever.

But it didn't last forever. His spasms slowed. The pleasure waned. The girl gave out a great sigh and her body relaxed, devolving into putty. He collapsed over her, his heart still thumping, his breath short and deep. "Ohhhhhhhhhhh, yesssssssssss!" he sighed softly.

His cock detumesced quickly and slipped from her crevasse. He ran his hands down her torso and over her hips. He knew that he should be elated. He had just had one of the best fucks of his life. But a feeling of dreadful loss came over him. His body felt chilled. He knew he had to do it. He had to do it! There was no other choice! He felt back to his pants and scooped them up. He slipped the Walther out of its pocket. It felt like it weighed a hundred pounds. He slipped off the safety. He loaded a round into the chamber.

All he had to do was place it quickly against the back of her head and pull the trigger. She wouldn't feel a thing. It would be all over. But the thought of it filled him with a soul wrenching sorrow. He had done many horrible things in his day. This would be one of the worst. For the first time in his life he had gained a conception of what it meant to snuff out the life force of another human being. If he did it, he would be wracked with guilt and shame for the rest of his days.

But he had to do it! What else was he supposed to do? If he put her in the trunk there was still the risk that someone would hear her moaning and groaning. Just her presence near him felt like a terrible risk. He had to gain his freedom! He had to! And she stood in the way! She had to go! She had to!

It was then that he became conscious of her body wracking sobs. She knew what was coming. He hadn't wanted it to be like this. It was like that girl he strangled so many years ago, the one he had been ordered to kill. Her desperate, hysterical pleas had haunted him just about every day since then, especially in stir where he could not drown it out by acts of cruelty or violence on others. He didn't want the pair of women haunting him. He couldn't take it. He had blown it. He should have pulled the trigger right away. Now her sobs would echo in his mind forever.

He looked at her. Her whole body was heaving. "Awwwwww fuck!" he exclaimed to himself. He closed the safety and tossed the Walther aside.

He rose from the girl. He fished around in his pants for his smokes and lit one up. He was a fool. He knew it. Never in his life had he allowed sentimentality to interfere with what he had to do. Something was changing in him and he was not sure that he liked it.

He got the soda and what was left of the sandwiches and the snacks out of the car. He sat down near the girl. She was still kneeling like he left her, crouched over, her legs spread. Her sobbing had subsided some. What was he going to do with her? Now that it was clear that the FBI knew where he was going, it didn't matter if he let her go and she was discovered. There was nothing that she could tell them that they didn't already know. He could leave her here all tied up to a tree. It would be hours before she was able to work herself free and go for help. It would take at least an hour for her to walk out of the park they were in and she would have to do it naked and in the dark.

But something inside him didn't want to let her go. It was the same something that wouldn't let him kill her. He wanted her for himself. He wanted to fuck her again and again. He wanted to own her totally and absolutely for all time. He had thought the other day about how great it would be if he could take her to Mexico with him. He would get a little place and keep her prisoner there. Maybe, after a while, she would get used to him and not want to run away. And if she didn't or if he got tired of her, maybe he would dig her a hole out in the back where he could visit her from time to time and put flowers on her grave.

He cursed himself for having these kinds of thoughts. There was no way he could bring her into Mexico with him. He wasn't sure how even he was going to get over the border. He would have to leave her with the boys in Alamogordo. They would do the dirty work for him. At least then he could say that it wasn't him personally who pulled the trigger.

There was also the fact that if he let her go, her life would continue. She would live on to think horrible thoughts about him. She would think of him with hatred all of her days. She would tell people what an animal he was. And she would go back to that insipid boyfriend of hers. They would love each other and marry and have kids. The thought of her loving someone made him cringe with anger. He knew she would never love him. He wasn't sure he even wanted that. He probably didn't. But the idea of her finding solace and gentleness and fulfillment in someone else's arms was too bitter to take.

He was lying back on the ground looking up at the sky. The girl was where he left her. The sun had begun to sink below the horizon and the bulbous, spare clouds above were turning pinkish against a graying blue sky. The moon was actually out, about 40 degrees up in the sky in the east. There was a slight breeze, just cool enough to foretell the chilly spring night to come. He was still naked, but he had retrieved the pistol and had his clothes piled up next to him in case he needed to put them on in a hurry. He had finished off one of the two remaining peanut butter sandwiches and the rest of the chips.

Tonight was the night. It was, by his reckoning, about a quarter after 6. It would be dark in about 20 minutes. It was about 4 hours to Tularosa, maybe a little more. He should get there by 10:30 or so, with plenty of time to spare. The problem was that if the FBI was scouting the likely places he might show up, they would be on alert for the Merc he was driving. He needed to get another car.

He looked over at the girl. She surely couldn't ride in the front seat with him from here on in. She would have to go in the trunk. He felt a little sorry for having to put her there, but there was nothing else to do. He also felt a little sorry that he hadn't let her eat all day. There was one sandwich left and he didn't need it. He decided to give it to her.

She was lying kind of perpendicular to him near his feet. He was just able to reach her with his left foot. He raised it and gave her a little shove on her hip. "Come here," he told her.

Carly had been kneeling still, as still as she could be. When she had heard the sound of the bullet entering the chamber of the gun, she had bit down hard on the rubber ball in her mouth and tensed all her muscles. She was already sobbing uncontrollably. She didn't want to be, it just came over her. Deep in her terror and misery, she kept thinking to herself, "Oh, god, don't let it hurt! Don't let it hurt! Don't let it hurt!"

When she heard the sound of the gun hitting the ground and the man's *sotto voce* curse, she knew that he had changed his mind yet again. And then the crying really started. It had taken her a long time to stop. She didn't know whether to thank God for saving her or to curse him for allowing her torment to go on. She knew that she could not go on like this. Sooner or later, she would go bizarrely mad. She had been with the man for three full days, not counting the night he had kidnapped her. And three times he had commenced the process of snuffing out her life only to pull back at the last moment.

She realized, ironically, that her decision to let herself go and relish in what she thought would be the last bodily sensations she would experience in this life had almost certainly turned the tide. The thing that she despised herself for, her trigger like sexual response whenever he touched her, had saved her life. He was keeping her alive because the enjoyment he got from fucking her was outweighing his instinct for self-preservation.

When her crying died down, she realized that he was lying on the grassy ground near her. He was quiet and unmoving and that suited her fine. She had no energy to do more than to remain motionless too. The sun was warm on her naked back and felt good. There was just a gentle breeze that chilled her skin as the sun waned, but, despite the slight discomfort, that felt good too. Her mind could do no more than relish the physical experience of being alive.

She had no idea what the scenery around them was like. She knew that it was remote. The ground under her knees and forehead was soft. She imagined it as a peaceful, beautiful place. She imagined trees and flowers and gentle rolling hills. From time to time she heard the sound of a bird's cry and pictured it soaring above her, its wings outstretched. She didn't know for sure where they were, but if he was going to Mexico they must be in Texas by now. She didn't know what kind of birds they had in Texas, but she imagined something like a hawk with its mighty wings held perfectly still as it circled them scouting the ground for prey.

If only she could fly, she would flap her wings and fly away far, far, far up into the sky where no one could touch her, no one could capture her, no one could tie her and confine her and hold her prisoner. Her hands were still tied to her sides and it was as if her wings had been clipped and she was condemned to remain as she was, grounded and at the mercy of a larger, harsher predator.

She was startled when she felt his naked foot push at her hip and his voice command her attention. He told her to come to him. At first, she was of a mind to disobey him. "Fuck you," she thought. "Fuck you!" But then she thought better of it. If she became too much trouble, the paradigm which kept her alive might shift. If she stopped giving him pleasure, either through his use of her body or from the satisfaction he got from controlling every move that she made, or didn't make, it would be so much easier for him to pull the trigger next time. For despite her revulsion at being still subject to his depredations, she wanted to live.

She rose up and shuffled on her knees until she was facing where the voice had come from. Then she shuffled towards it. She kept going until her knee bumped up against his thigh. She waited obediently for his next order.

She felt him reach behind her head. He removed her blindfold for the first time since she had gotten into the car that morning. She looked quickly around. It was almost like she had imagined it, the crystal blue lake, the green grass, the blooming trees. And then, after only a second or two, just the maximum amount of time that she had learned he would tolerate as a delay in obedience, she directed her attention to him.

The only good thing about that day while she was

blindfolded was that she didn't have to look at him. Now, here he was, inches away from her, his dark eyes glaring into hers. Here was the man who had been a split second from killing her. Here was the man whose every whim she had to obey to the letter if she wished to remain alive. His power exuded from him. His physical presence loomed over her. She shivered and the familiar by now queasy emptiness rose up from her stomach. He was sitting up, his mammoth legs crossed. He shifted his body so it was facing hers.

She once again felt conscious of her nakedness before him. While the front of her short, denim skirt covered her sex and thighs, her breasts were bare and presented for his depredations. She was kneeling with her knees together and he told her gruffly to spread them. As she edged her knees apart, her skirt rode up higher on her soft, pale white thighs. "Wider," he told her, and to kneel straight up. She spread her knees apart as wide as they would go and raised herself up. He reached down and lifted her skirt and tucked it into the rope around her waist like he had that morning. Her naked sex was now subject to his view. He slipped his large, rough hand over it and began to stroke it softly.

He was watching her eyes as he stroked her. She didn't know where to put them and tried to look away, at the trees, the grass, the lake, anything, but he told her to look straight at him and, unhappily, she looked him in the eyes.

His gaze was piercing her as he manipulated her sex with his usual, deft touch. Carly wanted to resist her arousal, but, besides the fact that she knew she couldn't, it was in her best interests not to. If he wanted her wet and passionate, then that's what she would give him.

She allowed the dancing fingers to stoke her desire. It

wasn't long before she felt them sliding easily along the inner portion of her crevasse. When he began to softly tickle her love bud, she sighed and her body softened. He continued until the sensations became so pleasurable that her eyes closed of their own accord, her torso bent forward and she groaned.

"Mmmmmmmmmm, what am I going to do with you?" Jack thought to himself as he recorded the girl's signs of arousal. He could feel his prick stiffening. Then he recalled his intent to feed her. He rubbed his thick fingers several times up and down her labial divide, drawing another moan from her, and then pulled his hand away.

He tapped her face. Not hard, but enough to gain her attention. Her eyes sprung open, soft, unfocused eyes, blue and starry. "I said to keep your eyes open," he told her. She nodded at him and her face exhibited a grimace as if she feared punishment.

He reached his hand for her face and, startled, she pulled it away just a little. He reached down and took hold of her nipples and gave them a twist that drew a loud whine from her. "Don't flinch from me," he instructed her gruffly. "Don't you know better than that by now?"

Tears had formed in the corners of her eyes. She nodded her compliance.

He released her teats and reached again for her face. This time she stayed still, although he could see the look of fear in her eyes. He pushed his fingers into her mouth and edged out the blue rubber ball lodged inside it. He put it down on his shirt. The sandwich was next to him, wrapped in a paper towel and he pulled it out. He tore off a corner and held it out to her. "Eat," he said.

He fed her the sandwich piece by piece. She chewed each piece carefully and thoroughly. He could tell that she was relishing it and that she must have been very hungry, although she showed no gratitude for receiving it. Her eyes just kept watching him warily.

He didn't blame her for being suspicious of his motives. He had put her through a lot. But he couldn't let thoughts of her sensibilities affect him. That defeated the whole purpose of owning her. And there was something satisfying about seeing the evident pleasure she got from so small a thing as a peanut butter sandwich. He had done her a favor really, he thought. Every sensation she was permitted to have was like a nugget of gold in the midst of a huge, sere desert. Without him, she would experience nothing, like on the ride today. He was reducing her to the bare essentials and she would appreciate them all the more because of their rarity.

She was so pretty, all naked and bound. Her breasts swayed each time he forced her to lean forward to receive another tidbit. Her hairless pussy was so bare, demure and available, it was hard to resist tossing away the rest of the sandwich and fucking her instead. Its soft folds promised hot delight within.

And her mouth. Each time she opened it widely to receive his beneficence, he thought of its deft playfulness and had to suppress the urge to feed her his cock instead.

When the sandwich was gone, he gave her some soda to wash it down with. She drank it greedily. The bottle was almost empty and he finished it off and tossed it aside. It was just turning dusk. The low light made the color of her short, red hair, seem soft and pastel like. Her pale skin was turned even whiter. The landscape had turned into mellow greens and browns. The sky in the west glowed a faint red. Her areolas had turned dark, almost maroon.

He reached out a hand and cupped a breast, squeezing it softly. His cock gave a little stir. He pinched the nipple lightly until it turned hard and then did the other. She was looking at him apprehensively. He couldn't decide whether to use her pussy or her mouth. She flicked her tongue out nervously, licking her lips. That decided it for him. Her mouth.

He raised himself up on his knees and took hold of the hair on the back of her head. He gave her head a gentle push downwards and she, understanding at once his intent, leaned over the rest of the way, nibbled on his cock to gain purchase on it and then slid her soft lips over it until it was subsumed within.

She sucked him slowly and purposively. His hands rested softly on her head. The hot moistness made his whole body soften even as his cock hardened into rigidity. She moved her lips up and down his length, making him sigh, and then suckled the end, running her tongue along his glans. His body shimmered with pleasure. Tonight, he knew, was fraught with danger to him. If he was spotted by John Law, he was fucked. But he would worry about that when the time came. For now, he was in bliss and nothing else mattered.

When he had caressed her breast with that look in his eye, Carly had known that he was going to do something. Her pussy gave a little burn at the thought of it. His hand was hot and her skin cool. Oh, she despised herself for the feelings his attentions gave her, but she could not deny them, a fault that had saved her life more than once. She hadn't meant to show him her tongue. It was a nervous reaction born of anxiousness and humiliation. She realized her error at once but it was too late to do anything about it. When he took hold of her hair, she didn't fight it. She lowered her head and took his cock in her mouth.

The moment it entered her, her body shifted gears.

That devil that had been haunting her emerged and took hold. The man's cock was large and strong, forcefully masculine. The feel and taste of it filled her whole consciousness. When she heard him sigh, she reveled in the sound. She could almost feel what he felt, sensed what he sensed. She gave a silent sigh of her own.

She could fool herself and think that she was merely doing what she needed to do to save her life. While it was true that her ministrations to his sexual need had done that, there was oh so much more to it. It seemed so right to serve him this way, her hands bound to uselessness, on her knees, his bulk towering over her. His manhood filled her so well, like her mouth had been made for it. His hands on her head, a controlling but not forceful touch, made clear whose desire was being fulfilled, who was the subservient, who was the user and who was being used.

Her pussy had turned so hot that she yearned to put her hand on it, to jiggle it into fruition, to accelerate her excitement. But the fact that she couldn't, that only he had the power and therefore the right to touch it, to caress it, to use it, made her lust burn all the more. She had descended into a state of pure functionality, a fuckslut, a whore, a trollop, a slattern, a bundle of nerves and sinews and flesh all wholly dedicated to the incitement of desire and the reception of its fruits.

It was a state so pure, so unidimensional that all of her prior conceptions of who she was and what she was were blasted away. It was as near to complete ecstasy as she could ever hope to attain. And even though she despised and hated the man rabidly for what he had done to her, she knew that without him she could never have experienced the total merger of her mind and body into a single, vibrating, exhilarating thought of pure, unadulterated lust.

She washed the man's prick with her lips and tongue lovingly as if it was a blessed object. She licked it, suckled it, kissed it, taunted it with her tongue. She pushed her head down as far as it would go, pressing it deeply into her throat as if with just a little more effort she could make it come out the other end, fuck her mouth and her pussy at the same time.

When she felt him tense, she relented. When he sighed with pleasure's suffusion, she sped up. When his hands tightened on her head, she drew her lips back as far as they would go and suckled and tickled the end until his accelerating lust forced him to push her head down again so he could feel her wet heat along its length.

When his hips began a relentless thrust back and forth, when he began to groan, when his fingers buried themselves into her hair, grasping it tightly until her roots burned, she knew that he was going to come. She firmed her lips tightly upon the shaft, pressed her tongue against it so that her mouth made a tight, little tunnel. He gave a rough shout and his instrument began to spasm and jerk inside her mouth. She moved her head back and forth, exciting it.

"Auuuuuuugh! Auuuuuuuuugh! Auuuuuuuuuuuugh!" she heard him groan. A split second later, her mouth was awash with his acrid cum. It was thick and cloying and hot. She let it slide down her throat as she relished the throbbing of his meat, triumphant that she had fulfilled her one and only function so obviously well.

He kept his cock inside her mouth until it softened. She continued to suckle it gently until he slipped it out. He held her there in place for a moment, bent over and breathing deeply. She closed her eyes and relished her satisfaction.

He finally rose and, taking hold of her hair, went to

his feet, taking her along with him. It was almost dark. Her status as his prisoner was resumed and she was, as always, filled with shame at the sensations and thoughts that he had engendered in her. He was a brute, an evil, remorseless, psychopathic brute. And she was at his mercy. And her life existed on a razor's edge. She was filled with fear and self-hatred. She was going mad, she knew it. How could she be so riven with lust, so utterly devoted to his pleasure at one moment, and so filled with hatred of him at the next? Yes, she was going mad.

Jack dressed quickly. The blowjob had been stupendous, a show stopper, but he had to hurry now. He wanted to be in Tularosa in plenty of time to make his contact. He had spent enough time here.

From a woodsman's habit he picked up the empty soda bottle and tossed it into the back of the car. He brought out the gag he had been using on the girl, filled her docile mouth with it and belted it tightly behind her head. He then pulled her to the rear of the car and bent her over the trunk. He untied the rope that had confined her hands to her hips, removed the remnants of her shirt and refastened them behind her back, clipping her leather bracelets together first. He fastened her ankle bracelets together so she couldn't run off and left her standing there while he went back to the front of the car, opened the driver's door and unlatched the trunk.

When he came back, the girl was crying. She knew where she was going. It was a poor reward for such a good blowjob, but there was nothing he could do about it. He took hold of the ring in the front of her collar and shook it harshly. "Listen," he said. "I don't want to hear a single sound out of you. If I do, I'll stop the car, open the trunk and put a bullet in you. Then you'll be quiet for good. Understand?"

Tears were flowing down her face. She nodded dolefully.

"This will be your last chance to piss for a long while. Do it now," he told her. He released her ankles, pulled her away from the car and held her arm while she squatted. When she was done, he took a remnant of her light blue, flowered t-shirt and wiped her with it. He brought her back to the car and turned her so that her thighs were against the bumper and bent her body over. Then he took hold of her lower legs and lifted her in. He maneuvered her until she was belly down, refastened her ankles and then lifted her legs, tying them off to her wrists with a triple knot. He went back to the passenger compartment of the car and retrieved two of the shorter lengths of rope. When he returned to the trunk, he used them to bind her elbows and knees together. She squealed when her elbows touched and he cuffed her, telling her to be quiet.

He went back to where they had fucked and retrieved the little blue ball she had worn in her mouth all day and the blindfold. He put the ball in his pocket and walked back to the trunk. She looked up at him miserably when he reappeared and her eyes cringed when she saw the blindfold. She issued a low moan of unhappiness when he put it on her. It would be dark in the trunk anyway, so maybe it wasn't necessary, but he might not want her to see what was going on when he finally got her out.

Before closing the lid, he took a moment to look at her. She was a treasure. His treasure. She looked so delectably helpless. Her little blue denim skirt had ridden up high on her thighs showing off just a little of her rounded rear cheeks. Her hands were flexing and unflexing in nervous frustration. He pushed her over so that she was lying on her side facing him. The light from the trunk shined down on her, as if she were displayed on some sort of stage. Her skirt had bunched up near her waist and he could see her delightful pussy and thighs. Her chest was heaving and she was sobbing, making her breasts bob. She was a treasure all right.

He leaned over and disconnected the trunk light and then shut the lid with a 'thump!' He got back in the car, fired up the engine and rolled the car back onto the trail.

CHAPTER FOUR

The parking lot of the shopping center was almost deserted. There were a few cars left, but the stragglers were coming out one by one. Already the floodlights from the more remote areas had been darkened. He was sitting behind the wheel of a shiny, new, dark red, Lexus GS 850. The cream colored seats were soft and padded. The interior was spacious and elegant. He was playing the car stereo and the sound was exquisite. When he had started up the engine, he could barely hear it and what he did hear sounded more like a purr. Cars had come a long way since he had been sent up. He had never been in a Lexus before, although he had heard of them, seen the ads on TV.

Next to him, kneeling on the floor of the passenger side, her torso spread across the seat, her wrists bound behind her, was the owner. She was stylish too. Jack had watched her emerge from the service exit from the mall and had followed her quietly to her car. When she took out her keys to open the door, he had been atop her in an instant, his bowie knife under her chin. He had considered using the Walther, which he had in his pants pocket. But women always found the prospect of being all sliced up much more harrowing. Within a minute he had gotten her into the car, bound her wrists and, in the midst of a piteous plea, had shoved the blue ball into her mouth and covered her lips with a 8" long strip of duct tape.

The woman looked to be about 38 or 39. She had fine, long brown hair that hung down almost to her waist. She was wearing a stylish, light tan, cotton skirt that went just below her knees and a luminous, dark beige satin blouse. Around her neck was a slim, golden rope chain with a diamond studded pendant. There were large, glittery stones in her ears too and a large one on her left hand embedded in gold. On her feet were 3" high heeled sandals of fine leather. Her toes were painted turquoise as were the nails on her hands. She had fine, quality features, elegant and sophisticated. Her makeup had been light, a little eye liner, dark red lipstick, maybe a little rouge on her cheeks, just a hint.

Jack had her figured for one of the store owners, probably a high end ladies fashion shop. Her key chain had about a dozen keys on it. And Jack had struck gold again. In her banana yellow, all leather Versace tote bag had been the day's cash receipts, about $12,000. She also had a petit, cute little .25 caliber Colt with an ivory handgrip and a can of pepper spray. The Colt was fully loaded. It was too bad for her that she didn't get a chance to use it.

He had parked the Merc on the outer edge of the parking lot near a stand of trees. Even with all the lights on the area had been shaded and dark. The girl was still in the trunk. He had warned her not to make a sound and told her that he would be back in a little while. He was waiting for the rest of the cars to leave, or at least most of them. Although the Lexus would probably stand out when he went to the bar in Tularosa, it was miles better than riding up in the Merc for which there were undoubtedly bulletins out all over the airwaves.

The woman had refined taste in music, not exactly Jack's cup of tea, but good to listen to. Right now he was playing a CD by some crooner and it was melodious and calming. For him at least. The woman kept sniffling and he could see that she was shaking. He hadn't decided what to do with her. He could slice her throat and leave her in the Merc's trunk, but it seemed a waste. She was grade 'A' material, although much older than what was usually put on the market, so maybe an A-. But she had fine hips and smooth, shapely legs. Her breasts were not what you would call large, but that was probably a good thing given her age. They would still hang firm and ripe.

And she had a marvelous ass. He had lifted the back of her skirt to take a look at it. She was wearing white, silk panties that gripped the contours of her firm, round rear cheeks and very light beige, self supporting stockings with lacy tops. He needed more barter material anyway. In a good market she would bring a good $10-$15,000, wholesale. On the street she would be worth a lot more, but he wouldn't have the opportunity to shop her around. In a forced sale, which was his situation, he estimated he could get anywhere from $5,000-$7,500. The boys in Alamogordo would give him at least that much, he was sure. They would know how to turn a profit on her. No, he would keep her.

There were only 2 or 3 cars left. More over-heads had gone out. They were down to a few around the outside of the stores. It was about 8:45 and he was about 40 miles outside of Albuquerque. He had spotted the shopping center from the road and knew that it was just what he was looking for. The wedding ring meant that she had a hubby at home, but he probably wouldn't report her missing for 3 or 4 hours at least. By the time a report was taken, and if he could convince the cops that she hadn't gone out bar hopping or was shacked up with a lover somewhere, it would take another few hours for reports to get out. A patrol car would be sent to the shopping center to scope out if her car was there, if the hubby hadn't checked that out already, and the cop might or might not spot the Merc. Even then, he might not make the connection. And by then, Jack expected to be safe.

He eased the luxury car into drive. He had been waiting in another dark, shaded area of the lot, in a position where he could keep an eye on the Merc. If anybody had gone snooping around it, he could have just taken off and left the girl behind. Having the two cars next to each other while he waited would have been too suspicious. And he didn't want to make the transfer of the girl and his goods until the possibility of witnesses had been reduced to about zero.

Lights out, he cruised slowly over to the Merc and backed in next to it. This way the transfer of the girl from trunk to trunk and would take place behind the cars where it would be harder for any onlookers to see what was going on. He turned off the engine. He had a longer length of rope in his pocket and he used it now to connect the unhappy woman's ankles with about 18" of lead between them. Before getting out of the car, he carefully removed her glittery earrings, the diamond wedding ring and the necklace and pendant. On her left wrist was a band of gold with a cameo silhouette of an elegant young girl embedded in it. It looked valuable so he took that too.

He popped the trunk and, grabbing the lady's handbag, got out and walked to the back. He fished around in the bag for her cell phone and put it in his pocket. He would get rid of it somewhere down the road. He tossed the handbag into the trunk. It only took him a few seconds to unscrew the trunk light. Looking around, seeing nobody, he went to the passenger side and opened the door. He took hold of her arm and told her to get out. She struggled, sniffling and crying, but she managed to do it. He hustled her to the back of the car, as fast as her bound ankles would go. When she saw the open trunk, she put 2 and 2 together and started to whine and moan. He slapped her and told her to shut up.

Once he had her in the spacious trunk, he untied one ankle and then brought them both together, tying them off. He then bound them to her hands. Taking a hold of the woman's chestnut brown hair, he pulled back her head. Her eyes were wide with terror.

"I'm only going to say this to you once," he told her gruffly. "If you make any noise, I'll stop the car and slit your throat. So if you want to live out the night, you'd better be quiet. Do you understand?"

The woman nodded her head up and down rapidly.

"Good," he said.

He lowered the trunk lid but didn't close it and then stepped over to the Merc. He didn't have the key so he had to open the driver's door and use the lever to open the trunk. He had turned the overhead light in the passenger compartment off. He shut the door and went around to the back of the car.

He had already taken out the trunk light for the Merc and he was just able to make out the girl inside. Her naked skin from her waist up gave off a slight reflected glow. After untying her ankles, he drew her out. Quickly, he brought her over to the Lexus and pushed her in. The Lexus' trunk was spacious and there was plenty of room in there for them both. He reaffixed the girl's ankles to her wrists and closed the lid. The girl had barely made a sound when he moved her. She was smart.

He had debated whether to bring the camping gear, but had decided against it. He brought the bag that held the chains he had been using on the girl, the bag of handguns he had stolen from the Army Navy store back in Wisconsin and the bags of clothes and the rest of his cigarettes. He put them all in the back seat of the Lexus.

There was an office park next door to the mall. He had thought about it and decided that it would be better if he parked the Merc somewhere else than in the mall parking lot. This would make it more difficult to link the woman's disappearance with him and would delay the law having the knowledge that he had switched cars.

He got into the Merc, turned over the engine and drove it to the office park. The parking lot went all around the three identical, six storey buildings. He parked the Merc in the back near the dumpsters and then walked back the 300 yards to the shopping mall lot. The Lexus was where he had left it. He took the car key off of the large chain and tossed the rest of the keys in the back seat. He started the car. In the console between the front seats were a few CD's. He picked out a Kenny Rankin album and put it in the player. As the perfectly balanced, quadraphonic sound filled the passenger compartment, he lit a smoke and resumed his journey.

Two hours later, he passed through the small town of Tularosa. There had been no sound from the females in the trunk. He had turned off the stereo from time to time just to make sure. The Lexus was sturdily built and they would have had to be shouting at the top of their lungs for any sound to escape. But it was best to be safe.

Tularosa was a quaint little town, with small shops along the main road and a few traffic lights. A cop was stationed in a cruiser at one corner. He looked warily at Jack as he pulled away from the light as it turned green, but he did not follow him. Jack had pulled the Walther from his pocket just in case. He remembered what the guy who called himself Moondog had told him. If he had to shoot it out with the cops, he should just keep going. Jack knew that if he had to shoot it out with the cops it was all over for him. Ten thousand cops would descend on the area. Eventually, he would be tracked down. Since he had already decided that he wasn't going back to prison, that meant he would have to make a last stand. His run, as sweet as it had been, would be at an end. So he wanted to avoid an incident with the cops at all costs.

About a mile and a half outside of Tularosa he passed the bar called Pete's. It was a small place with a well-lit sign like Moondog had said. Rather than pull in the parking lot, he drove past it. He tried to see if there were any cars with people in them watching who came in and out. He couldn't see anyone, but that didn't mean that they weren't there.

This was the most dangerous part of his journey. If Moondog was dealing out of this bar, the cops might have a good idea about it. They might just be biding their time before they rolled him up. And if they knew that Moondog spent every night here and he was a Rogues member, they would have the place staked out.

But all of this must have entered Moondog's calculations when he told Jack to meet him here. The guy wouldn't voluntarily put himself in the soup. So maybe it was safe.

It was a tough decision to make. The problem was that he had no other strategy for getting over the border. He had over $20,000 now. Maybe he could go to San Diego and buy himself a ride on a fishing boat or something. But he would have to go there and make contact with someone to lead him to the right guys. There was an LA Rogues chapter, but that was probably being watched as closely as the one in Alamogordo.

He pulled to the side of the road. His hands were sweating. He lit a smoke. He turned off the stereo and leaned back in the plush seat. He had already gotten much more than he had ever thought he would as a result of his breakout. He had had three days of rockin' and rollin'. He had breathed free air. He had decided where to go and when to go. He had cooked himself some great meals and had actual, fresh brewed coffee. And the girl had been magnificent. That went without saying.

This connection was his best bet for escape to Mexico. It was right here, less than a half mile away. He had to take a risk at some point. Even if he paid off some fisherman to drop him off in the Baja, the guys might just take his money and turn him in. Or he could find himself swimming in the Pacific with a bullet in him several miles out to sea. No, this was where he would make his move. At least he could trust Moondog as a fellow Rogues member. All in all, that was the deciding factor.

There was hardly any traffic on the road. A tractor-trailer was coming northbound and Jack waited for it to pass before turning the Lexus around. He was tempted to drive by the bar again, but the red luxury car was so conspicuous it would look very suspicious to anyone who was watching. He pulled into the gravel lot and drove to a spot in the back of the parking lot. He backed into a spot on the very edge so he could make a quick getaway if he had to. Also, it would be less likely that someone would walk by the car and hear anything in case the females in the trunk somehow got their mouths loose and started screaming. He popped the trunk and went back to take a look at them just to make sure. They were both as he had left them. They were both alive and as well as they could be. The new woman looked up at him with doleful, hopeful eyes. She began a whine when she saw he was going to close the trunk again. It was cut short by the lowering of the lid.

The bar was a one story affair. It was constructed of red adobe bricks with narrow, horizontal windows in the front and had a wooden porch. There were a few choppers in the lot along with five or six pickups of varying age and condition and a few junker cars. Two couples dressed in denims and black t-shirts were drinking long necks on the porch. Jack nodded to them nonchalantly as he passed. They nodded suspiciously back.

He went through the solid, wooden door and stepped into the bar. There were a few ragged looking guys playing pool and a couple of people of similar mien sitting at the large, round, polished wooden tables that sat over to one side. The jukebox was playing something from ZZ Top. The bar was about 30' long and several men and a few women were hunkered over it. There was a mirror in behind the bar, old and tarnished. Mounted above it was the pale white skull of a steer.

It was dark inside. Various stenciled signs on the walls established the rules of the place as it pertained to credit (none), spitting on the floor (not allowed), gambling (not allowed either) and fighting (take it outside). A poster on the wall near the pool table had a list of house rules. Four quarters were lined up on the table. The guy who had been shooting had stopped to watch Jack as he entered, but after a second or two went back to his game. He was a tall fellow with a bristly beard under his chin up to the end of his jawline. He was wearing a rolled up, red and white checkered bandana around his neck. Another fellow, shorter, with a bushy moustache was standing a few feet away from him leaning on his cue.

Jack bellied up to the bar. The bartender was a heavyset, tough looking chick who looked about 40 or so. She was wearing a faded red t-shirt with white lettering that spelled out in fancy script, "Pete's Place". Her oversized breasts pushed the letters out so far that it was hard to read them. She was wearing faded jeans and black cowboy boots. Her hair was stringy and yellowish. She had been leaning over the bar when Jack came in, talking to a man in the corner. He was just a little bit bigger and rounder than her and there were two 7 oz. glasses of draft and empty shot glasses in front of them. Jack figured the guy as a boyfriend. He slid onto a stool.

The bartender, after sharing a laugh with the fellow in the corner, strode lazily over to where Jack sat.

"What'll it be?" she asked him when she finally arrived.

"Gimme a short draft and a double shot of Jim Beam," Jack told her.

She went over to the beer taps and poured Jack a 7 oz. glass of Coors. She tossed a round, cardboard coaster on the bar in front of him and placed the beer on it. It had a 2 inch layer of foam on the top and the coldness made the glass start to sweat right away. She took an old fashioned glass and plunked it down next to the beer and filled it ¾ with Jim Beam. Jack threw a ten on the bar. She picked it up, giving Jack the once over and brought it to the register on the back bar. The register gave a little 'ching!' and the drawer popped out. She shoved in the ten and brought out 2 quarters, a single and a five and returned to Jack. She tossed the bills on the bar next to his drinks and placed the quarters on them one by one.

"How about you?" Jack asked.

She smiled. "Sure," she answered. She brought her beer glass over to the tap, drained it off and poured herself a Coors. She placed it down on a coaster next to Jack's and picked up a shot glass from a stack near the taps. From the back bar she brought over a bottle of Wild Turkey and poured herself a shot. After replacing the bottle, she ambled back to where Jack was sitting. She picked up the shot glass and proffered it to Jack as if making a toast. Jack picked up his Jim Beam and touched it to her glass. They both shot back their drinks. The woman picked up her chaser and downed it all in one swallow. "Thanks," she said. She picked up the five and the coaster.

"Keep it," Jack told her. She nodded and went back to the register. She rang up $2.75 and put the change in a shiny brass spittoon next to it.

"Another?" she asked Jack.

"Sure," Jack answered.

She poured Jack another double shot of Jim Beam.

"On the house," she said.

Jack expressed his thanks.

He nursed his drinks for a little while. There was a TV up in the corner with the sound off. It was showing some cops and robbers drama. The pool game ended. The tall guy with the beard won. The smaller guy came over to the bar and bought two Lone Star long necks and gave one to the winner. Another fellow, with curly, dirty blond hair and wearing a light yellow t-shirt under a denim vest picked up a quarter and placed it in the slot. The balls dropped and rolled noisily to the end of the table, clicking and clacking as they jumbled together there. The blond guy, he looked in his late thirties, racked up and the big fellow broke. The nine ball dropped in the corner.

"Big ones," the blond man said. The tall one nodded and began to scope out vulnerable striped balls. Jack watched as he skillfully dropped four of them and then missed on a tough bank shot on the 15 to the side pocket.

Jack was getting nervous. It was a long time to leave the women untended in the trunk. The Walther and a spare clip were in the pocket of his green camouflaged pants. He kept eying the door as if he expected John Law to come rushing in, blazing away. He finished his draft and his Jim Beam and asked for another round. He placed a twenty on the bar. This time, when the woman came back, he asked her if Moondog was there.

She looked at Jack suspiciously. She paused as if trying to decide whether she should acknowledge the existence of anyone with that name. "He went out," she told him finally.

"Do you know when he'll be back," Jack asked, trying to disguise his tension.

"By and by, I guess," the woman replied. She went back to the corner and her boyfriend.

Jack bided his time nervously, splitting his attention between the pool table and the soundless TV screen. The jukebox was playing a variety of rocker and country tunes going from Led Zeppelin to Waylon Jennings. There was a strung out looking chick at the end of the bar opposite from where the bartender and her boyfriend were having their conference wearing a halter top and short-short cutoff jeans. She was drinking a mug of Coke in which the ice had melted long ago. Jack saw a guy go up to the tall pool player with the beard, hand him some cash and then disappear with the woman into the back room. They came back out in about 15 minutes, the man looking happy and relaxed and the girl just a tad more dismal.

A heavy despondency settled about Jack. He had been so elated to have been able to find the bar and enter it undiscovered by law enforcement and now it seemed that it had all been for naught. The west coast option started looking better and better, except now he had two women to worry about getting rid of and was driving a car that stuck out like a sore thumb. He started ruing having left the camping gear behind. If he got enough provisions, he could set out into the desert and try to hike to the border.

If all these Mexicans managed to find a way in past the border guards, maybe he could find a way out.

Jack saw another guy who had just come in go up to the tall, bearded guy, speak to him for a second and then hand him some cash. This time, the tall guy brought the guy into the back room himself. When they came out, the tall guy went back to his pool game and the new guy left without having a drink.

Jack was now on his third drink. He was starting to get a little woozy, not a good thing. He had just about decided to leave when the bearded guy, having finally lost a game by scratching on the eight ball, came up to the bar and ordered two long necks and a shot of tequila from the bartender. He gave one of the longnecks to the victor. Jack noted that he hadn't paid for the drinks. The bartender went back to her corner. The big guy stayed standing next to Jack. The bartender had left a lime and a salt shaker with the tequila shot. The tall guy performed the ritual and downed his shot. He winced slightly as the liquor went down and then turned to Jack.

"I'm Moondog," he said.

"I kinda figured," Jack replied.

"I'm just trying to make this as subtle as possible. These people in here know who I am and where I come from, and most of 'em know what would happen to them if they dimed me out, but on something big like you there's no way to tell."

"Sure," Jack answered him. "But I'm getting kind of nervous here and I've got some goods in my car, if you know what I mean."

"You mean the blond? I saw her on TV, she's a hot little number. "

"And there's another one too. I had to switch cars, and, well, you know."

Moondog laughed. "You're a one man recruiting agency," he said. "We oughta let you drive around for the rest of the week and by then you'll have collected a truckfull."

"And maybe not," Jack said. "Listen," he added, "I'm as hot as a tin pistol out here. I need some sanctuary. I don't mind kibitzin', but maybe later, you know?"

"Sure, sure," Moondog said. "But I just gotta tell ya, the way you busted out and all that, I mean, you're the man, you know what I mean?"

"Thanks, but...."

"Okay, okay," Moondog replied. "I gotta lock up my bitch first or she might run off. Last time it took me three days to find her and then after I paid her back for runnin' off, she was out of action for a week."

Jack looked over at the girl. She looked maybe 24 or 25, but she had a lot of mileage on her. Moondog seemed to read Jack's mind.

"And anyways, I'm dumping her off to a guy who runs street whores in Santa Fe at the end of the week. I got a little Salvadoran girl all lined up. Less trouble. You know what I mean? My boys have been breaking her in for a couple of weeks. She's about ripe by now."

"Nice to hear it," Jack replied dully.

"I'll be right back," Moondog said.

Jack watched him go up to the whore in the corner. He spoke to her briefly and she got up from her stool. Moondog held the door for her as she walked unhappily into the back room. Moondog followed her in and came back out a few minutes later. "I'll be back," he said to the bartender.

Jack followed him out of the bar. "Where's your car?" Moondog asked. And then he said as they walked into the parking lot, "No, don't tell me. It's the Lexus, right?"

"Yeah," Jack answered.

"You do know how to go in style," Moondog said, "but you lack something in subtlety."

"It was the best I could do," Jack answered.

"The broads in the trunk?"

"Yeah."

"I'll bet its getting a little stuffy in there by now. Just make sure you don't stop off and pick up any more on our way outta here," he joked.

Jack was not in a joking mood. He just stared back.

"Okay," Moondog said, "here's the drill. I'm not taking you in. I don't rank that high, yet. I'm taking you to a guy, his name's Mouse. He'll take you in. So just follow me, okay?"

"Okay," Jack answered.

"Man oh man!" Moondog blurted out. "I can't believe it's really you! There'll be makin' songs up about you! Say hello to those *senoritas* down Mexico way for me. Maybe I'll get down there someday and we can toss back a few, huh?"

"That'd be fine," Jack replied impatiently.

"See ya around, partner," Moondog said, holding out his hand.

Jack took it and shook it.

He went up to the Lexus and popped the trunk. It was dark outside, but he could see his two captives squiggling inside. He reached in and checked their bindings to make sure they were secure. The older one was mewing and crying. The other was silent.

"It won't be long now," he told them, more for the younger one's benefit than the older. He chided himself for not remembering her name. It was Carolyn, he thought, or something like that. Her pocketbook was in the back seat of the car. He would have to look it up again. He would be damned if he would ask her.

He closed the lid, got in the driver's seat and started the car. Moondog had started his chopper and with a loud roar he advanced out of the parking lot turning right. Jack followed him.

"It won't be long now," Carly thought. Not long for what? Whatever it was, it wouldn't be good for her. Nor for the woman who was lying next to her. Carly assumed that she was the owner of the new car they were in. The man had solved the problem of everybody knowing what car he was driving pretty fast. And he had taken another prisoner. What did that mean for her?

The woman had barely stopped whining and sobbing since Carly had been plopped down next to her. She squirmed and jerked and moaned and groaned almost the whole time. Carly wanted somehow to shut her up. The only good thing about being shut up in the trunk had been the quiet and the fact that she could take her mind off the presence of the man for a little while. During the ride, when she had been alone in the trunk of the other car, she had, after a half hour or so of self pity and intermittent crying, deadened herself. It was the only way to deal with the solitude, the confinements and the looming unknown. Being with this other woman had prevented her from doing that. It made riding in the trunk twice as miserable.

She had had the feeling that they were close to some destination the man had plotted out for himself even before he had announced it. The car had been still and quiet for a long time. She had deduced that he was meeting someone, probably a member of the gang he was a member of, the Rogues, as the newsman had called it. She had never heard of them, although she had heard of others, the Pagans and, of course, the Hell's Angels. She assumed they were, as an aggregate, as cruel, corrupt and remorseless as her captor. What would they do to her once they got to their headquarters or hideout or whatever? Would he turn her over to them? Was she to be the price of his liberty, an exchange for their help in getting him to Mexico?

The presence of the other woman certainly raised that as a possibility. Her mere presence in the trunk of the car instead of dead in the trunk of the other meant that the man had kept her for some further purpose. He never did anything on a whim. It made no sense otherwise since, so close to his goal, he would have to dispose of her soon anyway.

Carly's blood ran cold. The ending she had so much feared was rapidly approaching. She had served her purpose, at least as far as the man was concerned. Now he would be getting rid of her. But what fate would she meet at the hands of his friends? Would they use her until they got tired of her and then bury her somewhere out in the desert? They couldn't keep her around forever. Sooner or later she would escape. They couldn't let that happen.

For the hundredth time, she struggled at her bonds and suppressed a wail of unhappiness. She had been in the trunk for hours, had endured utter loneliness and dismal fear for so long. Now, as she felt the car wheels running again along the asphalt beneath her, her destiny was coming closer and closer with each passing second. How long did she have? An hour? Two? Probably less. It was so horribly frustrating to think that their pictures were all over the news, the whole country was looking for him, and yet he had slipped by them, the police, the FBI, everyone, so easily. She had thought all day, while she rode up front all bound, silenced and blind, and later, riding so cruelly confined in the trunk, of all the cars they passed and which passed them. Normal, everyday people were in them, people who had control of their own lives, their own future, and her an abject prisoner, mere feet away from them, with none.

They undoubtedly listened to the news with a sense of outrage and sympathy for her, remarking to one another how awful it was that something so terrible should happen. They undoubtedly congratulated themselves on their safety, their immunity from such horrible things that always happened to other, less fortunate beings. In a week or two it would pass from their consciousness. "It's too bad they never found that girl," they would think, and then forget. "What a horrible thing to have happened," they would say to each other, and then move on with their lives. And the police officers and FBI men and women who had engaged in the search for her would move on to their next case and the details of her abduction and mysterious disappearance would be filed away in some cabinet to be looked at every once in a while wistfully. "It's too bad," they would say. "It's a shame."

More than once she had felt sorry that the man hadn't killed her. Her torment would be over. Neither the man nor the men he was going to deliver her to would be able to hurt her any more. And the worst part of it was that she probably was wholly without any power to force them to foreshorten her ordeal. She had no power to resist them. They would beat her and torture her until she submitted. And she would submit, just as she had submitted to the man who had captured her, so frightened of the violence he could mete out that she could not summon one iota of rebellion. And he was just one. It would be all the worst when there were many.

The woman next to her would not stop whining and moaning. It was driving Carly mad. Her only recompense was the knowledge that she would soon experience the things that she had. She would surrender herself too. They would use her and fuck her and whip her. They would strip her naked and bind her with chains and ropes. "Then she'll have something to cry about," Carly thought. And maybe, just maybe, they would pay less attention to her as a result.

Moondog led Jack along a series of two lane county roads, turning here and there. Jack kept a close watch in his rear view mirror for any signs that they were being followed. Every time a car appeared behind them, sooner or later it would turn off or they would turn off and the other vehicle would go on straight. Jack was so nervous his hands were sweating. Sanctuary was so close he could almost taste it. For three days he had lived on the razor's edge, fearing that any minute somehow he would be found out and the final showdown erupt. He wished he had asked Moondog how long it would take to get where they were going. He wanted to know how long he had to sweat it out.

And he thought of the girl. It had been a magical time he had spent with her, just the two of them in their own universe. Once they got to the safe house, all that would come to an end. The other men would see her and want her. That bothered him. He didn't want anybody using her until he was done with her. What happened to her after that was not his affair, but he didn't want to be thinking of the other men using her, fucking her, while he was nearby, where he would have to see her afterwards and wonder whether she panted and moaned and shuddered with pleasure for them as she had done with him. He would be expected to share her though. And though he had rank, and rank had its privileges, it was really former rank and maybe notoriety. That would only take him so far. And once he arrived there, he would be utterly dependent on them. If he crossed them, disrespected them, they could find a hole in the desert for him too.

About 40 minutes after they had begun their ride, Moondog veered his bike off the road and stopped in front of a small, run down diner. He pulled into the parking lot, stopped his bike for a second and waved. Then he edged the bike out to the road again and went back the way they had come. A few moments later, a man stepped out of the dark as if he had sprung up from the depths. He tapped on the passenger side window with his ring. Jack popped open the door locks and he got in.

"Mouse," he said. He was wearing a green military style jacket and jeans. He put out his hand and Jack shook it briefly.

"Turn right outta here. I'll tell ya where to turn," he said.

Jack followed his directions. He kept checking his rear view mirror to see if they were being followed. After a while, he noticed a beat up old pick up trailing them about 3 or 4 hundred yards behind.

"There's somebody behind us," Jack said.

"That's one of our guys," Mouse replied. "He's just making sure we don't have a tail. He'll drop off in a little bit."

Jack accepted the explanation and continued to drive. His heart was pounding and his mouth was dry. "Get a hold of yourself, Jack," he told himself. It was funny, when he had no future, or when the possibility of having one was still remote, resting largely on the chance that he would not be spotted by law enforcement, he had been almost calm, having overcome all of his anxieties. Having the girl to fuck probably had a lot to do with that. But now that there was a good probability that his life would go on, he was as nervous as a kitten.

How would he live? He didn't speak a single word of Spanish except for maybe *adios* and *via con Dios*. He had a little bit of money, and he would probably get more for the woman he had kidnapped, the jewels, the guns he had stolen and the car, but money had a habit of running out fast. He needed some form of transportation, preferably a bike. He needed a place to stay. He would need to have some social connections with somebody or he would go mad really fast. And then there were the Mexican police. If they thought there was more profit for them in turning him in, he would be gone in a New York minute. Somehow, he needed to be able to finance the cost of their inaction.

And pussy. He needed that too. He knew there was plenty of it down Mexico way, and it was cheap, at least as far as American standards went, but it still cost something. It had been a long time since he had had to pull his meat to get off. Even in prison he had had sex every day. These were all things that he hadn't really thought about until now. Maybe it was better to go out in a blaze of glory than to die a little bit more every day as he tried to scrounge out a living in a strange country. Maybe, after all, he would have been better off in prison where he had three hots and a flop, sex almost any time he wanted it and the respect and fear of everyone around him. Everything was certain. Each day was like the last. There were no decisions to make. You knew where you would be at the end of the day, every day, week after week, month after month and year after year.

Jack looked over at his passenger. He was staring out the window, not dully, but without expression. This guy Mouse was a lot different from Moondog, he thought. The exact opposite. He didn't chatter, he had no exuberance. He was all business. There was something a little creepy about it. On the other hand, he was so on edge that he wouldn't have been a very good conversationalist anyway.

They drove for about another 45 minutes. The roads kept getting more desolate and the signs of civilization more rare. They came up to an old, ramshackle, wooden building that looked like it had been abandoned years ago. Mouse told Jack to pull into the parking area in front of it. He told Jack to stop the car and put out the lights. They sat there for about 15 minutes, saying nothing. Then, without comment, the man got out of the car. He went up to what looked like a solid wall of the broken down building and put his shoulder to it.

To Jack's surprise, the wall rolled open. The man waved to jack, indicating that he should pull the car into the vacated space. Jack did as he was told. He watched from the rear view mirror as Mouse took a broom that had been laying against the wall and swept over their tire tracks. He then pulled the wall of the shack closed, sealing them inside the building. He walked up to the back wall and it too opened up. Mouse pushed it aside and waved to Jack to proceed. Jack pulled the car through the opening. It emptied onto the beginning of a packed down trail. Mouse closed up the wall, hustled back up to the car and got back in.

"Okay," he said. "Just follow the road. There's plenty of light so turn off your headlamps."

Jack did as he was told. The moon was sailing almost full at about halfway up the sky. It cast a soft light on the craggy and rough terrain. Deep shadows spread over the trail at parts and Jack was careful to limp the car along, peering intently ahead of him. The trail twisted and turned. At one point it turned right, but Mouse told him to get on a smaller, apparently more disused one on the left. When they had crossed into it, he made Jack stop the car again and, using a big tuft of tumbleweed, wiped out the traces of their passage.

Fifteen minutes later, the car came up over a rise. It was then that Jack saw it. The hacienda was nestled into a sort of box canyon. It was entirely invisible from the approach they had taken until you were directly on top of it. The windows were blacked out, but you could see just a peek or two of light emanating from the building. A small vent stack on the roof was emitting a tiny puff of smoke, probably, Jack thought, from a kitchen stove.

As Jack pulled down the hill, he saw a number of motorcycles and pick-ups lined up in an orderly fashion about 40 or 50 yards away from the building. They were tucked into a cut out made on the hill that formed a semi-circle around the house. They would be invisible from the air.

Mouse directed Jack to pull the car into a wide space between two pick-ups. Jack shut off the engine and issued a deep sigh of relief.

"Welcome to *La Casa Picaros*," Mouse said. He clapped him on the shoulder. "You're home, man!"

CHAPTER FIVE

Yeah, he was home. It was hard to believe. He had travelled about 1500 miles or more, the most wanted man in America, and he had made it. Home. It just sounded so nice.

Mouse opened his door and got out. Jack followed suit. "You can bring in your things later," Mouse said. "The boys are all waiting for you."

"Well, there's some things in the trunk I need to get out," Jack said.

"You mean the girl?" Mouse asked. "You still got her?"

"Yeah, and another one I picked up on the way."

Mouse issued something close to a smile. "Well, the more the merrier," he said.

Jack beeped open the trunk. Two men had emerged from the house. It was Rocker and Chaz. "Hey man," Rocker said exuberantly, "Let me shake your hand." Jack turned and extended his arm. Rocker took his hand and shook it vigorously. Chaz was next. Jack was starting to pick upon the excitement of the moment.

"What ya got in the trunk?" Chaz asked.

Jack stepped away so that they could see. The girl and the woman were squirming and sniffling. The woman's eyes were wide open with fear.

"Hey, lookie here, Rocker, the guy's brought his own amusement park," Chaz said excitedly.

"This the one that was on the TV?" Rocker asked, pointing at the girl.

"That's her," Jack answered.

"You cut off her hair," Chaz noted. "She was a cute little blond if I remember right. Now she's a redhead."

"It'll grow back," Jack said.

"Let's get in the house," Mouse offered. When Ike wasn't around anything that Mouse said was akin to an order.

Jack bent over the edge of the trunk and untied the girl's ankles. She was blubbering and crying as he lifted her out of the trunk. She could hardly stand.

"I'll hold her," Chaz said, taking hold of her arm.

Jack went back in the trunk and released the ankles of the woman. She was blubbering too. Jack pulled her from the trunk. "Hey, she's nice," Rocker said. He reached down and took hold of the hem of her skirt and lifted it up until her white silk panties were visible. "And she's got legs that go all the way up," he joked.

The woman, too, was finding it hard to stand. Rocker took hold of the hair behind her head and straightened her up. She squealed and he shook her head violently. "Shut the fuck up!" he told her. Tears were flowing down her cheeks. Her eyes were darting around the group of coarse looking men. The moonlight made it almost as light as day.

Mouse led the way. Jack felt a little uncomfortable having one of the men escort the girl, but he didn't want to say anything about it. Already his ownership of her was being diluted. He was intent though of ensuring one thing. Nobody was going to fuck her tonight except him.

Carly was frightened beyond her wits. She had heard the voices of the men. They could see her, but she couldn't see them, and they talked about her as if she were some prize that the man had won. She didn't want to get out of the car. She would have preferred to stay in the trunk, die there if necessary. She didn't resist being pulled out of it for the same reason she had failed to resist all the other dozens of orders, verbal or otherwise, the man had given her over the last three days. She was too scared to.

Her thigh muscles groaned when her legs were freed from her hands, and when she was brought out of the car, so near to the crowding men that she could feel the heat from their bodies, she had almost fallen, her knees were so weak. She heard the one man say that he would take her and she felt his tight, powerful grasp on her arm and she almost fainted. "Oh, god! Oh, god! Oh, god!" she thought to herself. "Save me! Save me! Save me!"

Her naked breasts wobbled and swayed as she stood there, shaking with fear. She knew the men could see them. She had no power to hide them. They would see them and desire her and then fuck her. Strange as it was, she craved contact with the man. She could hear his voice, but she wanted him near to her, touching her, owning her. If she belonged to him, then maybe the others would leave her alone.

She suddenly realized that she was sobbing. She didn't want to be. It made her feel like she was falling apart, that she was disassembling right before the men's eyes. She knew she would get no sympathy. It just made her seem more vulnerable and that was the last thing she needed. The other woman was crying too. She heard her squeal and realized that the men had probably done something to hurt her. It frightened her even more. "I'll do what they want," she promised her deity, "but please don't let them hurt me, please!"

They marched as a group to the house. She stumbled once or twice and the man who was holding her lifted her arm up so that her weight was on him and he kind of dragged her along. As they got nearer the house, Carly could hear music playing. It was some kind of rockabilly thing she had never heard before. They came up to some steps and the man who was holding her practically lifted her up. A door opened, the music got louder. Now it was mixed with the sound of a partying crowd. Men and women were laughing loudly. There was loud conversation. She could smell food.

Once through the door, she was pulled another ten or fifteen steps. The music and the crowd noise was right in front of her. One of the men who had come out to the car started to shout, "Quiet! Quiet! Turn that fuckin' thing off!" The music deadened and the crowd hushed.

"*Mi amigos and amigas,*" the voice shouted, "may I have the privilege of introducing to you, fresh from an engagement at Wolverton State Penitentiary, the one, the only, Jack 'Blackjack' Jackson!"

The crowd erupted into a series of raucous cheers. There were whistles and whoops and rebel yells. The crowd surged around them.

"Wait! Wait, my friends!" the man continued. "I would be remiss if I also failed to present our other guests, two lovely lady fairs!"

Carly felt herself pushed forward. The other woman was next to her. There were more catcalls and whistles and cheers. A hand went to the back of her short, denim miniskirt and unclasped it and then lowered the zipper. It fell from her hips and there was another round of applause and exuberance. Someone swept it from her feet. A hand circled one of her breasts and squeezed it.

People were massing all around. She heard the other woman shriek and then a slap and a cry from her followed by laughter. Carly was panicked. It seemed that the crowd had lost all control and she expected any moment to be thrown onto the floor and her dreaded assault to begin. Then, she felt a hand in her hair. It pulled it taut in a familiar way. It pulled her back and she felt him near her. It had to be him. She would know that touch anywhere. A wave of relief flowed through her. For the moment, she was safe.

Jack was overwhelmed by the surging crowd. There had to be fifteen or twenty men in the room with maybe ten or so women. Hands grabbed his, hands slapped his back. He began to feel overwhelmed. He would never have let anyone as close to him as this in prison, never mind a crowd of motherfuckers. And then he thought, "The girl? Where was the girl?"

He saw a small group of men surrounding her. They were poking and pinching her, laughing, enjoying her distress. They had stripped off her skirt. He quickly stepped to his left to where she was standing. He took hold of her hair with his left hand and pulled her to him. The crowd still pushed up on him. He felt ready to explode.

And then came a commanding, deep voice. "Okay! Okay! Let him breathe!" The crowd parted. A tall, broad shouldered man stepped up. He was dark and weathered looking. "I'm Ike," he said as he held out his hand. "Welcome to *La Casa Picoros.* The House of Rouges. As they say, '*Mi casa es su casa.*'"

Jack maintained a hold on the girl's hair with his left hand as he shook Ike's hand with his right. There was no question. Ike was the boss. He was being greeted as one *jefe* to another. Jack felt a surge of pride and relief. He had been afraid that he would be treated like some destitute refugee. But the man's face and hand bespoke respect. Yes, he was home.

"Now all you folks relax," Ike said to the small crowd. "You'll all get a chance to meet him."

Ike turned back to Jack. "How was your trip?"

"Hairy," Jack replied. "We got snowed in in Arkansas. I thought for sure they would get me then."

Ike looked at the girl. "Looks like you had a nice way of passing the time though," he said.

"Yeah, she's pretty fucking hot. And she's smart and does what she's told. Don't you honey?" he said shaking her head.

The girl released a muffled whine but was otherwise silent.

"Let me introduce you to some of the boys," Ike said. "This here's Rocker. He and Chaz were the ones who escorted you in." Jack gave a nod to the pair. Rocker had the other woman's hair still in his hand. He had unbuttoned her shirt and her lacy bra was pulled down, freeing her breasts, lifting them up. They looked bigger than Jack had thought.

"And this here's Stitch. He kind of runs the place. Anything you want, anything, you just ask Stitch. If he ain't got it, he'll get it."

"Hi, Stitch," Jack said. "Glad to meet you."

"My pleasure, Jack," Stitch returned.

They went around the room. There was Breaker and Hound Dog and Ice Man and Killer and many more. Jack said hello to each one of them. They all looked at him with awe bordering on reverence. Most of the women were with gang members, their girlfriends. But a few of them Jack could tell were property, owned by the club and brought in to round out the entertainment. He could tell from the familiar, sullen looks and their skimpy skirts and blouses. One of them had her blouse off already. There was a red tattoo on the top of her full, right breast, a 2" high, cursive 'R. Besides, the property were all decent looking if not good looking chicks. The girlfriends, paired off with gang members more for purposes of companionship and shared interests than sex, were as a rule a little scraggly if not out and out hefty.

One of the women, a girlfriend, asked if she could get a better look at the girl's face. Obligingly, Jack removed her blindfold and gag. The girl sputtered a bit and stared about the room wide eyed. The woman, half back sized with long, scraggly blond hair, a fat, flat face and wearing a stretched out yellow halter top and jeans took hold of the girl's nipples and shook them. "So what's your name, baby," she cooed at her. The girl looked at her sullenly. She had turned red from shame.

"C-C-Carly," she managed to stammer in a low, subdued tone.

"That's it," thought Jack. "Carly. I should've remembered." It was a little strange to hear her voice. He had denied it to her for most of 3 days and he had almost forgotten that she knew how to talk.

"You're pretty, Carly," the woman said sweetly while pinching her teats. "How do you like being Blackjack's whore?"

"She's not permitted to talk," Jack told the woman. He reinserted the gag into the girl's mouth and buckled it tightly behind her head. He left the blindfold off. It was a kick seeing her so flustered and humiliated at being naked and the center of so much not quite friendly attention. It made his cock rise.

There was a spread of charbroiled steaks, ribs and thick chorizo sausages together with a big pot of baked beans on a long table along with the usual utensils. Ike nodded towards it. "Feel free to load up," he said. "If I had to guess, I'd say you probably didn't get much to eat today."

"That's right," Jack replied. He could eat a horse. But he didn't want to let go of the girl. Someone would probably grab her and want to fuck her. Ike sensed his discomfort.

"I can see you want to keep your little honey to yourself for now. Bring her over here. She'll be safe."

Jack followed Ike to the side of the room, pushing the girl before him. He saw the four little cages lined up along the wall. Only one was occupied. It was a young, black haired girl. Ike unlocked one of the cages.

"There's two more, but they're upstairs right now getting some cock. Feel free to sample one if you want. Or you could use one of the whores we brought in from our house of delight in Albuquerque. They're highly skilled and very obedient. In fact, I'd say that just about any female in the place would be willing to give the infamous Blackjack Jackson a hummer."

"Maybe," Jack said nonchalantly. He knew that as soon as he used one of their girls, his would be up for grabs. There were some really good looking females, but he promised himself he would hold off.

He pushed the girl's head down until she had fallen to her knees and then gave her a little shove towards the cage. He didn't have to do more than that. The girl knew what to do. She bent over and crawled on her knees until she was inside. Her hands were still bound behind her back. The cage was big enough so that she could turn around, but just barely. She curled up into the smallest ball she could make. Ike swung the cage door shut and reinstalled the lock. He gave the key to Jack.

"When you're ready to crash, just come and get her. If you want, I'll have Stitch take her into the kitchen and feed her."

"Maybe a little later," Jack said. "It won't hurt her to wait." He crouched down and looked at the girl. Her face was turned away. "Get up," he told her crossly. "Get up on your knees and face me."

The girl struggled to come to her knees. It wasn't easy in the small confines of the cage. Finally, she managed to turn the right way and look at him. She wasn't crying, but she had tears in her eyes. Her knees were pressed together. "Spread your legs," he told her. And then when she moved them a few inches apart, he said, "Wider. As wide as they can go."

She pushed her knees to the sides of the cage. It wasn't very far, but it was far enough that her hairless slit could easily be seen. Jack took a moment to enjoy the view. There was something about seeing her all confined like that that was just perfect. "I want you to stay like that so everybody can look at you. I'm sure this crowd would enjoy seeing me give you a good whipping, so keep that in mind," he told her. He couldn't see her downturned mouth, but he saw in her eyes what he was looking for. They were about as doleful as they could be. It made him want to tear her out of the cage and sink his cock into her. But he would give her a round fucking later. For now, he wanted some eats.

Jack loaded a plate up and found a chair where he could keep an eye on the girl. There was a half keg and someone poured him a large mugful of the dark brew. A bottle of Jack kept circulating around and several times he had to interrupt his meal to do some shots. He got more than one offer of a blow job. One of the guys offered up his girl if he could watch. She wasn't bad looking and it was tempting, but Jack turned him down politely.

The music had started again and the crowd started back into enjoying itself. Some of the women started dancing. Two of the heftier ones took one of the property girls out to the middle of the floor and made her strip. She had the same tattoo on her breast as the other. They ordered her to start dancing and the girl began shaking her hips and swinging her breasts as if she were on stage. That gave the hefty women some laughs. It wasn't long before a small crowd of men surrounded the girl. Not long after that, she was on her knees with a cock in her mouth.

Jack had just finished his plate when one of the men came over to him. "Hey Jack," he said mirthfully, "I think your girl over here wants to say something to you."

He had just about forgotten about the older woman. He got up, tossed his paper plate into the trash, finished his mug of beer and stepped over to where a small group of partiers had gathered near the door. They parted for him.

The woman was on her knees. They had stripped her and she was completely naked. Her hands were still bound behind her back. One of the men was dangling a pretty severe looking flogger in front of her. She was staring at it wide eyed and trembling.

The one they called Rocker was standing in front of her. He had in his hand the blue ball that had been in her mouth. "Hey, Jack," he said. "Me and your babe here have been talking. I think she has something to say to you."

The woman looked up at Jack, misery painted across her face. Her eyes then darted around to the crowd that surrounded her. Jack had been right about her tits. They were full, but not heavy, and hung well on her chest. Her nipples were like little buttons and her areolas were small and dark. Her stomach was lean but not fully taut, just a hint of fat around her waist. She had trimmed her adult growth into a bikini cut, a little triangle above her mons. Her thighs were firm. There was a tattoo of a rose just above her right hip.

Jack approached the woman. "So what's so important?" he asked.

The woman's face cringed. The guy with the flogger, Jack thought that he remembered his name as Hound Dog, a kind of depressed looking fellow, waived it at her. "Come on now bitch, make up your mind!" he told her harshly. "Or I'll make up your mind for you!" He ran the tassels of the flogger over her breasts. The woman's body shuddered.

Rocker crouched down next to her. He put his arm across her shoulders. "Come on, now, honey," he said smoothly. "You know you can do it. You know you gotta do it. So tell Mr. Jackson what you want to say to him."

Tears were drifting down her cheeks. Her lips trembled. She looked at Jack. She started to mumble something. It was indecipherable.

"That's it man," one of the men said, the guy whose name was Billy Boots. "I've had just about enough of this shit! Give her the whip already! Enough fucking around!"

"You see?" Rocker asked her. "Time's running out. Give it another try."

The woman took a deep breath. She ran her eyes around the small crowd that had gathered. Then she looked at Jack. Then she blurted it out.

Her voice was strained and high pitched. It wavered. Her lips formed a little frown.

"M-may I p-please suck your cock, Mr. Jackson?" she stuttered, her voice cracking.

There was a round of rambunctious approval from the crowd. The woman stared at Jack unhappily. You knew that she wanted him to say no. But she should've known that if she didn't start with Jack, she would just start with someone else after she got her beating.

You could see that saying the words had taken a lot of energy out of her. She bit her lip and awaited anxiously the verdict. The eyes of the crowd were darting from Jack to the woman, to the woman and then to Jack and back again. They waited in silence.

"No," Jack said. There was a wave of amusement in the crowd.

"Sorry, honey," Rocker said to the woman, "Jack said no." He turned to the crowd. "All right boys, string her up."

The woman's face fell. Her eyes widened. Her body went limp. Two of the men went to grab her arms to lift her to her feet while Rocker stepped away from her.

"Noooooooooo!" the woman shouted. "Pleeeeeeeease no!" And then to Jack, "Pleeeeeeeease! Pleeeeeeeease let me suck your cock! Pleeeeeeeeeease!" She broke out into sobs.

"Okay. Okay. I'll let you do it," Jack said finally, getting in to the spirit of the thing as the woman was being pulled from her knees. The men let her back down. "But if it's not grade 'A', number one, it don't count," he told her. "Understand?"

She nodded her head desperately. The man who held the whip dangled it in front of her and said, "Make sure you do a good job, little lady. I'll be waiting for ya!" and laughed.

One of the women said, "Come on, honey, let's see what you can do!"

Jack had lowered his fly and slipped out his cock. It was rubbery and half filled with blood.

"Atta boy, Jack, let her have it," someone said.

The woman was crying. She was looking around the crowd as if seeking out a friendly face. She was trying to put off the inevitable.

"Come on, sweetheart," Jack said to her. "I'm starting to get a little impatient here. Come to papa and get to work."

The woman's lips formed into a frown and then she inched her way over to Jack who was standing a few feet away. Her face seized into a grimace and then she lowered her head, opened her mouth and took him in.

Her heat sent a warm rush through Jack's body. She had to arch her back and creep a little closer so that she could get a good movement going. She suckled his wand slowly up and down and up and down. She swirled her tongue along his glans and suckled the head. Then she slipped her lips down until he was fully sunk within her and then slowly slipped her lips up again careful to keep them tightly wrapped around the stem.

The crowd was giving her shouts of encouragement. Jack just kind of tuned them out and concentrated on letting her ministrations send him wave after wave of pleasure. He had closed his eyes. It was just like the old days. It was almost as if the twelve years in the joint had been only a bad dream. He had broken in, or seen broken in, dozens of unhappy women this way back in the day. They thought that they were performing the odious task to avoid more unpleasant eventualities, but they were really doing nothing but forestalling them.

Jack had no doubt that his was not the last cock she would suck tonight, just as he was sure that sooner or later, before her evening was through, she would make acquaintance with the long, stiff tassels of the flogger she had been shown a little while ago. But hope sprung eternal and the woman had undoubtedly acted with the expectation that somehow sucking his cock and doing a good job would alleviate her sufferings when actually she was just initiating them.

She worked his cock skillfully. Her hands twisted and turned behind her back in their bindings. Her long, brown hair recorded each movement of her head, swirling this way and that. Once Jack's cock had reached its maximum extension, she had had to edge herself back a little so that her mouth could accommodate it.

Jack reached down and seized her hair. On her next down stroke, he pushed her head down firmly until his cock pressed against the back of her mouth. "Go down all the way, honey," he told her gruffly. "Give me long, slow strokes like you like it."

He held her head down until her gurgling started to get frantic and then he released her. Tears were flowing down her cheeks. She pulled her head back slowly until the head lay just inside her lips and then lowered again slowly, this time making sure that she got in as much of his rigid pole as she possibly could.

The crowd had pretty much silenced now. There was an old Hank Williams tune playing. It was sweet and low and made the woman's predicament seem all the more doleful. Jack had to give it to her. She was really doing a good job. She was issuing little squeals and moans as she worked his dick. Her eyes were closed in an attempt to blot out everything around her.

One of the women shouted out, "Now I recognize her! That's Malinda Ramirez! I seen her picture in the paper. Her husband owns half the real estate in Albuquerque and a dozen or more car dealerships! She runs a string of these high class women's wear places. She's a millionaire!"

A couple of people seconded the woman's observations. The woman's eyes sprung open and she released a loud moan as if having been identified made her shame all the more woeful. She slowed down and released a sob. Jack tapped her harshly on her cheek. "Come on, little rich girl, get back to work," he told her gruffly.

With a sob, the woman went back to her odious chore. Jack closed his eyes again, relishing the friction of her lips, the agility of her tongue. He had to give it to her, she was putting her all into it. It made him happy that he hadn't ditched her.

But there was something wrong with what was going on, something slightly off kilter. There was something about being back in the milieu of so many years ago that was not quite satisfying. It was like his years of spiritual torment, the deadly years of confinement, had taught him to seek out the deeper, more pure essence of things. The people in the room, people who were getting their jollies from watching him humiliate the woman, seemed somehow puerile and shallow. It was a surprising discovery.

All those many years in the joint he had thought that this was exactly what he wanted, the approbation of his cohorts, his peers, indiscriminate access to alluring, subservient females. He had achieved that goal, no one in their merry band was more honored right then than him, and he had a helpless, much more than attractive bitch sucking his wand. To his surprise, it did not give him the thrilling charge he had thought it would.

And then he realized, it was the girl. He wanted the girl and no one else. He imagined that is was her mouth on his cock, her on her knees before him. The wavelength he had been seeking, that pure, unadulterated stream of rapture he had experienced with the girl came rushing back. It was her that he wanted, her that he craved. Something had happened between them in that isolated cabin buried in snow, or at least it had happened to him.

He felt his climax coming. A wellspring of exultation erupted within him. A wave of pleasure washed through him. He felt that peak building, that peak that presaged the eruption of his passions. He held himself there, wanting to preserve that feeling of immanence as long as he could. "Carly. That's her name. Carly," he thought. He knew that he should have saved himself for her but it was too late to do anything about it now. The crowd around had sensed his approaching crisis.

"That a boy, Jack!" "Go get 'er Blackjack!" "Give it to her!" "Fuck her face!" "Shove it down her throat!" the voices called out. He held himself there, held himself, held himself. The picture of his captive's doleful eyes looking up at him as she consumed his manhood sprung into his mind. It was perfect! Perfect! Was this love? Was he in love with her? What did it mean?

And then all thoughts of reflection left him as his cock exploded. He gave a loud, angry sounding grunt and he felt his cock throbbing and jerking in the woman's mouth. She gave a squeal and tried to back away, but his hand circled her head, grabbing her hair, and he pushed her down and up, down and up, down and up, as his juices flowed in rabid spurts from deep inside his balls.

"Arrrrrrrrrrrgh! Arrrrrrrrrrgh! Arrrrrrrrrrrrgh!" he groaned. His body was permeated with bliss. "Oh, yeah! Oh, yeah! Oh, yeah!" he thought.

As his cock's pulses waned, he pressed the unhappy woman's head down as far as it would go. He felt his prick pierce her throat and she began to gargle and cough and struggle. He kept it there while he wound down. "Ohhhhhhhhhhhhh!" he moaned. "Ohhhhhhhhhhh!" That was great.

The crowd of onlookers erupted with glee and mirth. Hands reached down and roughly pulled the grimacing woman away. An animated discussion arose about who was next. Then Ike stepped in. "I'm next," he growled sternly. The men and women hushed. He had been standing next to Jack.

He reached out for her arm and the others gave her up. The woman looked frantic. His hand easily enclosed her upper arm. He grabbed it tightly and pulled her to her feet. The woman winced. He stood about 8" taller than her and was twice as wide.

"I'm going to take her upstairs and see what million dollar pussy tastes like," he said. He turned to Jack.

"You don't mind, Jack, do you?" he asked. His tone suggested clearly that he expected no objection.

"Not at all," Jack replied. "Not at all."

Ike gave a yank to the woman's arm and he began to propel her to the stairs. She squealed and whined. Ike stopped and took her by the throat. "If I were you, I'd shut the fuck up," he told her.

Her eyes wide and her lips trembling, the woman gave a frantic indication of assent. "Please don't hurt me!" she whined.

Ike released her throat and took hold of her arm again. He passed by Hound Dog who was still holding the flogger.

"Give me that," Ike said.

Hound Dog handed him the cruel instrument.

"C'mon, Malinda, or whatever your name is," Ike said. "I'm going to give you a little lesson in discipline."

The woman sobbed and wailed all the way up the stairs. Only the closing of the door to the bedroom silenced her.

CHAPTER SIX

Carly hadn't witnessed what went on with the woman, but she had heard the crowd's excitement and the woman's pleas. Most of the time though she spent quailing in her cage enduring the unrestrained eyes of the people around her. A few of them came up to the cage to taunt her. Having received the command from the man, she didn't dare flinch as they perused her intimately, suggesting what they would do to her when they got the chance.

One of the women, harsh and butch looking, had practically salivated over her. Carly assumed that she must have some kind of rank with the gang since she held herself haughtily and none of the men came to stand over her. She was hefty, but not really fat, just built like a tank. Her black hair was short and messy. Her nose looked like it had been broken at least once, maybe more. She was wearing a black leather vest over a black, sleeveless t-shirt and had tattoos up and down her arms. On her upper right arm was the same cursive, bright red '*R*' she had seen on the breast of one of the women. Her face was broad and coarse looking, her features thick.

She had a blond companion, slim and a little weather beaten. There was a bright brass ring in her nose. She was wearing a short, yellow shift with cut out sleeves and a scooped neck. The butch woman seemed to have some authority over her and Carly assumed that they were a couple, of sorts.

"Heya, honey," the butch woman said, leaning over the cage and banging on it loudly. Carly had to bend her neck up to see her.

"Nice tits. How'd ya like to come out and play a little bit? I'd sure like to get my tongue up your sweet looking little pussy. Say hello to the little girl, fuckslut," she told the other woman. Carly noticed then the chain leading from the woman's nose to the butch woman's hand. The blond woman was pale and her skin looked as thin and as delicate as tissue paper. Carly expected her to cringe at the caustic appellation, but she just smiled.

"Hello, little girlie," she said in a high pitched voice. "You look kinda cute."

"I wonder whether she's ever licked a pussy," the butch woman said. "Maybe I'll ask Blackjack if we can have a turn with her tomorrow." Her eyes kept sweeping over Carly's flesh. It made her skin crawl and when she mentioned asking her captor for a turn with her, Carly's stomach went sour and a chill ran through her. She was fighting back her tears.

To Carly she said, "How's about it, honey? I'll be ya I could make you scream. Then I'd squeeze your pretty face between my thighs. Maybe I'll see what Blackjack's looking to get for ya. I'd love to put ya in my stable."

Fear shook Carly to her core. She was right about the man selling her off to the gang. To think that she could become this woman's property made her blood run cold. The tears she had been suppressing started to flow.

"Lookie, mistress" the blond woman said. "She's crying."

"Ain't that sweet," the bulky woman said. "I'd love to give her something to really cry about."

Carly shivered and she closed her eyes. The woman laughed. She apparently tired of her sport. "When ya talk to Blackjack next, tell him Big Betty wants to get a piece of ya." She laughed again. She pulled on the chain that led to the blond woman's nose.

"C'mon, fuckslut," she said. "Let's see whose cock needs suckin'. I don't want you getting all rusty on me."

Carly watched them amble away with dismay. "Don't let her buy me! Don't let her buy me!" she thought desperately. "What am I going to do? What am I going to do?" All the people who loved her were a million miles away. She had somehow fallen into hell. She couldn't imagine what it would be like to be in the butch woman's stable. It sounded like she ran a whorehouse or something. From the looks of her, it was probably a harsh, terrifying place. "I couldn't stand it! She thought. "I couldn't stand it!" But then again, someone was going to buy her! They were going to make her a whore! "Please, God, no! Please don't let it happen! Please! Please!" she prayed.

Her eyes started seeking out the man. She had seen him enter into a crowd of people and she assumed that he was the one that they centered around. Once, the crowd parted momentarily and she saw the man's face lifted up, his eyes closed as if in a trance. She deducted that he was taking pleasure from one of the women and worried what that portended for her. Her only hope was that the man would still want her enough to not turn her over to the gang. She knew it was a slim hope, and remaining the man's prisoner was harrowing in itself. But the prospect of becoming a common whore for the scurvy, conscienceless people she had seen so far was abhorrent.

At one point, one of the men unlocked the cage next to her and the frightened young girl was removed and taken upstairs. Another one, a thin blond, was brought down and locked in the cage the other had just left, but her sojourn there was brief as another man came and got her out within a few minutes. Carly cowered in her little cage, seeing firsthand her probable future.

She saw the big man, the one who had shown her captor where to lock her up, take the woman she had shared the trunk with up the stairs. The woman was wailing and sobbing and watching it made Carly shiver with fear. The man who was leading her seemed as ruthless and cruel as her captor. Maybe worse. He looked like their leader. If he was, sooner or later she would have to fuck him. The thought made her cringe with dismay.

The crowd dissipated and some of them began dancing again to the loud, twangy music. Two men seized one of the prettier girls and dragged her over to a couch and made her strip. The room smelled of pot, cigarettes and beer. One of the men had brought out a large bong and a circle of celebrants surrounded it and started taking hits. Part of Carly envied them. It would be good to be able to smother her consciousness, take her mind away to another state. She would smoke and smoke until her senses became so dulled she wouldn't care what they did to her.

Just then, the man reappeared in front of her cage. He was looking at her strangely. She welcomed the sight of him. She knew that there were bedrooms upstairs and she began to hope that he would take her up there soon. She would do anything to be beyond the eyes and reach of the partygoers. And she was hungry too. She had watched the man eat while she starved and she added it to the long list of things she had compiled to seek revenge on him for. But now, all her mind concentrated on sending him the strongest psychic message she could. "Please take me away from this! Please! Please!"

Jack looked down on the doleful and supplicative eyes. She looked so pretty in there, all caged up. This is exactly how he'd keep her if he ever got her down to Mexico.

She'd have no existence outside of her little world unless he gave it to her. He'd feed her and clean her and exercise her so she stayed lean and tight. She wouldn't be allowed to say a single word, ever. And he'd keep her naked, like this. He desired her so much that he could feel it under his skin. This was bad. He would do anything to keep her out of the hands of these vultures. But how would he do it? He didn't even know the next step as far as he was concerned. Tomorrow he would talk to Ike. They must have a way for him to get over the border. And maybe he could take her after all.

He remembered that she hadn't eaten. The first rule for a pet is that you had to feed them right. If he wanted her helpless, he had a responsibility to take care of her. There was a table full of food, but he didn't want her eating in here where all the others could watch her. They might get the wrong idea. There had to be a kitchen here. He would get a plate of food and bring her back there. Then, maybe, he'd head to bed. The partying would go on all night and he was hang dog tired.

Taking the key from his pocket, he unlocked the cage. When the door swung open, she looked to him for permission to exit. He motioned her out with his hand. When she had shuffled out and cleared the door, he took hold of the hair on the back of her head and brought her to her feet. He led her past some revelers and over to the table. He had her kneel while he filled up a plate with a nice sized hunk of steak and some beans. Then he brought her back to her feet and led her in the direction of where the kitchen might be.

The music was still blaring loudly. Couples were fornicating out in the open. Bottles of Jack were being passed around. The property girls were all naked now and in various states of use. He exited the room and saw a hallway. He brought the girl down it with him. There was a door at the end. He pushed it open and they were in the kitchen.

It was large with copper colored stone tiles across the floor and half way up the walls. A wide, long, wooden table sat in the middle of it. There was a nice sized, shiny steel, industrial type refrigerator and a commercial stove. Pots and pans hung on hooks on the walls. Wooden chairs were distributed around the table. At one end sat the guy who had been introduced to Jack as Stitch. He had a naked, black haired girl kneeling on the floor next to him and he was feeding her bits of food from his plate.

The door swung closed behind them, deadening the noise from the party room. Stitch looked up at Jack and smiled.

"Had enough?" he asked.

"Yeah," Jack answered. "Too many people."

"I know how you feel," Stitch replied. "I did a six year stretch at PNM, a max joint over in Santa Fe. Took me about a year to get used to being around people without watching to see who was going to jump me. I ain't never going back."

"Tell me about it," Jack said. There was a long, wooden, butcher block counter near the sink where he could chop up the girl's steak. He released her hair and tapped a spot on the floor with his boot. She gave him an unhappy glance and then sank obediently to her knees, spread them and put her forehead on the floor.

"Nice trick," Stitch observed. "You've got her trained good."

"Yeah," Jack answered. "You gotta show them who's in charge right away. Saves a lot of problems later."

He went over to the counter and pulled a butcher's knife out of a wooden block. He dumped the steak on the counter and then opened a few drawers until he found a fork. He started in to chopping the steak into little pieces.

Stitch just watched him. The girl he had been feeding watched him too, nervously. She had heard the others talking about him and how mean he was. She didn't want to go nearer than a mile to him. Stitch had to give her a little slap to get her attention. She looked at the piece of meat in his hand and opened her mouth. Her hands were confined to her collar by a small chain. There were a number of faded marks on her pale skin from a beating or two. She took the meat from Stitch's hand and started chewing.

Jack had the meat all cut up and started looking in the cabinets for a bowl big enough to mix the beans and meat together.

"Lookin' for a bowl?" Stitch asked him.

Jack grunted a reply.

"There's some bowls there on the floor by the wall," Stitch told him. "That's where we usually feed the girls."

Jack looked over. There were four large, stainless steel dog bowls all lined up near the wall. They looked good enough. He went over and picked two of them up and brought them to the counter. He dumped the beans and the meat in one and mixed them all around. He turned to Stitch. "Got any milk in that fridge?"

"Yeah, on the door," Stitch answered.

Jack went over to the refrigerator and opened it. There was a gallon jug in the door slot.

"All the comforts of home," Jack commented.

"Yeah, we like to keep it nice. Somebody makes a run for stuff every couple of days. We try and keep the traffic down to a minimum, especially during the day," Stitch said. "For obvious reasons."

"Yeah," Jack answered. He brought the milk over to

the counter and filled the other silver bowl almost to the top. He returned the jug to the fridge and then put the gleaming bowls on the floor. He snapped his fingers and the girl's head rose up. He pointed to the bowls and she shuffled over on her knees. She paused when she reached the food and looked up at him. He removed the gag from her mouth and gave her a nod. She spread her legs and leaned over until her mouth was by the bowl with the food and began to eat.

Jack watched her for a few seconds. It never ceased to give him a little charge to see her eating like that. Between bites, she looked up at him resentfully. It made him chuckle inside. He hoped she never got over the humiliation of eating like a dog. It would take the fun out of it.

He had seen some long necks in the fridge and went back and got himself one. "Get you one?" he asked Stitch. Stich nodded. Jack took out two bottles of Lone Star and brought them to the table, pulling out a chair. Before he sat down, he handed a bottle to the other man. Stitch nodded his thanks and twisted off the top. He told the girl to go stand in the corner. She got up from her knees and, giving Jack a fearful glance, scurried over to where the kitchen wall met the outside of the building and pressed herself into it face first.

Jack took a long look at her, admiring her firm posterior and long, graceful legs. He had to admit, she had appeal. He realized that he ought to fuck his balls off while he had the chance. Who knew how long it would be before he got himself all set up in Mexico, if ever. He might regret not fucking everything he could. But then he looked over to his captive. He had a good view of her from where he sat. He was behind her and her hot little slit peaked out between her legs as she ate. He promised himself to spend a little time there before too long.

There was a bottle of Wild Turkey on the table with a couple of glasses. Stitch poured them both a shot. They raised their glasses at the same time and clinked them together. "Here's looking up your kilt," Stitch said.

"Yeah," Jack replied. "To good times."

They both shot the rye whiskey back at the same time.

Jack was feeling a little high from all the drinking he had been doing. He wasn't used to it. Stitch poured them both another shot, but he didn't protest. He was starting to like the way it felt.

"So what are your plans?" Stitch asked him.

"Right now, the only plan I have is to get to Mexico in one piece," Jack told him.

"Ike'll take care of that," Stitch said. "One of our Mexican contacts is coming here tomorrow night to pick up some merchandise. I'm sure Ike'll fix you up with him. He could probably use a guy like you."

"That would suit me fine," Jack said.

"What are you going to do with the girl?" Stitch asked.

"I'm not sure yet," Jack answered. "I'd kind of like to take her with me, but we'll have to see."

"You could get a pretty good buck for her from our friend," Stitch told him. "She's right up his alley. You'll need some dough to get all set up. Or you could talk to Ike. We've got a few places where we could use her. But he'd probably give her to Big Betty. Did you meet her?"

"I don't think I did," Jack answered. "But I think I know who you mean. She's a 200 lb. bull dike, with arms like a prize fighter?"

"That's her," Stitch replied laughing. "She runs one of our special places, ya know, where you can get anything you want. We send all of our trouble makers there. Once

Big Betty gets a hold of 'em they aren't trouble any more. She keeps 'em all under lock and key 24/7. Once a girl goes there, well, there's no place to go after Big Betty's."

"I'll give it some thought," Jack said. "As to the money bit, I scored a little on my way here. But not enough to last very long. If this Mexican guy can give me work, that would be good."

"I'm sure he has work for you," Stitch assured him. He poured two more shots. "Here's looking at you," he said as he raised the glass again. Jack followed suit and they downed the liquor. They stayed talking for a while. They compared notes on prison life. Stitch told Jack he was wanted on a parole warrant, but that he'd shoot it out if they ever came for him. Jack agreed that that was the only thing to do. Jack started telling some stories from the old days and Stitch had a few of his own.

At one point, the girl had finished the food and started in on the bowl of milk. When she was done, Jack went over to her and wiped her sauce covered mouth and chin with a paper towel. He reinstalled her gag and told her to go stand in the corner opposite the black haired girl. When she was situate, he sat back down in his chair. Stitch had another shot ready.

Carly listened while he men swapped horrific tales of their depredations and of their lives as convicts. It was the most she had heard the man talk. It was a little strange to hear him go on. She had only heard short sentences from him since he had taken her, and sometimes he had said nothing to her for hours, using gestures or a snap of his fingers instead. From the stories he told, she confirmed for herself what a brute that he was. The other guy wasn't much better.

When she had heard the other man mention the bowls on the floor, she had quailed at the thought that she would have to eat that way in front of him and the naked black haired girl. When she saw the actual bowls, her heart dropped. They were clearly bowls meant for dogs. She obeyed though. She didn't have much choice if she wanted to eat. And she was very, very hungry. The steak and beans wasn't hot, but it wasn't cold either. Carly knew that if she ever got free she would never eat beans again. She hadn't liked them to start with, but since her captivity they had been virtually the staple of her diet. For now, though, it didn't matter. She would do what she'd been told. She gulped them and the small bits of meat obediently.

She kept an ear out for the men's conversation. As a prisoner, she knew that no one would ever tell her what was going on around her and so she would have to draw her own conclusions from the bits and pieces of conversation she was able to decipher. She heard the man confirm that he was heading for Mexico. That was no surprise. But the next thing he said had much more interest for her. The other man had asked if he was going to take her with him. Then about selling her to the Mexican guy. Then, he mentioned Big Betty, who Carly had already met. She had to pause in her eating when she heard that.

Liberation was clearly not in her future. The dismalness of her situation made her feel like breaking out into sobs all over again. There had to be some way out of this! There had to be! But what she had seen of the other girls told her that these men were practiced at keeping women prisoner. Dozens of women had probably passed through here. If they couldn't escape, how could she? The very fact that this strange slice of hell in which she now found herself existed meant that none of them ever had.

So one of the three possibilities the other man had

mentioned was her future. Of the three choices, she would choose staying with the devil she knew. But even the mere possibly being sold into slavery was horrifying. What life would be like imprisoned in a Mexican whorehouse she hardly dared imagine. And to be sold off to that woman, Big Betty, that was the most horrifying of them all. Men could get anything they wanted at her place. And she had had a sample of the anything they were talking about over the last few days. And from what the man said, they would keep her there until she was of no more use to them and then dispose of her. Throw her away. She would probably die an agonizing death at the hands of some psychopath. "Oh, god, please not that! Please!" she thought.

When she realized she had stopped eating, she quickly pressed her face down in the bowl. She had been ordered to eat and if he saw her slacking off from his order, he would punish her.

Now, standing in the corner, she realized that her only hope of avoiding the worst was to please her captor, to make him not to want to part with her. He was just one man and sooner or later he would become inattentive and she could get away. But if she were held prisoner in a brothel, the likelihood of her getting away would be much smaller. They would have systems and routines just for the purposes of keeping their property secure. Someone would be watching over her and the other girls all the time. No, she had to somehow convince the man to keep her, to bring her to Mexico with him.

But did he even have final say in the matter? Up to now, he had been the supreme authority over all things that concerned her. Things were different now. That man, the one who was the leader here, he had had a clear voice of authority. And while her captor did not cower before him, there was just a semblance of deference in his voice. If the other man wanted to take her away from her captor, he would order it. It would be difficult for the man to refuse. Only if he desired her above all things would he put up a fight. It was her only hope.

His desire for her had overcome his instincts for self-preservation three times in the last three days. It needed to work one more time. He was going to take her upstairs and fuck her soon. She needed to make sure that it was the best he ever had.

So she stood there patiently, even though the act of burying her nose in the corner, having her bare back and bare ass displayed, put away like you would a dog, made her shake with shame. And yet, the idea of her helplessness, the very fact of her shame itself, her fear filled need to give abject deference to any of the man's humiliating whims, coupled with the fact that in a short while he would place his hands and lips on her again, pierce her with his steely, remorseless cock, made her lusts begin to burn.

After about the fifth shot, Jack started feeling very woozy. He was not used to so much booze. Stitch was still going strong, but Jack had had enough. He looked over at the girl. She was standing still, silently, just as she had been ordered. Her conjoined hands rested just atop the demarcation of the divide between her pale white buttocks. Her fingers rested, intermingled. She was still wearing the sandals he had adorned her with this morning. They made her ass rise up nicely. Her short, fiery red hair blended nicely with the copper colored tiles of the floor and walls.

In the other corner was the other girl. She had a fine ass too and slender legs. Her whole naked back could be seen since her hands were joined in front of her. Her black hair came down to the middle of her back. Jack had only gotten a short glimpse of her, but he recalled her being stacked well. Her ass was plumper than the girl's and begged for the kiss of a riding crop or a lash. Fucking it would be heaven.

For a moment, he toyed with the idea of making a swap with Stitch. He could take the girl, Carly, see, he could remember her name now, and Jack would take the black haired girl. It might be fun to fuck someone new.

But no, there was really no contest. He would be a fool not to fuck the girl again. This might be his last night with her. Probably would be. Although maybe, just maybe, he could talk the Mexican who was coming tomorrow to let him bring her with him. There were all kinds of practical issues with that like where would he keep her until he got set up an all, but it might be just possible.

Part of him wondered what it would be like to let go of her. She had epitomized everything right about his escape until now, had been the physical embodiment of it, the grand prize he had seized. Would his luck run out when she was gone? Would he pine for her like some love-struck fool? Or would he come back to his senses, remember that she was just one cunt among a long line of cunts from the past and, hopefully, in the future?

Why should he feel about her the way he did? She was hot, yeah, but there were plenty of hot young sluts out there. He bet that he could make the black haired one screech with passion before the night was out if he picked her instead. No, it was more than just the fact that she was hot. It was the way she looked at him when she was eating on her knees, that look that combined sultriness and hostility. It was the way she sobbed when he was done with her, so vulnerable and destitute. It was her obedience, so complete, and how she couldn't bear to look him in the eye, but did so when he ordered it, filling up with tears and her body trembling. It was the precise size and heft of her breasts and the taste of her pussy. She was the one who could not be replaced. No other woman would be just like her. No woman could ever be better. It would be a shame if he lost her. A real shame.

"Hey," Jack told Stitch, "I'm hitting the hay."

Stitch looked at him. "You want Maureen, here?" He asked Jack. "She'd make a great threesome."

"Not tonight," Jack answered. "Which room should I take?"

"The first one down on the right. It's usually my room, but I got it all fixed up for you. There's all the amenities, a shower, a nice big, fully supplied bathroom, towels, toothbrushes and a king sized bed. There's even a cage in the closet if you don't want to sleep with your honey there. Just shut the door and it's, 'See you tomorrow!'" He laughed.

Jack ignored the humor. He was going to ask where Stitch was going to sleep but decided he didn't give a fuck. He eased the chair back and then carefully pushed himself to his feet. The room didn't spin so much as kind of wobble. It took him a second to catch himself. He went to the corner and took hold of the girl's hair, pulling her back and then pushing her forward. They went back through the swinging kitchen door. The music from the party became louder right away. Jack tried to scoot by unnoticed over to the stairs, but it was not to be. One of the men called out, "Here's Jack!" and several pairs of eyes turned to look at him.

"Hey Jack," the man he remembered as Chaz said enthusiastically. "Ya gotta come here and see this!"

A syrupy country song was playing. Here and there

people were passed out. A few of the men were still ensconced with the party girls. A group of four of them were circled around a woman bent over a hassock with a man who Jack recognized as Billy Boots on top of her. Jack drew closer. The couple was facing him. The woman had her wrists fastened to a ring in the front of a leather collar around her neck. She had short blond hair. Billy Boots was easing himself in and out of her rear entrance. She was moaning unhappily.

"Jack, meet Special Agent Linda Kramer of the FBI," Chaz said. "She's been detailed to capture you." There were laughs all around.

"Ike caught her nosing around his bar yesterday. I don't think she'll be nosing around anymore," Chaz continued.

Jack looked at the woman. A surge of anger went through him. Here was one of the people who were trying to put him back in a cage. She issued another moan as Billy pushed his cock deep into her bowels. He looked up at Jack. He had an evil smile on his face. He hadn't bothered to undress. His cock was protruding from his unzipped jeans. "Give me a few minutes and you can have a turn with her, Jack," he said. "Her bung hole is nice and tight."

He leaned back and took hold of the hair behind the woman's head, lifting her face up to look at Jack. "Hey, fuckface," he said, "say hello to Blackjack Jackson. I think you were looking for him. Now you've found him."

The woman looked at Jack miserably. Her face was awash with tears. To Jack, she epitomized the forces that were trying to hem him in, to return him to captivity and, if not, to kill him. A fierce impulse within him made him want to smash his fist into her. It was sure tempting. He held himself back and let the surge of anger subside. He had better things to do than to fuck with this cunt, he thought. "Maybe tomorrow," Jack said. "Right now I've got something else on my mind. Just save me a little piece of her."

"Sure, Jack," Billy said, amused. "We won't use her all up. She's going to Mexico tomorrow and we want her all in one piece for that." He shook her head. "Ever been to Mexico, honey?" he asked her sarcastically. "I'm sure you're going to love it." He laughed and released her hair. Her unhappy face fell. Billy resumed his traverse of her ass, picking up the pace a bit.

"Hurry up, Billy," one of the other men said. "I want a shot at her."

Jack stepped away, bringing the girl with him.

As he led her up the stairs, Carly thought unhappily about the fate of the FBI agent. Here was someone who had been sent to try and rescue her. And even she was powerless to resist the men's depredations. If they were audacious enough to kidnap an FBI agent, what hope of rescue or escape did she have?

They came to one of the doors at the top of the stairs, the one the man down in the kitchen had talked about. The man opened it, pulling the door outwards and then brought her in.

The room was large, about 20' by 30'. There was a king sized bed head into the wall on their left. It was covered with clean looking, light blue, satin sheets. In the middle of the headboard, just above the large, fluffy pillows, was an embedded brass ring. A chain led from it to a little pile in the middle of the bed. There were rings in the footboard too, two of them, near each corner, and chains connected to them led to the floor.

Straight ahead was a wide and tall, boarded up window. Underneath was a long, dark oak credenza. In the corner, a chain dangled from the ceiling. Several whips were mounted on the wall behind it. Just seeing them made Carly cringe with fear.

On the right, across the room from the bed, was a low slung dresser with a long, wide mirror over it and next to it a door which opened into the bathroom. Her captor led her there right away. The floors and walls up to about 5' were covered with aqua colored tiles. The walls above it were painted white. There was an elegant, modern looking sink embedded in a polished, wooden vanity. Carly got a glimpse of herself in the mirror as her captor pushed her past it. She looked away quickly, not wanting to be reminded of her destitute state.

She was led over to the toilet where the man made her pee. When he was done, he wiped her and made her stand by while he did the same. He then took her over to the bathroom sink where he released her gag and her arms behind her back. He found two brand new toothbrushes in drawers there and gave her one. There was toothpaste too and after squeezing a dollop on her brush, he ordered her to get to work. He did the same.

Carly couldn't help but look in the mirror. "Here we are, like some married couple on vacation," she thought. It was too absurd. But after being down in that big room with all those people, it was somehow comforting. The grotesque bond they had formed over the last few days was being reestablished. They were alone now. It was just them. Soon he would fuck her. She looked up at his reflection in the mirror. He was huge next to her. His face was scarred and scary looking. He had a day's growth of beard on his face. His deadly eyes caught hers and she looked away. He spat out and cupped some water to rinse with. Then he ordered her to do the same.

He grabbed her gag with one hand and the hair at the

back of her head with the other. He pushed her from the bathroom and over to the bed. At his instruction, she climbed up onto it. He connected her hands in front of her and then to the chain that led from the headboard. Then he told her to lie down. When she had obeyed, he stepped back and began to get undressed.

She watched him warily as he stripped off his clothes. When he was done, he stood above her, looking at her. She was lying on her right side. The chain that confined her hands had plenty of play to it, being intended to confine a prisoner there while allowing her to be moved about the bed as the need arose. It could be shortened when needs be by pulling on the other end and hooking it off. So her hands, while bound, were free to roam about her body. She felt the urge to cover herself, at least as much as her bound hands could afford, but abandoned the thought as soon as it entered her head. There would be a punishment for that, for sure.

He stood there staring at her for the longest time. He seemed wobbly on his feet and she recalled her early fears of what abuse he would rain down on her if he ever got drunk. That fear seemed so naïve now. There was hardly a thing he could do to her now that he had not already done, except, perhaps, for beating her senseless with his fists. But she felt somehow confident, as confident as she could be about anything that is, that he would not do that unless, perhaps, she committed some sin that was beyond forgiveness. He craved her flesh too much. He enjoyed her humiliation and shame too much. He reveled too much in the heights of passion he could drive her to.

"Come to me," she thought. "Come and partake of me." She knew that tonight was perhaps the most significant of all of the nights that they had spent together. Tomorrow he would decide her fate. She would need to demonstrate to him what he would be missing if he let her go. If she didn't, she would meet some uncertain fate.

What would be worse, being a whore in some scrofulous Mexican bordello or being under the harsh tutelage of the woman who called herself Big Betty? It was hard to tell. On the one hand, she might spend years and years as a ten peso whore until she was too worn out and useless for even the most lowly peon. On the other, she might suffer untold abuse and cruelty, cruelty so ferocious that it would quickly squeeze all of the youth and pleasure from her body so that her travails would be harsh, but her path to eternal rest swift.

All in all, she would rather remain with the man. It was funny, really, in a way. She had so quickly become used to being the man's plaything that she had almost become comfortable in her role. They had washed and brushed together like some old, married couple. She was awaiting him in their bed, knowing, like she knew the back of her hand, what was soon to come, yearning for it in a way. Some kind of bond had formed between them. Outside, at the party, they had drifted apart. And from the looks she had seen on his face, he had been as uncomfortable and unhappy about it as she, although for somewhat different reasons. Now, the world was again excluded from their bizarre relationship. It was just them again, like it had been. It was almost comforting to know that he would soon come to her.

"Come," she thought. "Come to me now." She leaned back and drifted her bound hands down her body, flitted them over her nude pudendum. She spread her legs wide and lifted her hips, proffering her denuded lower lips. "Here it is," she thought. "Come and take it."

Jack watched the girl's display. It didn't surprise him.

It had been the whole point of the training he had been giving her. She had entered a zone of total need and total reliance. She had one purpose, and she would find meaning and satisfaction only through performing it. He had taken everything else away from her.

Her bare pussy was so inviting. He realized that he had forgotten to shave it again. It was too late now, he was too far gone in his passion. His cock had been filling with blood and her last movement had stiffened it. But he didn't want to partake of her flesh just yet. He wanted to savor the sight of her. Her body was a circus of pleasure, an engine of delight. Her moist, faraway eyes were fixated on him, two starry, blue sapphires set amidst shimmering pools of entrancement. She didn't need to look away any more. She knew what she wanted.

Her breasts, recumbent as she lay back, shimmered with her excited breaths. Her nipples were stiff, her chest already a shade more pinkish than the pure white skin that offset her maroon areolas. Her lips had puffed out. Her inner thighs glimmered with a sheen of perspiration.

He was a little woozier than he would have liked. His desire for her was tinged with a yearning he was unfamiliar with, as if the alcohol had pried open some deep well of need in him. What would tomorrow bring? Would he lose her forever? Was this their last night together? The thought of it filled him with an emptiness he hadn't known since he was a very young boy.

He could smell her scent. It entranced him like the most fragrant perfume. It was a scent only hers. The thought that he might never smell it ever again roiled his mind. The unfairness and cruelty of life came home to him. After all these years he had found the only woman who had ever captured his soul, and he was going to lose her. It would have been better, far, far better if he had put her to sleep way out there in the desert somewhere. The idea of someone else possessing her was driving him to the edge of madness.

The bed was slung low, the bottom only a few inches from the floor. He lowered himself to it. The girl took a deep breath as he approached her. Her lips parted and her tongue did a little dance along their edge. He lay down next to her, so close he could feel her body's heat. He wanted her so badly, it was as if he had been struck with some powerful virus. He raised himself on one elbow and stroked her face. His hand tingled with excitement. He leaned over, brought their lips together and kissed her.

Her mouth was hot and receptive. He couldn't help the sigh he released as their tongues intermingled. There was a softness to her lips that bespoke tenderness. His body pressed up against hers. It was smooth and soft and warm. His hand found her breast. Its weight was comforting and exciting all at the same time. Its resilience to the gentle squeeze he gave it caused an ache to run all through his body. And then the girl moaned and he was lost.

As in a daze, he began to swim in her flesh. He ran his hand down her torso to her hip and over her thigh. He broke their kiss and lowered himself until he could subsume one of her nipples in his mouth. He suckled on it gently, running his tongue all over it. The scent of her flesh was now overwhelming. Part of him wanted nothing more than to ravish her, to sink himself within her and seek apotheosis. But he wanted the blissful sensations of consuming her flesh to last. He lowered himself further. He kissed her belly while squeezing her breasts, more firmly now. He pinched her nipples, stiff as pencil points, and she groaned. Her torso squirmed under him and her hands, bound together like those of a supplicant, came to rest on his head, caressing it, stroking it.

He went lower, running his tongue around and inside her navel, sliding his hands down her sides. He had maneuvered himself between her legs. Her thighs were spread out virtually perpendicular to her body. Her mons brushed against his chest. Her heard her moan again and her hands dug themselves into his hair and took hold. He lowered himself further until her could place his hands on the insides of her widespread thighs. His face was even with her swollen pudenda. There was a glistening between her enflamed love lips. The aroma of her arousal almost made him swoon. He lowered his head, and as he ran his stiffened tongue between her outer labia, the girl's back arched and she issued a long, impassioned hiss.

He labored at her cunt, reveling at the smell, the taste, the heat. When he suckled her rigid love bud, the girl sighed deeply and she pressed her hips up, mashing her pussy up against his lips. He scoured her tender, inner thighs with his hands, rubbed them across her belly, reached up and took hold of her breasts, giving them mighty squeezes. He pressed his tongue deep within her hole, flitting the tip up against the roof of her tunnel. She ground her pussy up against him, arched her back and moaned, "Ohhhhhhhhhh! Ohhhhhhhhhhh!"

She was squirming and moaning. He circled his arms under her thighs, slid them down to under her ankles and lifted them up. He kept pressing on them until her legs were bent up against her, her ankles touching her breasts. Then he delved his head back between her thighs and began to suckle and lick her sex with rabid passion.

"Oh! Oh! Oh!" she cried as her lusts were pushed past tolerance. "Oh, yes! Oh, yes! Oh, yes!" she cried. "Oh! Oh! Oh! Oh!"

And then her whole body shuddered. Her back arched

and she groaned loudly and deeply. Her eyes rolled back and she began to thrust her loins up and down as if she were fucking his agile, rapidly flitting tongue.

"Ohhhhhhhhhhhhh! Ohhhhhhhhhhhhh! Oh! Oh! Oh! Oh!" she cried out as she came.

Carly's mind was short circuiting with pleasure. The man's tongue and lips were driving her mad. She had wanted to drive him wild with pleasure and instead, he was doing it to her. She had no choice but to accept it. And there was no part of her that rued that choice. This was the payoff, the just deserts, the rewards, the compensation for her cruel bondage to the man, and she intended to collect each ecstasy laden instant of it. Her hips were raised high in the air and her thighs folded wide. His hands had circled her ankles and he was pressing them hard against her chest. She was held in place tightly. She could not have frustrated his assault on her even if she wanted to. And she wouldn't if she could, forestall the eruption of her lusts and a battering array of soul shaking throbs and contractions of her cunt.

When he sensed that she had crested, Jack leaned back and brought her ankles down. He pushed her thighs apart and raised himself until his cock was level with her dilated, ooze laden crevasse. He took hold of his thick, rigid meat and directed it to her gash. Its head found her yawning hole and he plunged himself inside it.

He groaned as her soft, moist heat surrounded him. He had wanted to take his time, to fuck her long and slow, but he had lost control of his passions. He began a rapid series of thrusts into her. He took her mouth and plunged his tongue inside. She groaned and met him. Her ankles crossed his back and she pressed him inside her deeply. At each downward stroke of his cock, she thrust her hips upwards, greeting him. His felt his peak coming.

He wanted to prolong it, delay it, but he couldn't control the thrusting of his hips. His needy cock was in command and it was seized with a rabid demand for fruition.

"Arrrrrrgh! Arrrrrrrrrgh! Arrrrrrrrrrrrrgh!" he groaned. His cock began to throb and spasm. His balls were tightened and a rush of pleasure flowed through his body, piercing his brain. The girl's hands were circled around his neck and the chain that connected her to the bed was jingling and jangling against his shoulder. He thrust his cock down so hard that he felt his hip bones collide against hers. "Ohhhhhhhh! Ohhhhhhhhh! Ohhhhh-hhhh!" he called out. Her pussy had erupted again and was clasping him hard each time it contracted. The girl was moaning wildly into his mouth. He gave her one, two, three, four more savage thrusts and he was done.

He lay atop her for a while. It felt like the girl had melted underneath him. He moved his hips slowly back and forth, just enough so that the mind numbing, sweet friction of her tunnel's walls eased out the last few small spasms of pleasure. When his cock had softened and slipped from her slit, he rolled off of her onto his back. His mind clouded over and he was asleep.

Carly lay there for a long time. It took her a while to get her breathing under control and to quiet the rapid beating of her heart. Her pussy was still purring from its eruptions. Her body was covered with sweat. She felt weak, as if she had just finished swimming a roaring river. She could hear through the closed door the faint sounds of the music they were playing downstairs.

The room was darkened, but the man had left the bathroom light on and its soft glow spread across the bed. She could hear the man breathing long and rhythmically. She looked over at him. His hands were lying across his belly, his mouth was parted slightly and his closed eyes were fluttering. She had never actually seen his face when he was asleep. The cruelty had faded away. It was at rest, at peace. It was not the face of a tormentor, of the cruel man who had done those things he had told the man downstairs in the kitchen.

She realized that this was the most freedom she had had in three days. She was neither under his watchful eyes nor bound virtually motionless. She pulled on the chain that connected her hands to the head of the bed. It had substantial play in it. She looked across the room. She had seen the man place the key to her confines on the dresser opposite the bed. Her eyes did a quick, hopeful calculation. If she scooted down the bed as far as the chain would let her, and she extended her leg as far as it would go, she might just be able to touch the top of the dresser with her foot.

She sat up. She could see the key lying there. She looked at the man. He was dead to the world, made almost comatose by the combination of sex and drink. If she could get the key and unlock her hands, she might be able to sneak down the stairs and make a break for freedom! She could wait until the music stopped, when everyone downstairs had either passed out or gone to a bedroom to fuck. She could be miles away before anyone noticed!

She crept slowly down the bed until her hands had tugged the chain taut. Her waist was by the foot of the bed. The dresser was about three feet away. The top was about four feet off the floor. If she could touch the key with the tip of her foot, she could drag it onto the floor and pick it up with her toes.

Turning to her right side so she could see the dresser and keep a watchful eye on the man, she lifted her leg high. Her big toe just touched the edge of the counter top. The key was only inches away. She dropped her foot silently. "Oh, please! Please! Please!" she prayed. She stretched her body so that she felt the sockets of her shoulders strain. Her leather bracelets were jammed up against the heels of her hands. She lifted her foot again. She stretched her leg out to the fullest, pointing her foot like a ballerina holding her foot *en pointe*. Her other knee was on the floor. She stretched and strained with all her might. She could just feel the edge of the key with her toe. "Please! Please! Please!" she prayed again.

She pulled on her arms to get just one more fraction of an inch out of them. She stretched her foot until her hip joint screamed. Her extended leg was shaking and vibrating and she tried to steady it.

"Just a little more! Just a little more!" she screamed inside. She felt her big toe touch it again. It moved a little over it. She pressed down with her toe as hard as she could to get traction. Suddenly, it moved! But it moved the wrong way! It moved away from her. The downward pressure had made it slide along the smooth dresser top. "Oh, god! Oh, god! Oh, god!" she called out in her mind. She was just touching it. She pressed her toe down again. And, to her eternal dismay, it slipped away.

Carly collapsed into a heap at the foot of the bed. She suppressed a woeful sob. She had been so close! So close! And now the key was out of reach. A wave of despair flowed through her. Tears were flowing from her eyes. She looked at the man. He was still sleeping soundly. The only good thing was that he had not seen her escape attempt. He would punish her cruelly if he ever found out. Slowly, in dismal agony, she climbed back onto the bed. She slid her body until it was again next to the man's. She pressed her face into the mattress and cried and cried and cried.

It took a long while for her to stop. Her mind had been going through the horrible, alternative futures which loomed over her. She lifted her head and looked over at the man. Her only hope was that he want her more badly than the money the others would give him for her. As much as the thought revolted her, she knew that she had to please him.

He was lying on his back with his legs spread. She wiped the tears from her eyes and crept closer to him. She moved opposite his thigh. His cock lay soft and loose, slightly leaning to his left, towards her. She had never touched him without permission. How would he react? Would he be enraged that she took an action on her own, outside of his control? Would he beat her and punish her? Her stomach turned queasy. She knew she had to do it.

Slowly, carefully, she crept over his leg and settled herself between his thighs. She reached out and took his soft cock into her bound hands. It seemed so harmless now, a limp, tired instrument. But she knew that she needed to bring it to life. She carefully held it poised between her fingers, lowered her head and took it into her mouth.

It tasted of sweat and cum and her own juices. It was still slippery from their fucking. She suckled on it gently, letting her tongue slide over the head slowly, lightly. She heard the man's breathing stutter for a moment and his thighs shifted. She stayed utterly still for a moment, his manhood lying atop her tongue. When his breathing began to become steady again, she resumed her supplication to it, suckling, kissing, licking ever so gently.

The soft appendage was beginning to fill with blood. It was getting warmer in her mouth. She kept suckling it until it had lost its softness and became rubbery. He moved again, just slightly, and issued a small moan. She stopped. When it was clear that he had not awoken, she resumed.

Her hands were no longer needed to hold it still. She moved them away, careful not to let the chain drag across the man's body. She placed the heels of her hands on his belly. He groaned. His cock had grown to stiffness now. What had commenced as a dreadful chore had become exciting. Just the thought of his manhood hard and ready was enough to make her feel that urge way down below. She issued a moan of her own, lowered her head as far as it would go, until his cock was pressing against the back of her throat, and then, keeping her mouth clamped tightly against the shaft, drew her head back up slowly and steadily, relishing every millimeter as it passed along her lips.

Jack was struggling to consciousness. He felt a wonderful sensation in his loins. His body was shimmering with delight. It took him a few moments to realize what was happening. And then he felt the girl's tongue trace a line under the engorged helmet to his prick and then subsume it again in her mouth.

The thought flitted across his mind that he should be angry that the girl had taken it upon herself to presume to make contact with him, especially of such an intimate nature, but the warm softness of her mouth quickly dispelled any notion that he should cause her to stop. Skillfully, she swirled her tongue around the head of his crank. She kissed its tip, running her tongue over the little slit and then let her mouth descend yet again, causing a river of pleasure to flow through him.

The cautious, reptile part of his brain wondered why the girl had taken this task upon herself. The reason became clear to him in a moment. She had heard the talk downstairs about selling her off and she was making her bid to get him to keep her. She was smart all right. It was precisely the right thing to do.

He let his musings fade as the girl maintained a steady churning at his loins. He rubbed his hand in her short, burnt orange hair. He closed his eyes and let the pleasure flow through him.

Carly had realized that he was awake when she felt his hand on her head. At first, she had steeled herself for the blow she half expected, but when it did not come, she relaxed and went on with her work. Sucking his cock put her in a kind of a daze, her mind swimming with contrary emotions. There was no getting around the fact that having his hard meat in her mouth was exciting and lust inducing. But there was also that familiar feeling of shame that she had been reduced to a mere mechanism to giving the man pleasure. And now she had taken it upon herself to do it rather than opening her mouth and receiving his maleness under threat of cruel, painful correction if she did not.

His hips began to rise to meet her lips as they descended down his tool. His hand gripped her hair. His breathing was becoming labored and shallow. His legs spread wide and he drew back his heels. He moaned deeply. His cock was rock hard. She washed it with her tongue, suckled it, stroked it with her lips, tickled its tip. She did everything she could think of to maximize his pleasure. When she sensed him about to commence his climax, she eased off a bit, letting him cool before started again. She did it once, twice, three times. Each time she relented her efforts, he groaned and his hips shifted.

And then his upward thrusts became more insistent. His grip on her hair grew tighter. Her heart was beating wildly. She knew that the moment of his eruption was at hand. She lifted her head from his prick and swiftly moved her hands so that they were below her chin and cupped his large, tight balls. She took his manhood back into her mouth and began to move her head up and down rapidly.

He groaned loudly, once, and then again. Then he shouted out a roaring grunt and his cock began to throb and spasm in her mouth. His jism came spurting out, coating the back of her mouth. She swallowed it readily and continued her assault on his prick, giving his scrotal sac gentle encouragement with her hands.

"Arrrrrrrrgh! Arrrrrrrrgh!" he called out. He pushed her head down until his cock popped into her throat. His body stiffened. She began to gag and cough, but she held her head still, did not resist.

As his spasms ebbed, his grip on her hair loosened. She was able to draw her head up and she took in a deep breath. She continued to slide her lips up and down his stem as the rigid pole gave off a series of post orgasmic shudders.

His cock was softening when she felt him pull on her hair. She followed the pressure on her scalp, releasing his now limp manhood from her mouth and slid her body upwards over his. He kept pulling her until she was lying next to him, their heads level. He took hold of her chin and placed his lips upon hers, kissing her deeply. She was filled with a strange satisfaction that she had brought him so much pleasure. He stroked his hand down her body, caressing her breasts lazily and running it across her belly and over her hip. He broke their kiss and caressed her face, looking deeply into her eyes. She looked back at him, hoping desperately that he would see the humanity within.

She was special, that was for sure, Jack thought. She was a treasure worth keeping. As his head cleared, he chided himself for falling asleep without securing her. One slip was all it would take for her to be gone. He didn't want to take that chance.

He gave her another, small kiss and got up from the bed. He stepped over to the dresser and retrieved the key to the chain that led to her wrists. Back on the bed, he released her wrists from the chain and, after kissing her again, pushed her over to her belly. He pulled her arms behind her back and connected them. Then he affixed the chain to the front of her collar and pulled it taut, securing it in place. He slid his hands down her rear and thighs until he reached her ankles, which he joined. There was a chain identical to the one from the headboard at the foot of the bed and he connected it to her ankles and drew it taut. He got up from the bed and went to the bathroom where he emptied himself. His cock felt soft and satisfied.

He turned out the light before he went back to the bed. It was completely dark without the bathroom light and he had to feel his way. He was about to lie down when he remembered something. He fished around by the side of the bed on the floor and he recovered what he was looking for. He moved back to the girl and took hold of her hair, bending her neck back. He then felt with one hand for her mouth and, with the other, guided the prong of her gag to the opening. She gave a muffled whine when it sank home. He buckled it tightly behind her head.

Laying down bedside her, he stroked her rear and the back of her thighs. "What a treasure," he thought. He then rolled over and in a few minutes was fast asleep.

Carly had been dreadfully unhappy when the man began to bind her. For a short while, she had had relative freedom. Having her hands immobilized behind her felt horridly familiar. When he pressed the gag between her lips, she felt despair flow through her once again and she began to cry silently. "It's okay," she thought after a while. "I did what I had to do." She felt sure that the pleasure she had brought the man had done its work. She had seen it in his eyes. He wanted her badly. And she wanted him to want her badly. Soon, she soothed herself and let the darkness take her.

Sometime later in the night, she felt her ankles being freed. The man's strong hands maneuvered her onto her knees, her forehead down on the mattress, and spread her legs. His hand toyed with her sex until she was wet and hot. When he slipped himself inside her, she groaned with pleasure.

Just last night, a mere twenty four hours ago, she had been filled with anguish as he forced her to pleasure again. Now, it was different. The very act which had driven her to despair the night before was now welcomed as a sign of his fevered desire for her. And as long as he desired her that way, there was hope.

She let the waves of pleasure from his fat, thick cock flow through her and she began to thrust back at him madly. "Yes! Yes! Yes!" she thought. "Fuck me! Fuck me! Fuck me!"

CHAPTER SEVEN

Jack awoke late. Only a slight sparkle of light filtered into the room through the slim spaces between the boards that covered the windows. It made the room glow dimly. The thin shafts of light were filled with little motes of dust making them look like tiny spotlights. He awoke, like he had for most of the last twelve years, with a start, but he was quickly calmed when he realized that for today at least he was not on the run. He was among friends in a hideaway that the cops had been looking for for years but never found.

Today was the beginning of a new life. Hopefully, by tomorrow he would be in Mexico. Hopefully, the amigo that the Rogues did business with would have a spot for him. Hopefully, the girl would be with him and he could look forward to countless days awakening with her bound and gagged by his side.

She was still asleep. He thought of waking her and tearing off a piece before he went downstairs and had breakfast, but he decided to let it slide. Not that he didn't want to fuck her, but, for the first time, there didn't seem to be the urgency about it that it had. He would get to fuck her plenty of times with any luck.

Carly, that was her name. He wondered idly whether he should maybe get it tattooed on her chest in large, ornate, blue letters so he wouldn't forget it again. He could get one of the Mexican artists to do it and set in amidst a fancy, elaborate drawing of choppers and weapons and naked, big breasted women and various other totems of his life. He could make it colorful and interesting and he would show her off to his many visitors. Maybe cover her whole body. Then it would make sense to keep her naked all the time so that she could be properly displayed. But no one else would fuck her. That would be for him and him alone. Sure, it might be fun to watch her do a lesbo thing with some Mexican slut from time to time. And special guests might get treated to a blow job now and then. But no cock other than his would ever penetrate any of her lower orifices. That was for sure. They would be reserved for him and him alone.

He crept off of the bed. He had a little headache from all the booze he had consumed and his mouth tasted like a dry gulch. He felt a little skeevy too and needed a shower. That would help with the hangover a little as would a nice big breakfast.

It was going to be a great day, he just knew it.

He remembered that all of his clean clothes were still in the car. That and the rest of his gear, the guns he had stolen, the cash. He didn't worry about anybody stealing it. It was more than just honor among thieves. Anybody ripping off another gang member would reap a whole world of shit. And stuff like that just had a tendency to get out. Besides, he was Ike's guest and anything that was stolen from him while he had that status Ike would be honor bound to make up to him.

So, he decided to wait for the shower. He padded barefoot into the bathroom and emptied his bladder. He flicked on the light and took a look at himself in the mirror. He needed a shave. If he wasn't mistaken, some of the worry lines on his face were gone. Prison had a way of aging you before your time and he had begun to look a lot older than his 44 years. But there wasn't an ounce of flab on him and he was sure that with a little sun and rest and recreation, he would regain at least a little of his youth in no time.

He went back into the bedroom and dressed quietly. He would get some breakfast and then get his stuff from the car. Just before he left, he saw the keys to the girl's bonds on the dresser. He had put them back there last night after he had chained her up for the night. He realized that he must have had quite a load on to forget to put them somewhere that they would be way out of the girl's reach. He decided to put them in his pocket. There was little chance the girl could get to them they way she was bound and all, but there was no sense in taking chances.

Stepping from the room, he closed the door softly behind him. He walked the short distance to the stairs that led downstairs and began to descend them. He was surprised at the activity and wondered what time it was. Two of the girls who lived in the cages in the playroom, one of the black haired ones and the blonde, were busily cleaning up from the night before. Naked still, their legs hobbled by 18" long chains, they were shuffling along, picking up empty bottles, glasses, paper plates. The one they called Rocker was sitting in one of the easy chairs supervising them. Two large, dark green plastic garbage cans sat by the entrance to the foyer full of bottles. The woman he had kidnapped yesterday, the elegant and rich Malinda Ramirez, was ensconced naked and gagged in one of the cages, looking out gloomily.

Jack gave Rocker a nod and turned to go into the kitchen. Stitch was there, in the same place as the night before, like he had never moved. The third girl was standing by the kitchen sink, her feet connected by a short steel chain, washing the serving trays from the night before. Stitch was drinking a mug of coffee.

"Mornin' partner," he said when he saw Jack. "There's coffee in the pot. Maureen here will whip up some bacon and eggs for you if you want them."

"Sounds good to me," Jack replied.

"Hey, slut," Stitch barked, "you heard the man. Get to it."

"Yes, sir," the dark haired girl replied sadly. She put down the tray she was washing and shuffled over to the refrigerator. She opened it and retrieved a carton of eggs and a package of bacon.

"Three eggs, over easy," Jack told her. "And don't break the yolks. And half a dozen strips of bacon and some toast." He turned to Stitch. "You got bread, don't ya?"

"Sure," Stitch replied. "Anything you want."

Jack went over to the stainless steel coffee maker. From the cabinet above it he retrieved a cup. He poured some coffee. It smelled strong. There was a carton of milk on the table. He sat down and poured some into his cup. He took the first sip and sighed. It was a thousand times better than the sewer water they served in the joint. When you could get it, that is.

He watched the girl toss some bacon in a big frying pan. A second or two later, it started to sizzle.

"I'm going to miss this one," Stitch said, nodding his head at the girl. "She's a pretty good cook. She and the other two are moving on tonight. There'll be new ones in in a couple of days, and I'll have to break one of them in all over again. It's a pain in the ass, but these ones have been here for about five months now and Ike's gotten tired of them."

Jack kept his eyes on the girl, gauging her reaction to the news that she was going to be sold off into sexual slavery that night. Tears were running down her face and she was shaking. But she kept up at her job, demonstrating the good discipline the gang had instilled in her.

He and Stitch sat there silently while the girl cooked Jack's breakfast. When she was done, she delivered the plates to the table along with a set of utensils. She brushed up her arm against Jack's as she set the plates down in front of him. He reached around her and ran his hand down her bare back and over her ass. The girl froze in place. "Spread your legs," he told her.

When she had moved them apart, he slid his hand along the inside of her soft, white thigh up to her crux and then ran his fingers over her mons tantalizingly until she had moistened and he was able to slip two fingers inside her. She gave out a deep breath as he entered her and she swayed in place. Jack was watching her face and he could see the turmoil building up inside her. "Maybe I can get her and the girl to do a threesome," he thought idly. He would enjoy the opportunity to watch the girl's face as this one ate her pussy. When he did it, he couldn't see it. He kept running his fingers in and out of the black haired girl's crevasse until she released a long sigh. Then he laughed, patted her on the ass and turned his attention to his meal.

The girl went back to her chores.

The meal went down quickly. When he was done, he told the girl to clear his plate and refill his coffee cup. She approached him warily. Jack was tempted to put his hands on her again, but he let her alone.

When he had finished his second cup of coffee, he announced his intention to go out to the car and get his gear. Stitch told him that Ike had had a couple of the boys bring it in last night. "The dough and the pieces you had Ike put away for safe keeping. The rest of the stuff is in the foyer by the front door," he said.

Jack was a little piqued that somebody had touched his stuff, but he knew that he didn't dare make a fuss about it. Hell, when it came right down to it, they could take it all as long as he and the girl got a ticket to Mexico tonight.

"Ike had the Lexus taken care of," Stitch continued. "We got some guys who'll run it across the border and unload it. It's better to take care of that kind of stuff right away. The cops'll be combing the countryside for it soon, if they're not already. Ike'll make sure you get your cut, don't worry about that, but we probably won't get more than fifty cents on the dollar for it."

That sounded okay to Jack and he said so.

"He'll be back in a little while. He said he wants to talk to you. He's got some plans for the Ramirez broad he wants to work out with you. And the other one too. He thinks our Mexican friend will go for her in a big way and if you sell her to him it'll put you in right with him."

At this, Jack blanched. He knew that Stitch was right, but he would do all he could to prevent it. If the Mexican guy wanted, he could get a hundred girls like her. Somehow, he would work it out.

Jack finished his coffee and gave the empty cup to the black haired girl to deal with. He excused himself from Stitch and went out to the foyer to retrieve his bags. A few seconds later, he was trudging back up the stairs to his room.

When Carly heard the steps outside the door, she knew that her captor had returned. She had awoken about 40 minutes or so before, just as the man had closed the door to go downstairs. When she had been startled into wakefulness, it had taken her a few moments to recollect where she was. It all came home to her in a moment as she experienced the dismal reality that she had begun another day of captivity. She remembered from the night before how close she had been to finding a way to escape and a deadly dreariness enveloped her.

Just like the prior times when the man had left her alone, she felt like he had left behind some evil spell that kept her bound and silenced while he was gone. Even though not physically present, he nonetheless still exercised his absolute, remorseless power over her.

She had tried to get used to the presence of the long, thick, insulting gag in her mouth, but it was an intrusion, an extension of the man's will, that could not be ignored. She tried to put out of her mind the harsh bindings that left her there on her belly frozen in place. For a brief time last night she had experienced some relative freedom, but now she was back in what had become her natural state, bound into almost total immobility, able only to wriggle her fingers and toes or turn her head from side to side.

She fought hard not to cry. She realized that this would be her permanent future if the man took her to Mexico. He would never let her go and never let her resume the life of an independent human being. She knew that the experience of having her helpless and under his total, strict control was a source of great pleasure to him. Part of her rued the passion which she had let herself experience last night. Was it really better to be this man's abject prisoner? Mighten there be some saving grace in the other dismal alternatives?

She quickly dispelled that notion. No, remaining the prisoner of the man was the least dreadful of her futures. As much as she felt shamed and degraded by her show of lasciviousness, she knew that it was all done for a greater purpose. She had to make the man desire her above all else or she was doomed.

So she awaited the man's return resignedly. She

resisted the urge to scream and rage against her fate, her miserable bondage, her loss of personhood. She pulled slightly at her bonds, not in any hopes of freeing herself, but more out of habit than anything. Her plight was so unreal, so outrageously bizarre and dreadful that her mind needed the assurance that her bindings were actual and not the product of some torturous, psychotic nightmare. "Be strong, Carly," she said to herself. "Be strong and survive."

When the man's steps stopped outside the door and she heard the click of the lock signaling his immanent entrance, Carly steeled herself for whatever ordeal the man had next planned for her. She pledged herself to an enthused obedience. And not just because she wanted to ingratiate herself more thoroughly to him. His cruel punishments still engendered a rabid fear in her.

Her stomach turned over when he came through the door. She turned her head to look at him. He was carrying the stuff from the car. He looked well fed and satisfied. He placed the bags on the floor and, giving her a mere glance, began to disrobe. Carly prepared herself for another round of his callous use, but she was wrong. He quickly stepped into the bathroom and a few seconds later she heard the sounds of the shower. She knew that it meant that she would have to wait for liberation. It made her anxious. She had to pee and was hungry. She would have to await the man's pleasure before she could get relief from either.

Jack reveled in the sensations of the shower. The bathroom, like the bedroom, was decorated in the art deco style of the twenties. It was spacious and kept, like the bedroom, very clean. The fittings were of gleaming brass and there were rococo designs on the door lintels. The shower was affixed to a pure white, sparkly clean porcelain tub. The sink and toilet were stark white and shiny too. Jack imagined the series of naked young women over the years who must have tidied and cleaned them, and the bedroom, under Stitch's meticulous direction. It made sense to have the girls cleaning the place. Otherwise, they would just sit in their cages all day waiting for somebody to come by and use them.

Maybe he would have the girl do some of the cleaning up when he got his place in Mexico. He would make sure that it was done under the strict supervision of a harsh *momasita*, all beefed up and strong as a bull. And if she made any mistakes or was disobedient in any way, she would whip and abuse her, and when he came home he would punish her too. His cock stirred at the thought of punishing her. She had such sweet flesh and large, doleful eyes. She was made for it.

When he was done with the shower, he shaved. "A face only a mother could love," he thought as he scraped away the bristly growth. Not his mother though. He wondered idly if she were still alive. She would be in her 60's. Not many skank addicts made it to their 60's, although it was possible she had cleaned herself up at some point. He tried to push those thoughts out of his mind. Too many bad memories. He knew that an armchair psychologist would make much of his disdain for his mother and his harshness towards women in general. Maybe there was some truth to that. But if it was, it was deserved.

He had never met a woman who he could trust. The ones that didn't run from him in fear only stayed because they wanted something. Like the girl. He knew that she wanted to go to Mexico. That was the explanation for her randiness last night. At least that's what she probably thought. But it was only partly true. He was sure that three or four days ago she would have rebelled against the idea that she should encourage him to use her in any way. Now she was trading sex for perceived safety. Soon she would be trading it for mere approval, the only joy she would ever get. She had started down the road to complete surrender, and once you got started on that, you didn't stop until you reached the end. She would display herself and crave his attention. She would find joy in serving him, satisfaction in her debasement. He had seen it happen dozens of times.

He rinsed off his face and dried it off. The bathroom was stocked with luxurious, fluffy, white towels. Just like a fancy hotel. The boys here didn't stint themselves on anything.

He went back into the bedroom. It was time to get the girl all washed up. He knelt near the bed and released her ankles and collar from the chains that affixed her in place. Taking hold of her hair, he guided her gently to her feet and brought her into the bathroom. He sat her on the toilet and let her pee. Then he removed her gag and unfastened her wrists from behind her back and had her step into the tub. He turned on the shower and indicated to her to get to work.

He left the shower curtain open so he could watch her. He sat on the toilet with the lid down. His smokes were in his pants pocket and he lit one. It was relaxing and enjoyable to watch the girl touch herself all over, giving him sideways, unhappy glances all the while. She did turn to him, without instruction, while she washed her breasts, covering them with soap and then caressing and massaging them much, much more than necessary while she rinsed them off. When she did her pussy, she turned her back to him, bent over and spread her legs. He watched appreciatively while she stroked her mound with her graceful fingers. She put two fingers on her love button and gave it more than a few gentle rubs before she straightened up to do her hair.

It was just what he had been talking about. She knew that seeing her touch herself pleased him, knew that arousing him would garner her his attentions. She couldn't stop herself. It was becoming ingrained, like from the first moments they were together when he sat her down in a chair and made her spread her legs and push out her breasts. All she had belonged to him. Nothing belonged to her. The concept of privacy had fled her mind. She was permanently and irrevocably his.

He ordered her to finish up. When she stepped from the tub onto the thick, soft bathmat, he used a fresh towel to dry her off. He scruffed her short, orange red hair until it was almost dried and then brushed it straight. He hadn't decided whether to keep her as a redhead or to let her blond hair grow back in. There was something appealing about how she looked when she was blond, but making her hair red had been an indicia of his ownership of her and demarked the creature she was now from the one she had been. He didn't need to decide that now, though.

He took hold of her dried hair in the back of her head and guided her back into the bedroom. He made her lie down on the bed, on her back, and connected her hands to the headboard, pulling the chain tight so that they would stay over her head and out of his way. He took a pillow and shoved it under her hips, raising them and told her to spread her legs and raise her knees. Her pretty little coosh was displayed nicely. He patted it affectionately and then grabbed her love lips between his thumb and forefinger and gave them a little squeeze. Not enough to hurt her, but just enough to establish his proprietorship.

She looked at him dolefully, her lips pressed tightly together and her chest rising and falling.

Jack went into the bathroom and came back with a shaving mug he had found there and a shaving brush. He had rinsed the mug with hot water and he used the brush to establish a thick lather. He covered her mons with it. He had also brought out the razor he had used on his face, a double bladed safety razor with sharp, new blades.

He sat on the bed between the girl's legs and used it to scrape away her three days' growth, cleaning the razor on a towel whenever it became thick with shaving cream. He pushed her mons this way and that to get all the little bristles hiding in the crevices on the sides, scraped up to the insides of her thighs and all over her lower belly. He made sure that the whole area from her belly button to her thighs was as soft and smooth as a baby's face. When he was done, he saw that her pussy was glistening. The activity had been pervaded with lust driving sensations for both of them. He couldn't resist placing his thumb over her hard, little bump and rubbing it until he sensed her body shift into sensuous mode and heard her release an irrepressible sigh.

He did her legs and under her arms too, making her smooth and soft all over. She kept her eyes on him the whole time, watching him warily. She was now hairless except for the mop on her head. Someday, he decided, he would do that too and make her go around bald for a while. He would wait until some moment when he felt she was in need of some deeper humiliation to remind her of her status.

He brought everything back into the bathroom and returned with a small hand cream dispenser. He pressed some out on his hand and rubbed it into everywhere he had shaved. When he did her pussy, the girl closed her eyes and bit her lip.

Finally, he was done. The intimate contact with her flesh had raised his lusts. His cock was jutting out in display mode. He wanted to fuck her, but not yet. He lay down next to her, leaving her hips raised in the air by several inches. He pressed his body up close to hers and leaned over her, kissing and caressing her heavy, pure white breasts. Her nipples stiffened obediently and, in a short while, she issued a moan.

Carly let the man's mouth and tongue ease her into a state of bliss. There was no longer any sense in resisting him. She no longer wanted to. Her surrender was complete. She had cast her lot with him and the bodily joy he brought her was her only compensation.

Earlier, in the shower, while he sat and smoked and watched her, she had felt compelled to caress herself in front of him. She wasn't sure why, but there it was. Part of it, she knew, was the fact that her ability to feel and touch her own body had been so limited in the last few days that the urge to take advantage of her brief respite from confinement was irresistible. And, she knew instinctively that to do so in his presence out of his view, hiding it, touching herself surreptitiously for her pleasure and satisfaction alone, would merit fierce punishment.

But it was more than that. It just somehow felt right, part of the natural order of things. These parts of her body that brought her pleasure seemed to belong more to him now than to her. And the thought that what she did would bring his eyes to where her fingers touched, would fixate him, draw him in, deepen his desire for her, gave her a peculiar, incongruous, ironic, shameful pleasure. Somehow, his fixation on her body, its orifices, its erogenous zones, its softness, curvature, resilience, femaleness, had sparked in her a dark, salacious need.

As his desire for her grew stronger, so did her compulsion to receive his attentions, as if the two forces were acting as an accelerant for each other, like two massive storms feeding on each other's energy. And the fact that this symbiosis could result only in, finally, a cataclysmic orgy of destruction, did not, could not, deter her determination to feed it. The more he shamed her, the more callous his use of her, the more helpless she was to resist him, the deeper and darker her need to be shamed, humiliated, used seemed to grow.

And just as his presence, his attention, drove her desires, his absence or inattention brought her only despair and unhappiness. Not just at what he had done to her, how he kept her, wrapped up and bound like some property temporarily put aside, but at how right and deserving that humiliation, shame and unhappiness seemed.

It was like a cavity deep in her soul that wracked her body with pain, but pain so delicious and intense that it served to foster an unfathomable craving for it. Something had happened to her mind. She knew it. She knew it was wrong. But her life now vibrated with an intensity so overwhelming that she could not bring herself to rue the change. The cocoon of security and happiness and self sufficiency in which she now realized she had been enwrapped before this ordeal had begun had been exploded and had produced not a butterfly, but a fiercely burning ball of fire.

So as his lips subsumed her teats, his hot, heavy hand wandered her body, she felt her need begin to grow. She closed her eyes and let the sensations fill her with pleasure. His hand stroked her inner thighs, lightly, deftly, delicately, as if her body were a fragile construct that too much pressure might collapse. It was tantalizing and lust inspiring. As was the thought of her powerlessness to resist him. Her thighs were fixed open like the pinned back wings of a butterfly in someone's collection. Her hands were stretched out tautly above her. She was utterly powerless to resist his ministrations.

The hand came back up, drifted over her mons, ceasing only to draw a thick finger between her already distended, blood filled labia and flick lightly across her tender pleasure bud. It stroked her belly up to her breasts, then seizing the one not being suckled luxuriously, took hold of it, squeezing it, caressing it, massaging it. She issued a long, impassioned sigh. Her hips squirmed as the ache of desire in her loins grew exquisite. His hand rose further, turned her cheek towards his face. His head rose from her breast and the next thing she knew, he tongue had forced entry between her lips.

A wave of passion swept through her. She kissed the man back madly. His hand floated down her torso once again, stopping to caress each of her breasts, to stroke her belly, and then took hold of her puss, squeezing her labial lips together forcefully, harder and harder until she moaned from the pain.

Satisfied with her response, while his hot tongue slipped and slid and probed and turned over hers, sending her exhilarating messages of pleasure, the hand began a passion inducing dance on her mons. It stroked it. Its fingers delved inside it. It caressed her clit, thrust itself in and out of her crevasse. It squeezed the lips again until she squealed and then slipped over her taut, distended thighs, stroking and caressing them only to return to her steaming fulcrum to drive her lusts ever and ever higher.

She squirmed and moaned. Her body shuddered. Her mind spun in a dizzying vortex. The hand knew its business well. Her hands, writhing and twisting in their bonds were useless. He was driving her into a frenzy of lust, forcing her to teeter on the edge of a raging completion. If only she could use her hands. But what if she could? Would she try and drive away the tormenting fingers, or press them more firmly into her sex to force the issue?

Either one would serve to relieve her of the virtually agonizing want that permeated her mind, if only for a few seconds. But she knew deep down that even if her hands were free, she would do no such thing. To disobey the man, to impinge on his privileges, to challenge his ownership of her flesh was beyond her capabilities. Not only because of her rabid fear of the harsh consequences that would result, but more so that she knew that she had no right to. She was his to enjoy, no matter what form that enjoyment took, no matter how excruciating the pain or pleasure she suffered, no matter how deeply her vulnerability to his designs shamed her.

Jack broke their kiss. His cock was a steely, rigid pole and his balls were tight and aching. He would fuck her, but not yet. The thoughts he had had while downstairs in the kitchen, the vision of the girl succumbing to the black haired girl's ministrations while he watched, had sparked his need to see her face while she came. She was primed now, ready to explode. When he abandoned her lips, the girl's mouth remained open, parted into a limp 'O'. Her face was soft and flaccid as if she no longer had the strength to pose it. Her eyelids, loosely closed, were fluttering. Her nostrils were dilated. Her cheeks were reddened, her eyebrows bent into a worried looking frown. She had wholly abandoned herself to her passions. There was nothing in reserve, nothing hidden away. He burned the image into his mind.

His two longest fingers were rubbing her clit, moving

in little circles, pressing down on it. Then he plunged them deep inside her, thrusting them in and out in a rapid piston motion. Then he brought them back up again, this time flitting them over the hypersensitive appendage again and again and again until she arched her back and groaned. She was so close to the top that it would take but little more to send her into a delirious explosion. This time, he didn't stop. He flicked the little bud back and forth *rapido*. Her knees spread ever wider. Her chest was rising and falling in a desperate effort to catch her breath. Her eyelids opened and her eyeballs rolled back into her head. Her face contorted into a simulacrum of agony.

And then she came. She shouted her pleasure into the room. "Ohhhhhhhhhhhhhhh! Ohhhhhhhhhhhhhhh! Ohhhhhhhhhhhhhhhhhh!" she called out. Her body jerked and shuddered. Her hips ground against his hand. He thrust his fingers deep into her cavern while continuing to worry her pleasure nubbin with his thumb. "Oh, god! Oh! Oh! Oh!" she called out. "Fuck! Fuck! Fuck!" she yelled. "Ohhhhhhhhhhhhh! Ohhhhhhhhhhhhhhh! Ohhhhhhhhhhhh!" She went on and on and on, as if he had launched her into cataclysmic eruption that would not end until all of her flesh was consumed.

When her orgasm finally crested, her whole body seemed to collapse as if her innards had liquefied. He continued to massage her messy, hot cunt gently, coaxing out of her several intense shudders of post orgasmic pleasure. It had been enthralling to watch. She was one in a hundred thousand. Her capacity for lust seemed endless. It was the image he would hold in his mind now whenever he thought of her, whenever he fucked her.

He drew his hand away. It was his turn now. He crossed between her spread out thighs and positioned his cock at her oozing gate. When he pressed the head just past the entrance, she looked at him, wonder, fear, surrender and eagerness on her face all at once. He shifted his hips and sank himself slowly home, reveling in the soft, moist heat which pressed on his cock from all sides. Her hips rose to meet him and her legs crossed over the backs of his thighs, pulling him in. He groaned with delight as he fucked her.

* * * * * * * * * * * * *

He did not know how long later he awoke. Their bodies were still intertwined. She was still asleep and he took time to enjoy the feel of the rhythmic rise and fall of her chest, the heat of her body. He had never felt like this about anyone. He needed her so badly that the thought of losing her made his blood turn sour. It was like had had contracted some disease, become addicted to her flesh. He thought of Ike and the Mexican drug lord who was coming tonight to purchase merchandise. Somehow, he would talk his way out of selling the girl. He just had to.

Rolling off of her, he grabbed his shorts and started to dress. His actions made the girl stir. She looked up at him apprehensively. She knew that he was going to bring her downstairs now. She would be naked again in front of all those strange men. They would cast their lustful eyes on her. It pleased him to show her off, and it pleased him to see her discomfiture. It was only the beginning of what he had planned for her. All he had to do was hold onto her for the next 24 hours and she would be his.

When he had donned his boots, he leaned over the bed and released her hands from the chain and pulled her to her feet beside the bed. He unbound her hands from each other and, after making her turn around, fastened them behind her back. The gag was on the floor and he picked it up and presented it to her mouth. She spread her lips and accepted it, looking intently into his face. "Don't worry," he thought. "I'll protect you."

She seemed to catch his thoughts and her anxious face calmed. He took hold of the ring in the front of her collar and pulled her towards the door.

Downstairs, the girls had finished their cleaning. Chaz was there and a couple of the other boys. They were binding and gagging the party girls from last night. There were four of them, all near model quality, all naked as jaybirds but for their 3" high high heels. One of the men had a cluster of black satin bags in his hands and as each girl was gagged and bound, he slipped it over her head, drawing it tight around her neck.

"Heya, Jack," Chaz said. "Sleep good?"

"I guess the fuck he did," one of the others said. "It's just past noon."

"If I had a little honey like that, I wouldn't be getting out of bed too early neither," Chaz replied.

"Hey, Jack," he added as Jack was about to pass him on the way to the kitchen. "Want a blow job or something from one of our girls here? We're getting ready to send 'em back to the house they work out of. You'll be missing something special if you don't."

"No thanks," Jack replied. He paused though, to look them over. They were all eminently desirable and would look good on their knees between his legs. All but the one on the end had a black bag pulled over her head. She looked about 24 or 25 and had a nice, pale, round face with sparkly, green eyes. Her legs were long and her long, plump slit was devoid of hair. She was shapely, with a nice set of breasts. Her hair was dark brown and hung down thick and wavy just past her shoulders. She wore the club's two inch high, bright red insignia tattooed on her right breast. She was looking at Jack with daggers in her emerald eyes.

Chaz noticed it. He took hold of a nipple and squeezed it hard. The girl moaned and her eyes turned soft and wet. Chaz just kept holding her teat, turning it harder and harder until she squealed and fell to her knees. Chaz released her tit. "That's enough of that, cunt," he told her. "You've earned yourself a good whipping when we get back to the house. Now bow down to Jack here and kiss his foot if you don't want to make it worse."

Tears were flowing from the girl's eyes. She bent over quickly and edged herself on her knees to where Jack was standing. When she reached his feet, she murmured something pathetic sounding from behind her gag and settled where her mouth would be on his boot. Jack took note of her narrow, curved back and her delicious rear orbs.

He took pity on her. "Okay, that's enough," he said. And to Chaz, "Why don't you let her off the hook this once?" he asked. "After all, it was only a look."

"No chance, Jack," Chaz replied. "Rules is rules. She knows better. She's been a little trouble lately and she's about due for a good whipping anyway. You gotta keep 'em in line. But I don't have to tell you that."

"No, you don't," Jack answered.

Chaz took hold of the girl's hair at the back of her head and pulled her off Jack's boot, bringing her to her feet. Her eyes were dour and glistening. The guy with the bags approached her. "Now you'll have something nice to think about on the way home," he said. He pulled the bag over her head, shutting her into darkness. Jack thought he heard a muffled sob.

"None of my business," he thought. He turned to go into the kitchen, pulling the girl Carly behind him.

There were a couple more people in the kitchen. One of the bikers from last night was sitting at the kitchen table, the one they called Killer, if Jack was not mistaken. Rocker was there too as well as the woman who they called Big Betty. Her slavish companion was kneeling up along the wall to the left of the table along with the three girls from the cages. Last night she wore a yellow shift, but this morning she was naked like the others. All of their hands were bound behind their backs. Before two of them were the large, silver, metallic dog dishes filled with what looked like Beefaroni. Stitch was standing by the stove ladling out portions into bowls for the other two. As he finished them, he placed them in front of the girls.

"Got room for one more?" Jack asked him.

Stitch looked up. "Yeah, there's an extra bowl in the cabinet. The more the merrier. Just have her kneel down next to Vida there."

By Vida, Jack assumed he meant the skinny blond haired that belonged to Big Betty. She was on the end. He brought the girl next to her, removed her gag and motioned for her to take her knees. A moment later, Stitch put a brimming bowl of noodles and beef in front of her. None of the other girls had started eating yet as if they were awaiting some signal. It appeared that they were since when Stitch clapped his hands, four pretty heads bent down to begin their meals. Jack looked down at the girl and gave her a nod. She immediately joined them.

Jack went around the table and took a seat between Big Betty and Rocker. From that vantage point he had a good view of the five women, their rear cheeks all pointed up and their legs spread as the bent over their meals. There were some bowls on the table and a large casserole dish with Beefaroni in it, the same as the girls were eating. Jack spooned some out for himself. There was a jug of deep red wine on the table and he poured himself a glass and then started to eat.

There was a constant banter between the gang members as they consumed their lunch. Rocker had a few jokes to tell and Big Betty was describing a few of her johns who came to her place for whatever turned them on. Across the room there was the sound of the girls giving out slight sighs and moans as they ate. Someone had removed the boards from the windows and the room was almost what you might call bright and cheery.

"Hey, Jack," Big Betty said at one point, "what's your price on the red head? I sure could give her a nice home."

"She's not for sale," Jack told her.

"Come on," Betty replied. "Everything's for sale. I'll give you top dollar for her, say, $25,000. That's a nice chunk of change for you to take to Mexico."

"No deal," Jack replied. "But thanks. I'm taking her with me."

Jack noticed that Stitch gave him a concerned look. He realized that he was throwing out a direct challenge to the gang's leader, but he figured he might as well get his position known right away.

"Come on, Jack," Betty continued. She was a woman who was used to getting her way. "Pussy's a dime a dozen down in Mexico. Your gal would be a big hit with my clientele. We'd keep her working a few months so they could all get to know her and then give her a grand send off. My people would pay a lot to see that. I tell you what. I'll even send you a DVD. They'll be selling for 5 grand a pop."

"I said, no thanks," Jack insisted.

"I'll cut you in on the house cut, say, 10% on top of the 25. What duya say?"

"I don't think that would be what Ike would want," Stitch said ominously. Betty gave him an angry look. Then she smiled.

"Okay, okay, I get the message," she said. "But I'm looking for a girl and I need to get her from somewhere. It's a special order."

"Talk to Ike about it," Stitch said.

Carly had been just about ready to burst into tears. $25,000 was a lot of money. When she heard the lesbian slavemaster make the offer she thought for sure that the man would take it. He would need money in Mexico, a lot of it. Her whole body soured and cringed in the split second that it took for the man to turn down the deal. Relief swept through her like a hurricane. Her stomach twisted and she became afraid that she would throw up. But she held it in, pausing in her meal for a few seconds, and then continued the task set before her by her master.

She, at first, couldn't decide whether it was better or worse to be eating like this alongside the other enslaved females. She cast sidelong glances at the other women as she chewed the soft food. They were casting glances back at her. She could see the shame in their eyes.

One of the girls, the blond headed one, was crying. It was then that she decided it was worse to be eating alongside the other women like an animal. She was able to see what the men were seeing, saw herself reflected four times. And it made the callousness of the gang, and her owner, seem so much more evil. They were laughing and joking, swapping stories, enjoying life. They were human beings. She was part of a class of human like creatures that were not.

It made her reduction into less than personhood seem so much more permanent. And it emphasized the essentially fungible nature she had acquired. She was just like the other women. There was no real difference between them. If the man, when he rose from the table, decided to trade her off for a few hours use of one of the other girls, no one would mind. And they could pick her to fuck. And she would do it, that was the worst part. She would be too terrified not to.

She hoped and prayed that the man would not do it. Somehow she sensed that his enthrallment with her was dependent on his total and complete ownership of her, his exclusive right to her. If one of the other men fucked her, the bond between them would be shattered. She would become just another cunt to fuck. No, she knew that the minute one of the other men used her, she was finished. He would sell her and buy five Mexican girls when he crossed the border. She would lose her luster, her appeal to him. She prayed and prayed that it wouldn't happen.

When each of the women finished her bowl of food, licking it clean as they had been trained, she rose and knelt back on her heels and waited. Carly was the last one to finish, maybe because she hadn't had as much practice as the other women in eating this way. She rose up like the other ones and stared at the wall in front of her. She hated being in the presence of the other men. She wanted to go back up to their room, even if she had to stay locked up there all day. If the men couldn't see her, they wouldn't be tempted to try and fuck her. "Please! Please! Take me upstairs! Please!" she thought hard in the desperate hope that her mental message would somehow get through to him.

It was Stitch who noticed that the women were all done eating. He got up from the table, went over to the sink and picked up a dirty dishtowel. He wetted it in the sink, squeezing it out, and then went down the row of women wiping their mouths. When he did Carly's, he leaned a little over her and she could feel the heat of his body, sense his unquestionable manness, feel the power that emanated from him. She was glad when he stepped away.

He came back a moment later and poured some of the wine into their bowls, filling them up from the gallon jug. When he clapped his hands, Carly leaned over and began to lap it up. She could tell that it was cheap stuff, but the smell and taste of it were more than welcome. And, she knew, so would the sensations that the alcohol would bring. Anything to ease her almost constant sense of terror and foreboding. She and the other girls lapped it down noisily.

She didn't finish last this time. When she was done, she rose back onto her heels and awaited her master's further disposition.

Jack sat at the table enjoying the company of his own kind. Stitch made the one he called Maureen get up and start washing up. Rocker pulled out a huge joint and started passing it around the table. The wine jug made a number of journeys. Jack started to get a little buzz on. At one point, Stitch brought the jug back around to the kneeling, silent women and filled their bowls again. After a while, Killer, a guy with a granite jaw and chiseled face, got up and took the blond girl called Julie upstairs. Two of the other gang members came in, new ones who had not been at the party. They were introduced to Jack and then joined the group for a while until Big Betty offered to let them take Vida upstairs and play with her a while. Rocker had the other black haired girl kneel between his legs and suck his cock, to everyone's amusement.

Jack hadn't felt so relaxed and comfortable for a long time. He kept looking over at the girl just to assure himself that she was there and being obedient. At Big

Betty's request, he ordered her to come to the table and walk slowly around it so everyone could get a good look at her, feel her tits and ass. Big Betty, while stroking her hand over her pussy, renewed her offer, and offered to throw in Vida as a sweetener. Jack said no and pulled the girl to him until she was free of Big Betty's clutches.

He could see the girl's discomfort. Part of him enjoyed showing her off. She was so clearly humiliated at being passed around that it made his cock stir. But the other part of him realized that if he kept showing her around, sooner or later one of them would ask if they could fuck her and he would have to refuse. He didn't want to have any bad feelings, so he pushed himself up from the table and announced his intension to go upstairs. There was some good natured ribbing as he applied the girl's gag and led her from the room. He didn't mind.

When they got upstairs, he took her to the bathroom and let her pee and then he made her lie down on her belly on the bed. He clipped her ankles together and affixed them to her wrists. Then he went to the bags from the car and pulled out two of the shorter ropes. He used them to tie her knees and elbows together tightly. Someone had put the blindfold into one of the bags and he took it out and draped it over the girl's eyes.

He stepped back for a minute. She looked so luscious like that that it made him want to untie her and fuck her. He had a desire, though, to go outside and take a walk so he could look around to see what the desert looked like. He could fuck her later. And the thought of her so securely bound and helpless in here, waiting for him, while he was outside taking in the sights was too exquisite to resist. By the time he came back, he would be well primed too.

It was perfect.

CHAPTER EIGHT

Jack went downstairs and out the front door. He had to shade his eyes from the bright sunlight. A couple of gang members were sitting on the porch drinking beers. He gave them a nod and went down the steps. He took a long walk. The landscape was more or less desolate with rocky outcrops and here and there a patch of desert grass or wiry scrub plants. There was a path that passed over and around a rocky hillock and very soon he was out of sight of the house. He started to sweat right away. The sun was very strong. The dry heat seemed to soak up the moisture from his body almost as soon as it was released.

He thought of prison, of the girl, Mexico. He thought about the long list of terrible deeds he had performed. After a while, he climbed a hill and found a place where he could sit and look out over the desert-like environs. He lit a smoke and just sat there, letting the sun warm his body.

There was nothing to look at as far as his eye could see except sparse vegetation and rocks. Every once in a while, the wind would lift a pirouette of dust into the air. Several small tufts of clouds were floating lazily in the azure blue sky. Three hawks circled seeking out prey. It was as peaceful a place as any he had been in in many a year.

As he sat there, it occurred to him that he did not deserve to be where he was, enjoying the fruits of liberation, a new life awaiting him. He wondered if his life could have been any different. Was there a single moment when he made the conscious decision to cast his lot with the darker forces? Once he made that decision, was there ever a time when he could have gone back? They had tried to rehab him when he was a juvie, in and out of detention centers. He remembered one night his mother was teary eyed drunk and high on skank. She begged him to be a 'good boy' as she called it, promising to straighten her own life out.

He was probably about 12 when that had happened. He had laughed. He was already earning good money running dope for the Rogues. He wasn't a full-fledged member, you had to be a lot older for that, but he was on his way. All the guys liked him. He had been invited to the clubhouse a few times and what he had seen made him eager to grow old enough to join. He had had his first sex there, a little later, at 14. One of the girls, a pretty girl with curly black hair, took him up to a room on the 2nd floor, stripped him naked and did a job on his body.

Her name was Honey, or at least that's what the guys called her. After that, every once in a while, when he came by to drop off money or pick up more dope, she would take him upstairs again and they would fuck. She was kind of a house whore and most times when he went there she was with somebody. But when no one wanted her, she would blow him a kiss, take him by the hand and they would go to her room. It went on for about 8 months, until she was sold to a pimp from Chicago for $1,500 and an ounce of horse.

That was the last time he had had any real emotional connection with a woman. He had fallen heads over heels in love with her. He would grind with jealousy and hatred as he saw the gang members order her upstairs or made her blow them there in the common room. When she was sold, right there in front of him by the club president, he ran all the way home, buried himself in his little shit hole bedroom and cried. When he emerged from his room the next morning, his heart was as hard as stone.

After that he never let himself get into a position of vulnerability with a woman again. He sold his first woman when he was 16. An 18 year old college girl was into him for $2,000 for dope. She was a sweet, young thing, a hippie type from the suburbs who had gotten strung out after trying heroin one night at a party and quickly developing a voracious jones. He got her loaded up with skank one day and drove her into Milwaukie where he sold her to a Latino pimp for $5,000, a $3,000 profit.

He eventually moved up the food chain in the drug business earning himself entry into the gang. He graduated into strong arm stuff, and murder soon afterwards. When he beat to death a member of the Cajuns, a rival gang in the Wachovia area, he was given his own crew. Five years later, he was club president.

And now, after all these years, he had let a woman get under his skin. How had it happened? It was a mystery to him. But he could not deny it. He lusted after the girl with a rabid hunger. He had kept her alive when it had been in his clear interest in disposing of her. He had her now, ensconced in their room, so no one else would touch her. He couldn't think of going to Mexico without her. He would die first.

Did this mean that he was going soft, that he had lost his edge? If he was going to be of any use to the Mexican drug lord the Rouges did business with, he would have to be ready to do some really cold blooded things. He had read about them in the newspaper while in the joint. The South and Central American drug gangs made the Rogues look like Boy Scouts. He would have to be prepared to do whatever it took. Could he still do it?

He thought of the guy he had killed in Wisconsin, the two guards he had slit open. He had been able to do what needed to be done then. But that was before the time he had spent with the girl, before he had become infected. Could he still do it now?

He watched as one of the hawks made a steep dive about 40 yards away from where he sat. It dove behind a row of scraggly bushes. A second later, it was back up in the air, a small rabbit in his claws. "Nice work," he thought to himself. He was definitely on the side of the hawks in this world. He had to maintain his confidence in himself. The girl was the problem and the solution. Without her, he would have never doubted himself. But he knew too, that he would do anything he had to do in order to keep her.

He sat there for a full hour, maybe more, smoking cigarettes and thinking. He was laying back and looking at the sky when he heard a noise behind him. He turned to look and saw one of the gang members coming up the trail. It was Chaz. He was probably just back from dropping off the whores. He was carrying two beers.

When he got close, he waved at Jack and lifted the beers in his hand. Jack waived back. When Chaz came up he handed one of the beers to him.

"They told me they saw you go out. I had a hunch you might be up here. It's quite a view, isn't it."

"Yeah," Jack replied. "It looks like some painting that should be in a museum."

Chaz sat down next to him. They clinked beer bottles together and took a drink.

"I like to sit up here sometimes," Chaz told him. "Reminds me of when I was a kid."

"Yeah?" Jack answered.

"Yeah, I grew up about 45 miles from here on a

hardscrabble ranch run by my pa. It was tough. I got out as soon as I could, or as soon as my pa could run me out, depending on how you look at it. But for some reason, I still think about that place as a kind of heaven. It was nowhere near heaven, but somehow I always think of it that way."

"That's a problem I don't have," Jack responded. He took another swallow of beer and put out his cigarette.

The two men were silent for a time. Then Chaz spoke. "Ike's back and he wants to see you."

Jack looked at him. He knew that he would have to deal with Ike sometime today, but being summoned like this was a bit ominous, sending a messenger and all. And with a bottle of beer to soften the blow.

"Okay," he said. "Now?"

"Yeah, now," Chaz replied.

Jack took a deep drink of the beer, swallowed and finished it off. "Okay," he said. "Let's go."

They walked slowly back to the hacienda. Jack had collected his cigarette butts both for security reasons and because he didn't want to leave the place worse off than when he found it. One of the older Rogues had taken him under his wing when he was a little over 15, and imbued in him a deep respect for the outdoors, taught him how to hunt and fish and to survive in the wild. He was doing a life term now in Nevada where he and another Rogue had got caught robbing a bank in broad daylight. A security guard and the other guy were killed. Jack's friend had tried to shoot it out too. He had received three slugs in his chest but they rushed him to the hospital and saved his undeserving ass. Jack had always figured that the two guys had been intent on suicide. Too bad it didn't work out for his friend.

As they approached the house, Jack's stomach began

to turn over in little somersaults. He would have to confront Ike and he wasn't looking forward to it. He was under no illusions. If Ike wanted him wasted, Chaz here would do it in a minute, or any other of the gang. Jack didn't think it would come to that, but that's how close he would have to play it.

When they reached the house, the three guys on the porch had been replaced by two others. Inside, Jack saw one of the gang members leading the young blond girl down the stairs at the end of a chain. When he reached the bottom, another guy was waiting. He took the chain from the first guy and turned the girl around, leading her back up to the bedrooms. The cages were empty, leading Jack to conclude that the other two girls were busy as well. Word had apparently gotten around that this was their last day. He wondered where the Ramirez broad was or the FBI agent. He figured that they must have a dungeon somewhere.

Chaz led him into the kitchen. Ike was sitting at the end of the table drinking a mug of coffee. The guy Mouse was standing a little behind him to his left. Stitch was standing to Ike's right, leaning up against a counter. Rocker and Big Betty were there. Her slave, Vida was kneeling on the floor behind her. Killer was sitting at the table opposite them. The girl Maureen was standing with her face in a corner her hands bound behind her. There was a bottle of Jim Beam on the table and a few shot glasses. The seat at the opposite end of the table from Ike was empty and Jack assumed it was for him.

He sat down. Rocker proffered the bottle to him, but Jack declined. Chaz took up a position to Jack's right, behind him, standing by the door. It looked like Ike had assembled the brain trust of the gang all in one place. Jack swallowed nervously.

"Hiya, Jack," Ike said. Jack returned the greeting.

"I wanted to sit down with you and go over a few things before tonight when our man gets here," Ike explained.

"Okay," Jack answered flatly.

"First of all, I'd like to say that we're all thrilled with your escape and all hope for the best for you when you get to Mexico," Ike started. Jack knew when he was being set up, and this was as good a set up as any.

"Thanks, Ike," he replied. "And I'd like to say that I appreciate all that you guys have done for me."

"That's good, Jack," Ike said. "Because I'm going to tell you a few things and I want you to listen very closely. I counted up your dough and you've got about $18,000. We're going to pick up about 25 grand for the Lexus, and half of that is yours."

"That's generous, Ike," Jack said.

"It's business, Jack. I think that you are going to be a big factor in some plans of ours and I want to be fair with you from the start. I had a long conversation with Mr. Morales today, our Mexican contact, and we think that there's a place for you and your particular abilities. Mr. Morales and, frankly, me, were impressed both at your skill in navigating all across the country with the whole world looking for you and the way you singlehandedly brought Mrs. Ramirez into our hands."

"Thanks," Jack said. "I appreciate that." He was waiting for the axe to fall.

"Mr. Morales intends to take Mrs. Ramirez over the border tonight. He's going to ask for a $1,000,000 ransom. You see, the one problem in doing a kidnapping is getting away with the dough. In Mexico, that's not a problem at all. Mr. Morales owns half the law enforcement in Monterrey and the other half lives in daily fear of him. So, the exchange will be made in Mexico."

"Sounds sweet," Jack said. "But what's my end?"

"Mr. Morales figures that Mr. Ramirez's people will negotiate him down to about $750,000, which is still a nice piece of change. Your end will be 20%, 150 G's."

Jack whistled. That was a lot of change. It would go a long way to setting him up pretty.

"And that's just the start. We figure you could make a score like that 4 or 5 times a year. You do the snatch, we hold her here until she can be brought over to Mexico and Mr. Morales does the switch. Half a million or so a year will set you up real good, Jack."

"I'll say," Jack replied. Half a million! It sounded too good to be true. But he could do it. He had the nerve and the ruthlessness to make off with a dozen pretty, little rich girls a year. A sensation of exhilaration swept through him. He tried hard to disguise it. But he knew that Ike knew what half a million a year meant to him. He would be living in Mexico like a king. He could have anything he wanted. What was the catch?

"But everything depends on you being a team player," Ike continued. His voice had gone from warm and friendly to stern and insistent. "Mr. Morales wants to know that you are in this all the way. He wants a little show of, well, let's call it respect. He wants the girl."

"No fucking way!" Jack spat out. The room bristled with tension. Nobody spoke like that to Ike. His word was law. Jack looked around. There were no players on his team in the room. That guy Mouse was standing on his toes, balanced to make a move against him if need be. Chaz was blocking the door. Rocker and Killer were sitting at the table to either side of him, eying him warily. Big Betty lit a Lucky Strike and blew a big, gray cloud across the table. Stitch shifted his weight nervously.

Ike waited a while before responding.

"I'm going to pretend I didn't hear that, Jack," he said ominously. "It's not a very good start to our friendship. There's only a couple of ways that this could work out. The first is you go along with the program and you live a long, happy, rich life in Monterrey, having anything you want, a dozen cunts at your beck and call, the finest booze, dope, a beautiful, new hog. Everything. Mr. Morales says that he would want you holding on to the merchandise until the switch takes place so you could have a lot of fun there too.

"Or," he continued, "we could take you out of here tonight and drop you off with your 18 G's and the clothes on your back in the middle of Albuquerque. You'd probably get picked up in about 5 minutes. But then, you've seen our little hideaway. Maybe you'd be pissed because we dumped you. Maybe we wouldn't want to take that risk. That brings up the third alternative.

"There's a nice little spot about 15 miles from here, way out in the scrublands. It's a quiet place. The scenery is magnificent. When the sun sets, the skies are so beautiful, you'd think you were in heaven. But we all know that that's not likely where you'd go. It is hot, though, and it has that in common with the place where you will end up. You'd have a lot of company out there. When there's a full moon, maybe the devil will let you come out and play with all the other ghosts.

"That's about the limit of the possibilities here, Jack," Ike said. "And none of them include you taking the girl to Mexico."

Jack was seething. His hands had drawn into fists. If he had his hunting knife which, like a jerkoff, he had left up in his room, he could probably leap across the table and bury it in Ike's heart before anybody could do anything about it. He might be able to take a couple of the others too. But even if he had his knife, he wouldn't be able to take them all. Mouse was carrying a Glock in a shoulder holster. The guy, Killer, had his own Bowie knife stuck on his belt. Chaz was behind him and could be on top of him in a moment. And he bet that Big Betty had something or other in her boot.

Ike gave him a few seconds to get himself under control.

"And then there's this, Jack," he said slowly and deeply. "You've caused me a whole shit load of trouble. The Feds knocked over five of our joints today. I spent the whole morning down at the FBI office being interrogated. So did Mouse. They had nothing on us so they had to let us go. But the heat's going to be on us for a long time on account of you. I would take it real hard if you repaid our hospitality by disrespecting Mr. Morales. He's seen the pictures of your sweet, little cunt on TV and he likes her a lot. He's doing you a big favor. You're going to be living under his protection down in Mexico. We value his participation in our enterprises. So it's yes or no, Jack. Yes, and we'll all have a nice drink and you can begin planning how you'll spend all that dough. No, and we'll have a drink all right, but it will be your last. So what do you say?"

Jack was seething with anger. For the first time in his life, he felt like he was going to cry. She was being taken away from him. No, not being, had. She was already gone. He knew that he would not leave the room alive if he said no. He looked around at the stone cold, hard faces. They had as much sympathy for him as he had had for a thousand others during his lifetime. As he had had for the girl, torn away from the ones she loved. Love. Yes, that was what he had been feeling. It was awful. He should be able to write the girl off, just one more cunt in a long line of cunts. But he couldn't. And now she was destined for a cruel captivity. He didn't know this Morales guy, but if he dealt with the Rogues and the Rogues were careful, if not afraid, of offending him, then he must be one mean motherfucker.

Anger and self-hatred filled him. He knew that he was going to give in. That had been the whole purpose of escaping, hadn't it? Hadn't he dreamed of just what was being offered to him? How could he let his feelings for this girl stand in the way of it?

He thought of her upstairs now, bundled and bound for his pleasure. But now it was for someone else's pleasure. He thought of her sweet body and the fierce fire he had seen in her eyes more than once. He thought of her warm, creative mouth, her soft, malleable breasts, the way she moaned when she was excited. He thought of her face. Above all, it had been her face that had done him in, its forlorn aspect when he bound her, the vision of her fear that flashed across it when he punished her. And last night, he had seen that face in the throes of passion, abandoning all artifice, overwhelmed with ecstasy.

Would he ever see it that way again? No, not if he could help it. He had lost her, that was clear. It was better that he blot out all memory of these things. He would steel himself, cast a mold of iron around his heart to replace the one that she had dissolved. He was Jack Blackjack Jackson, the meanest motherfucker who lived. That's what everyone had said, what the judge had said when he sentenced him, what the newspeople were saying, what each one of his countless victims had thought.

He dared not show his weakness before Ike's assembled crew. He needed to save face. He had to act like the girl meant nothing to him, except, perhaps, a point of pride in her ownership, a pride which he would, on this one occasion, sacrifice for the group. This was his tribe, his fellow travelers, his cohort. He couldn't separate himself from them. He could not be what he wasn't, no matter how much his heart ached at his loss. This was the life he had chosen for himself. He had told himself that when he was sentenced to consecutive life terms. He had borne the brunt of the loss of his freedom then, he would bear it now, without shedding a tear, without remorse, without feeling. He would forget her. He knew that he could. He just had to.

Jack let his face relax. His body, which had tightened, coiled, ready to strike out, relaxed. The fire left his eyes. His outward appearance was calm, accepting, cooperative, but he could not dispel that feeling of lonely emptiness he had inside.

"No problem," he finally said. "She's just a piece of ass anyway. He can have her, but he's gotta pay. I've been offered $25,000 for her."

Ike cast a fiery glance at Big Betty. "Hey, I didn't know," she said to him, shrugging her heavy shoulders. "I think she's worth it."

Ike turned his harsh visage back to Jack. "That's between you and Mr. Morales. But whatever he offers, you better take it."

Jack had no reply. It was a point of pride now for him to get the 25 large Big Betty had offered him. His stomach felt like there were a hundred spiders crawling in it. He wanted to explode in a fit of rage and destroy everything around him. At the same time, he had a hurt so bad it made him want to break out bawling, an emptiness so fierce that nothing in the world could ever fill it. Twice he had felt it before, once when he witnessed his slovenly, drunken mother be beat to a pulp by that trucker when he was a kid, and then again when he lost the whore, Honey. Now it was back, and with a vengeance.

"How about a round of hooch to salute our new partner?" Rocker suggested. He grabbed the bottle of Jim Beam on the table and started pouring shots. Stitch got a few more glasses out of a cabinet so there would be enough to go around. He put a rocks glass down in front of Jack and Rocker poured him a double shot. When all the glasses were full, Ike raised his glass and said, "To success."

All the glasses were raised and emptied. Jack relished the burning sensation as it went down his throat and the momentary headiness it gave him.

"One more," Rocker insisted. The bottle made another round. This time, it was Rocker who made the toast. "To those who, for one reason or another, can't be with us here today."

There was a general murmur of approval at this. Jack thought of all his boys still locked up in the joint doing 20 or 30 years or life sentences. He thought of mates who had been killed doing this or that, knifed in a bar fight, gunned down by rivals, killed on their bikes, some who had caught the skank habit and had o.d.'d. He raised his glass in communion with his fellows and downed the ounce and a half of rye in a single swallow.

The glasses all went down. There was a moment's pause. And then Big Betty spoke up.

"This is all well and good, but what about me? I need to pick up some sweet, new pussy for a special customer. I was going to buy Jack's little honey, but I guess that's out of the question now."

Ike looked at her. Then his eyes moved over to

Maureen standing in the corner quiet and unhappy. "What about her?" he asked.

Big Betty looked over at the girl. "Well, she's got a nice ass. Nice and plump like it was made for a whip. What's the rest of her like?"

"Come over here, slut," Ike called out. Maureen shivered in place, but did not move. Ike turned to Stitch. "What's her name?"

"Maureen," Stitch told him.

"Hey, Maureen, get your ass over here!" Ike barked.

Maureen had been listening intently to the conversation. She had been listening earlier that day at lunch when Big Betty had described the fate of the girl she was going to acquire. The last thing she wanted to do was have the crass, cruel woman assessing her virtues. "Please, no! Please, no!" she thought desperately. She tried to pretend that she was locked in place, that if she didn't move they would forget about her, that she could disappear into the walls that surrounded her on two sides.

"What the fuck?" Ike cursed. "What's the matter with her? Hey cunt!" he yelled. "Get the fuck over here right now or I'll beat your ass until you bleed!"

At this, hands locked behind her back, Maureen slowly turned. She was crying and her lips were quivering. She edged her way over slowly. She passed the table on the other side from where Big Betty was sitting. When she got within Ike's range, he took hold of the ring in her collar and pulled her towards him. Then he gave her face a solid crack with his open hand. Maureen screamed and her head jerked back. When she turned it back she was sobbing.

"Hey, Ike," Big Betty said. "She's no use to me all marked up."

"Don't worry, she'll heal real good," Ike replied. "She's

just gotta learn to do what she's told."

"Oh, she'll learn that all right," Big Betty replied, laughing. "Hey, Rocker," she said, "pour me another shot, will ya?"

Rocker smiled and fulfilled her wish, and then filled everyone else's glass too. Jack was glad to have it. He shot his back with the rest.

Ike took hold of one of Maureen's pale, melon sized breasts and squeezed it hard. Maureen squealed.

"She's got what it takes up top," Ike said. His other hand was still on the ring to her collar. He made her turn away from him. He ran his hand down her sloping torso and down over her plump rear cheeks. "I'd say she's got everything you need."

"Let me get a good look at her," Betty said.

The girl was to Ike's right and Betty to his left. He pulled her by the collar until she had gone around him and handed her off to the bull dike.

Maureen's face was a mask of woe. Her body was shaking. Big Betty held her at arm's length for a few moments. "She looks all right," she said, approvingly. She grabbed her by the chin and turned her face right and left. "Not bad looking either." She made her turn around and rubbed her hand over her ass. "Not bad," she said. To the girl she said, "Bend over and spread your legs."

Maureen hesitated. Big Betty's hand flashed out and she gave her a mighty slap on her rear cheek.

"Ohhhhhh!" the girl cried out.

"Bend over, cunt!" Betty told her harshly. "Or I'll fuck you up good!"

With a sob, Maureen folded herself at the waist and spread her legs. Big Betty snuck her hand between her thighs from behind and took hold of her shaven mons. "Her pussy's nice and plump too. I wanna see how tight she is, or did you assholes drive a truck through her?"

There was general laughter around the table. "We only took her out on Sundays for a ride back and forth to church," Rocker said, laughing. "Honest!"

This was followed by more mirth. Big Betty ignored it. She was stroking the poor young girl's pussy, waiting for it to lubricate defensively. Ike reached out a hand and took hold of a breast and began to caress it. "I'm trying to remember what fucking her was like," he said. "If I recall, she was pretty hot. Or was that the other one?" he asked Stitch.

"No, it was her," Stitch said. "The other one takes a lot more warming up."

Rocker pulled out a fat joint and lit it. He handed it to Jack. Jack took a deep toke and handed it to Stitch.

'Ooouu, baby," Big Betty said softly as she caressed the girl's crevasse. "What a sweet little honey pot. Make it wet for me, baby. Come on, loosen up for Mama, make it good and wet.... There you go.... There you go...." she urged her slowly as she worked her fingers expertly up and down the line of the girl's denuded love lips. "There you go....That's better," she murmured as the divide began to moisten. "Just a little bit more, my little whore, just a little bit more.... More.... More.... That's it....That's it....Yeah, right in!" she exclaimed as her two thick fingers slipped easily into the unhappy girl's now lubricated tunnel. Maureen issued a groan of dismay.

"Nice and tight," Big Betty said. "Looks like you were right, Rocker," she added mirthfully.

Maureen's hands were squirming behind her back. Her long, black hair was hanging down the sides of her head, covering her face. She was sniffling and moaning as Betty continued to stroke her fingers in and out of her purse from behind. Finally, she pulled them out. "Let's see how tight her ass is," she said. Maureen released a whine of dismay.

She placed two thick fingers, slimy with her discharge, at the entrance of the girl's bowels and squiggled them around until they began to descend within her. Maureen groaned and whimpered. Betty sank two fingers in way past her knuckles. "Oooooouuuu, nice," she said. "Either she's pure as the driven snow or all you guys must have small dicks," she said, laughing.

The boys took it good naturedly. They all knew that Maureen had had plenty of use and put down her relative freshness to her youth.

Betty withdrew her digits. "Here," Stitch called out as he tossed a soapy washcloth to her. "I don't want your shitty fingers on our joint." More laughter.

Maureen stood as she had been left while Betty wiped off her fingers. She tossed the washcloth back to Stitch and then slapped Maureen on the ass.

"Turn around, honey," she told her playfully.

The black haired girl rose and turned to face the bruising biker. Betty took hold of the ring in her collar and pulled her close. Maureen's face was sour with dread. Betty wrapped her thick arm around the girl's waist and fastened her mouth on one of her teats. Maureen's lips tightened into a grimace. The joint was still being passed around and Jack took another big toke. Rocker's stuff was not like the stuff in the old day, it gave him an immediate, mind numbing rush, a rush that was welcomed heartily.

The girl emitted little whines as Betty suckled her breast. She shifted to the other one for a while and then emerged. Taking hold of her right breast, she squeezed it tight and then flicked her finger over the taut, rigid nipple. Maureen's nipples were long and fat. Her areolas were small and dark maroon. "Nice," Betty murmured.

She shifted her attention to the other one and flicked that too. "Very nice," she said. Then she took hold of the girl's teat and gave it a vicious twist. Maureen screeched in pain and tried to withdraw from the cruel woman, but Betty held her tight. Her other hand snaked out and clamped over Maureen's other teat and began a vicious twist of that one too.

"Ohhhhhhhhh!" Maureen called out. "Pleeeeeeeae don't! Pleeeeeeease! Pleeeeeeeease!"

Betty pulled the girl close again. "Don't ever back away from me, bitch," she snarled sternly. "You'll find yourself in a whole world of trouble real fast, got it!"

"Yes! Yes! Please let go! Please!" Maureen yelled.

Betty turned to Ike. "She'll do fine," she said.

"Ohhhhhhh, no! No! Please don't sell me to her! Please! Please!" Maureen screamed, all decorum and training forgotten. "I'll do anything you want! Pleeeeeeeease! Pleeeeeease!"

"I think we need to shut you up," Betty said. She twisted her nipples harder. "If you don't shut up, I'll twist these fuckers right off! Understand?"

"Yes! Yes! Oh, yes!" Maureen responded. "Ohhhhhhhhhhh!" Then she pressed her lips together. The effort to remain silent filled her whole face. But, except for a small whine, she was successful. Betty loosened her grip on her nipples. She turned to Vida, her slave girl.

"Go get my bag, pig," she told her sharply.

The scrawny, blonde leapt to her feet and ran from the room. Betty released one of Maureen's nipples and wrapped her arm around her head, pulling it towards her. She brought their lips close. "Open your mouth, slut," she told her. Maureen obeyed. Betty pressed their lips together and thrust her tongue into the girl's mouth.

Maureen struggled and writhed, but she did not pull away. Her whines and moans could be heard arising from her throat.

Betty released her other teat and put her arm around the girl's waist until her bare breasts were pushed up against her own, heavy, fat mammaries. The girl looked like a toy in the bigger, heftier woman's arms. Betty kept up the insulting kiss until some moments later when Vida came rushing back through the door. She was carrying a large black gym bag with a worn out, silver Oakland Raiders' insignia. Vida put the bag next to her mistress, opened it and then knelt down in her former position.

Betty released Maureen from her kiss. "I'm going to have a whole lot of fun with you, kitten," she told the panting girl. "I hope you like pussy, 'cause you'll be licking mine two or three times a day. We'll try you out in a little while, but first I think we need to get you outfitted."

Holding on to the hair on the back of Maureen's head, she leaned over and fished around in her bag. She emerged with a jumble of straps. It had a metal studded prong on one end. "Get up and hold the cunt still," Betty told Vida. Vida sprang back to her feet and circled behind the distressed Maureen. She took hold of her shoulders and pressed her body up against her back.

Betty struggled briefly with the tangle of straps, straightening them out. When she had managed to sort it out, she held it out to the group and said, "This is what I call my persuader." She then took hold of the prong and presented it to Maureen's lips. "Open up, sweetie," she told her.

Maureen's lips turned into a piteous frown, but as the prong was moved forward, she opened her mouth and received it. The prong was long and fat and the metal studs had pointy tips. Betty glided it in over her tongue and then, when it was in, wrapped a leather cup that hung underneath it around the girl's chin and pulled it tight.

Maureen's eyes were widened as if in wonder. Jack was sure that she was experiencing the sensation of the sharp points digging into her tongue. She was holding her mouth open as wide as she could and tears were flowing down her face. She started to struggle, but Vida, with a fierce grip on her arms just below her shoulders, held her still.

Betty began to wrap the straps around Maureen's head. One went up over her nose between her eyes to the back of her head and another around her head just above her eyes. Betty pulled on and adjusted them until they began to be drawn tight. Straps went along the girl's jaw line and, from the corners of her mouth, just above her ears and behind. As Betty tightened them, the girl's mouth began to be pulled closed. She squealed and struggled and moaned. Her eyes were as wide as saucers. Betty gave the straps another little tug and Maureen's body stiffened and she shrieked.

"There you go," Betty said releasing the straps. "That's much better. No more talking, understand? Not ever, ever without permission. From now on."

Maureen nodded her head up and down frantically. There was a brass ring on the front of the gag. Betty took hold of it. "'Cause all I have to do is give this a little shake and I'm sure you will be very unhappy." She did as she said, jiggling the ring. Maureen's eyes lit up and she shrieked again. She moaned, deep and long.

"Catch my drift, cunt?" Betty asked her sinisterly. Maureen dared not nod her head while Betty had hold of the ring. She tried to make her acquiescence known with her pleading eyes.

"Okay then," Betty said. "Go stand there in the corner

like you were before. I'll take you upstairs in a little while and we'll see how good you are around a pussy. And, for your sake, you better be damned good."

Maureen gave the woman a distressed look. Then she looked around the table to see if there was anyone who would give her aid or succor. There was no one. Rocker was busy pouring another round of shots. Stitch had the joint and he took in a deep draught. The others, including Jack, were just looking at her, wondering off handedly if they would get a shot at her before Big Betty took her away forever.

With a forlorn moan, the poor black haired girl moved to obey her new evil mistress. She stood in the corner, her hands clasped tightly together behind her back, sobbing heartily.

Betty raised her shot glass and the others followed suit. "To pussy," she called out. Everyone laughed and threw their liquor back.

Jack was welcoming the deadening feeling he was getting. He had always rejected drinking as a weakness, but now he was getting to like it. But his hurt was not yet over.

Ike rose from his chair. "I'm going upstairs to fuck your little cutie, Jack," he announced pointedly. "I wanna see what makes her worth 25 g's in case Mr. Morales asks me. You don't mind, do you?"

Jack's blood ran cold. For a second he wondered whether he could get Killer's Bowie knife off of his belt and drive it into Ike's chest. He knew that Ike was testing him. If he said yes, then all bets would be off and he would be back where he started, a deep hole in the desert awaiting him. If he said no, Ike would befoul the only female he had cared about in 30 years.

He looked quickly around the room. When Ike got

up, Mouse, who had not been drinking but rather watching over events solemnly, had come to alert. The others were looking at him expectantly. Jack felt his belly fill with bile. He had just barely accepted the idea that she was to be taken from him, but the thought that he would have to sit here and stew while Ike was fucking her upstairs less than 100' from where he sat, was another thing entirely.

But what choice did he have? He had already sold out. He had to face it, the girl was no longer his. What did it matter in the long run? In a day or so, maybe even sometime tonight, the Mexican would be fucking her and maybe his boys too. And for every day from here on out until her uncertain future came to an end. His mind was boiling with helpless rage. He gripped his glass tightly. He realized that he would have to answer. And answer soon if he wanted to retain any semblance of pride. "No," he finally managed to mutter. "I don't mind. Help yourself."

"Thanks, Jack," Ike said slowly, as if in emphasis that Jack's permission was no longer needed, that the question had been a mere courtesy. Ike was the leader here, not Jack. And as the leader he got whatever he wanted, whenever he wanted it and no interloper has-been, like Jack, would ever stop him.

Ike took hold of the remnant of the joint that had just passed Killer's lips. He took a toke off of it and then tossed the tiny butt into the ash tray on the table. "I'll let you know what I think of her," he said.

He walked past Jack to the door and exited the kitchen. Mouse stayed, his beady little eyes fastened on him.

CHAPTER NINE

When Carly heard the footsteps outside the door to the room, she knew right there and then that something terrible had happened. They were not the footsteps of her captor. She would know his tread anywhere. These were heavier, more plodding, than his. His boots had soles of rubber and these sounded like they had hard, leather heels. And when the door opened and the man came in, she sensed a malevolent presence looking down at her. It made her body sour with dread.

She had been a long time bound and still. The man had left her this way so many times now, you would have thought that she would have developed a strategy for enduring it, but she hadn't, not really. When the man had left, she knew that she would remain there imprisoned into motionlessness, silenced, blinded, for a very long time. She tried to prepare herself for the wait. For a while, it worked. She thought of songs that she knew, she revived memories of her childhood, she tried to remember the names of all her teachers, she, in essence, tried to ignore where she was and how she was for as long as humanly possible.

But it did not last long. It couldn't last long with her arms pulled back tightly, her legs in the air, her elbows bound together, that rude, invasive instrument in her mouth. Despair kept raising its ugly head. And fear. And shame. And self pity. She passed through these emotions in stages, overcoming one by sheer will only to have another creep into her consciousness. She couldn't count how many times she pulled at her bonds uselessly, knowing it was useless, but needing desperately to try all the same. She tried not to cry, but at times her carefully shored up psyche would collapse and she would break out into heartfelt sobs.

"Why me? Why me? Why me! Why me!" she kept repeating over and over and over again to herself. If she were not the man's prisoner, at this very moment she would probably be home getting ready to have Randy over for dinner, or to go to his place or maybe out. They would make love tonight and, if they ate at his place, she would probably bring her things and stay over. She thought of her friends at work, the girls she worked with, none of them had had to experience what she had. None of them had ever been hogtied and gagged and blindfolded and abandoned for hours on end. None of them had had to submit to scurrilous use by a man who probably didn't even remember her name. Only her! Her! Carly Walker! It wasn't fair. It just wasn't fair.

Like before, when he had tied her up and then left her, she felt like she was under some evil spell that he had cast on her. His iron will bound her wrists and her knees and her ankles and her arms. He had promulgated some dark wizardry to fill her mouth with a thick, stifling, unignorable force reminiscent of his prick to ever remind her of her mouth's new, superior purpose, that of giving pleasure to him, serving as a moist, hot, energetically compliant sheath to his fleshy sword. He was there even when he wasn't there. She could not stop thinking of him and his supreme power over her.

The minutes dragged on remorselessly. She tried to count the seconds off, but whenever she got up to four or five minutes, her mind would wander down one of the many dark pathways engendered by her fate, and she would lose count. She strained her ears for some sounds from the house to remind herself that she was not alone. A couple of times one of the bikers must have taken one of the girls to the room next door because she could hear through the walls exclamations of passion in a deep, male voice and shrill, unhappy, feminine wails and cries of abuse.

She knew that becoming the fucktoy of a group of callous men was one of the possible outcomes of her present predicament and she thought of the poor girl who had probably had to fuck dozens of the coarse men at one time or another, many of them multiple times. "That's me I hear through the wall," she thought. "That's my future. That's what I will sound like when the men maltreat me." Her body would shudder and her belly would churn at the thought of it.

And she listened to the men coming up the stairs or walking the hall, thinking that it could be him and knowing that at any moment he could return, wanting and not wanting it at the same time.

But when it finally happened, that is, when the feet finally stopped at her door, she knew it wasn't him and a sharp stab of fear pierced her belly.

The feet came in the door. She heard the door close and the lock restored. She felt evil intending eyes wandering her body. She tried desperately to wish herself away, to disappear before the man's very eyes, to where, she did not care. Even the ultimate darkness seemed preferable to what she knew would happen now. A chill went through her body and she could not help the escape of a whine from her throat.

The man didn't say anything at first. But she knew who it was. It was that dark, fearsome man, the leader of this pack of degenerate slavers. She recalled the vision of him leading that woman up the stairs last night. She had felt sorrow for the woman then. And she felt sorry for herself now knowing full well that whatever that woman had suffered last night she would suffer the same now.

Or worse. She had sensed the powerplay last night between her captor and the man who was in the room with her now. She had known then, as much as she tried not to believe it, or, rather, as much as she hoped she didn't have to believe it, that her captor would give in to him. The other man was the alpha dog, the A number one. There could be only one of those and the alpha dog always made sure that any dog that could challenge it was put in its place. And there was no better way for a man to put another man in his place than fucking his woman.

The man stood there for a moment. She could feel his eyes running over her and, like some kind of perverse telepathy, for a moment, she saw what he saw, her bound, helpless limbs, her pale, soft skin, the contrast of her shocking red hair, the roundness of her curves, the lines of her graceful thighs, her long, delicate fingers, the plumpness of her rear and her breast as it peaked out from underneath her. It was a lust inspiring vision, a naked, comely, helpless woman at the full and complete mercy of anyone who wanted her.

Then, without ceremony, she heard the distinctive sounds of him stripping for action. He kicked of his boots. She heard his zipper fall. She heard the slide of cloth and his heavy steps as he lifted first one foot and then the other. There was the sound of clothing hitting the floor. And then he sat on the bed, almost certainly to remove his socks.

He was so close to her that she could hear him breathing. She whined again, though she had tried to force it down, and a sickness pervaded her body. When she felt the bed sag as he edged himself closer, she strained and pulled desperately at her bonds and her mind and psyche rose up in frantic, hopeless, agonizing revolt. A protest rose up within her so strong that she felt like her body might explode. "No! No! No! Don't let it happen! Please! Please! Don't let it happen! Pleeee-eeeease!" she called out in her mind.

For she knew that the moment this man put his mark on her, befouled her, polluted her, her bond with her captor would be broken. It was all she had left. There was nothing else. And while she had suffered mightily in achieving it, she had developed a powerful, perverse need for it. "Please don't! Please! Please! Please!" she screamed inwardly. "Please!"

And then she felt his hand on her. It was hot and strong and rough and large. It snuck in under her outstretched arms and slid down her back, rubbing over her naked rear cheeks. She bit down hard on her gag and her inner self cringed in piteous despair.

His body was so close she could feel its heat. She could smell its smell. She could sense the vicious aura of malevolence that surrounded it. She knew she was doomed. She knew that no power in the world could stop what was going to happen now. She gave one more, fierce, hopeless pull at her bonds releasing, at the same time, a forlorn groan of self-pity. And then she was done.

"There, there, little lady," the man said calmly, his voice deep, gravelly and low, his hand rubbing up and down her plump, rear orbs. "We're going to have a little fun together. I'm not going to hurt you, unless, of course, you disappoint me. Then I'm going to come down upon you like a whole world of hurt. But that's not going to happen, is it? You're going to be a good little girl, aren't you?"

Carly had no answer for him. But, of course she

would be good. She was so frightened that her stomach had turned into a knot. Her body shivered. Her heart commenced a dreadful pounding.

The man shifted next to her and she felt his hands go under her, one under the tops of her thighs and the other across her chest. In a moment, he had lifted her and rolled her to her side, exposing her belly and breasts. He pushed her until she was leaning back on her bound arms, slanted away from him.

"Mmmmmmmmmm," he hummed. "You're a lovely little lady. Now I know why old Blackjack didn't want to share you. You could become a habit."

He ran a hand over her breasts, caressing and massaging them and then down her taut belly and across her joined together thighs. He moved closer to her, placing his naked body up against her thighs and then she felt his mouth take hold of a nipple. His mouth was hot. He began a gentle suckle, his tongue playing with the tip of her teat. His hand ran down her torso and over her hip. She bit into her gag and tried to fight off the sensations of desire that were arising in her.

"Please don't! Please don't! Please don't!" she repeated in her mind. But she was not speaking to him this time. Her prayer was not to him, but to herself. To her body. To the nerve endings and synapses and primordial urges that lurked within her. She knew what was going to happen and she hated herself for it. Hated him for lighting the fuse that would set her body aflame. "Please don't do it! Please!" she begged.

His mouth left her one teat and fastened on the other. He suckled gently at first and then harder and harder and harder until she released a squeal.

"Mmmmmmmmmmmmmmm, you like that, don't you, you little slut?" he asked tauntingly. "What a little whore you are. We're going to have a real good time together. I can just tell."

He leaned back and she felt his hands go behind her head. They fumbled for a moment and she felt the straps to her gag being released and then a pull on the gag itself until it cleared her mouth. She realized at once that her gag, the source of so much agony and shame to her, had been, up to this minute, a shield against the man's depredations. Now it was gone and her mouth felt vulnerable and empty and she was terrified at the certainty that he intended to fill it.

His hand took possession of her face. He squeezed her cheeks harshly, forcing her mouth ajar. She felt his lips touch hers. She could taste his dry, hot breath. And then, his tongue slipped slowly and easily across her lips. It entered her mouth and a wave of heat passed through her body. "Ohhhhhhhhhhh!" she moaned unhappily. She tried to open her mouth wider, to pull back her tongue, to draw her head away from his, but he held on to her face harshly.

"Don't fucking do that," he said sharply. "Don't pull away from me! I have a lot of experience making little girls like you howl. And once I snap, I never know how far I'm going to go. So, if I were you, I'd pretend that I'm your favorite lover boy and kiss me like you were hungry for it. You understand? You got that?" His tone was cruel and heartless, filling her with dread.

She issued a forlorn whine and attempted a frantic nod of her head. Her body was cold with fear.

"No!" he said loudly and gruffly. "Say it! Say, 'Yes, Mr. Ike. I understand.'"

Carly squealed again and the hand squeezed her cheeks harder. "Say it!" he demanded. "Say it or so help me god, you'll wish you had!"

"Yesh, it-er Ike, I unnerstan!" she responded desperately through her distorted mouth, her voice whiney and pleading, her blood running cold.

"Say, 'Please kiss me, Mr. Ike.'"

"...ease ish ee, it-er Ike!" she responded at once, frantic not to displease him.

"Say, 'Please fuck me, Mr. Ike!'"

" ...eashe uh ee, it-er Ike!" she sobbed.

"Say, 'Please stick your dick in me, Mr. Ike!'"

Carly could hardly talk from her forlorn sobs, but she forced the dreadful words out.

"...eeese it ur ick ih ee, it-ir Ike," she repeated through her sobs.

"Now, are you going to be good?"

"...essh, it-ir Ike," Carly answered desperately.

"Are you going to fuck me like you mean it?"

"...essh, it-ir Ike," she repeated tearfully.

"Am I going to have to tell you again?"

"...oh, it-ir Ike," she replied weakly.

He released her jaw. She was sobbing uncontrollably. Her whole body was shaking. "There, there, now," he said sweetly, rubbing her head. "I'm going to give you one more chance, okay?"

"Yes, Mr. Ike," she forced through her sobs.

"Okay, then. Now catch your breath and calm down, Okay?'

Carly nodded and took a deep breath, holding it for a few seconds. Then she released it slowly. Her lips were trembling. He was still rubbing her head softly. He ran his hand down her side and over her hip and over her joined thighs. He ran it back up again over her belly and over her breasts, gently squeezing each one. The hand was hot and heavy and sure of the liberties it was taking, asserting dominion over her flesh.

He took her nipples in his mouth again, suckling them gently while rubbing her belly. Despite her revulsion at his touch, she felt herself calming. He suckled her for a long time, until she felt the surge of her lust. She bit her lips but could not prevent her moan from escaping. He raised his head again and his hand seized her breast. His lips touched hers. His tongue entered her mouth. He pressed his lips against hers. His tongue was hot and thick and was moving gently, slowly in her mouth, capturing her tongue and curling over it and around it and against it. Her loins began to burn and she knew that she was lost.

She whined fretfully as his hand, his right, free hand, wandered her body, bringing a tantalizing excitement everywhere it went. He kissed her hard, forcefully, but his hand was as light as a bird, hopping from this place to that, running itself over her breasts, caressing her belly, rubbing the fronts of her thighs. She had no choice but to endure the caresses, which were bringing her closer and closer to where she did not want to go. Then his hand seized a breast, her left one, and squeezed it hard. His thumb and forefinger took hold of her nipple and twisted it until she moaned. Then the other, caresses, then a mighty squeeze and then a voracious twist of her teat that made her cringe and cry out. His hand became heavier now, forceful, an assertion of his will and dominion.

Cary couldn't help but moan and sigh. She felt the urgent need to twist and turn her body, but her bindings held her still. Her legs pulled firmly on the connection to her hands, stretching out her wrists. Her fingers splayed and unsplayed, pulled together, rolling up into little fists and then unrolled again. They were the only parts of her body that could move and she couldn't keep them still. She had a terrible sense of the immediacy of what was happening. Her mind could go nowhere else. Her lusts were growing so fast that they were forcing everything else out of her brain.

Then he drew his hand down to where her thighs joined, forming a little triangle of space with her sex. Her thighs were jammed together and it was tight, but he was still able to sneak a finger into the gap and, when it found her stiffened love button, began to stroke it. A surge of pleasure went through her. "Ohhhhhhhhh," she moaned into the man's mouth. His tongue kept up its lust driving dance and now, in combination with the friction on her clit, made her squirm and twist and pull on her bonds.

Her breath was coming fast and heavy when he broke their kiss. He ran his hand down and up over her belly and breasts once again, pinching and pulling on her teats, circling his huge hand around them, kneading them. He kissed one, and then the other, suckling on them hard, biting at them, subsuming them into his mouth. Carly gasped with a fierce arousal. When satisfied that she was on the razor's edge, he drew his hand away and began to slide his body up. Carly's body was near the end of the bed and so there was room for him to slide up all the way until his loins neared her face.

Carly cringed and close her mouth. He was going to fuck her there, she knew it. His cock was unseen to her; she was still blinded. But she imagined it, knobby and swollen, thick and long, pink and red and veined, jutting out arrogantly from his loins. As he adjusted his position, a chill went through her, a chilly ache brought on by a wave of self-pity and shame that she had no power to stop him.

Shamed by her fear of resistance. Shamed that she knew she would do whatever he said, whatever he wanted, that he should have the power to force these things on her. Shame because she knew that there was something inside her lying in wait, and as soon as the man's cock breeched her lips it would come roaring into fruition. Her captor had sparked it. He had sensed in in her and had drawn it out. That being used so felt so right was so wrong. She knew it, but there was nothing she could do. That demon would arise and her lusts would go off the scale. To her shame, she had found her rightful place in the universe, the place where she fit best, bound and powerless, forced to endure the unendurable. Forced to pay obeisance to her true lord.

His hand went on the back of her head and took a good grasp of her hair. He pulled her to her side. She whined.

"Open up," he said. "Make a tight little hole with your mouth."

Carly obeyed. She was trembling and her belly was rolling over and over and over, making her nauseous. He shifted himself closer on his side. His cock brushed up against her lips. It prodded gently at the opening, just a tad larger than the hole that she had formed with her pursed lips. Then it pressed forward. Her lips pressed up close against the shaft as it slipped into her mouth. The bulbous head brushed against the roof of her mouth and her tongue. It kept going, going, going until it met the barrier of her throat. She could feel his wiry hairs against her nose and face. She issued a piteous whine, but held her lips tight as she had been told.

"Ahhhhhhhhhh," he said, low and soft. "That's good, whore. That's good. Keep it nice and tight. Don't make me have to tell you again."

He began to rock his hips. His thick member began to slide in and out of her lips. He met every outward thrust with a thrust downward of her head as if he were jerking himself off with her mouth. Slowly, back and forth, long, leisurely strokes. He was in no hurry. He moaned and sighed appreciatively. "Ohhhhhhhhhh, that's nice, whore," he hissed. "That's nice. Keep it tight. Nice and tight. Just like that. Yeah. Yeah. Ohhhhhhh, yeah."

He kept going on and on. Carly was overwhelmed with shame, but her blood was beginning to boil. The soft but rigid object, forced upon her, ruling her, filling her, was an insult to her psyche. "Stop! Stop! Stop!" she prayed uselessly. "Oh, please, please stop!" But it kept going and going. She could feel the fire burning in her loins. She squeezed her thighs together. "Ohhhhhhhhhh, don't do this! Don't do this! Don't do this!" she thought.

And then something snapped in her. A rush of passion flowed through her. Her mind went on overload. A need so intense, so powerful came over her. Her defenses collapsed and the demon took hold of her. "Oh, yes," she began to say. "Yes! Yes! Yes! Fuck my mouth! Fuck it! Fuck it!"

The only noise was her assailant's heavy breathing, his grunts of pleasure and her occasional whine and groan. It seemed like he could go on for hours. Carly's lusts kept burning and burning. "Mmmmmmmmmmmm!" she moaned. "Mmmmmmmmmmmmmm! Mmmmmmmmmm-mmmm!"

Then she heard something in the next room. Someone was in there fucking. She heard a deep, male voice. It sounded loud and angry. There was a high pitched female shriek and then another followed by a woeful sob and more of the angry voice. Then a faint, continuous, anguished whine.

"Oh, god! Oh, god!" Carly thought frantically. "That's me in there. That's what they are going to do to me! They'll hurt me and use me and make me sob and cry with pain. Oh, what's going to happen to me! What's going to happen to me! Oh, god! Oh, god!"

As the sounds were the trigger for her despair, so it was the trigger for her assailant's lusts. He began to push and pull at her head harder and harder. His hips came faster and stronger. His grunts became louder and more determined. "Ohhhhhhhh, yeah! Oh, yeah!" he growled. "Oh, yeah, you're good, whore! You're good! Take my cock! Take it! Suck it! Suck it hard! Harder! Harder! Harder or I'll make you scream!"

Carly suckled with all her might. Terror ran through her. Her whole being concentrated at her task. And the demon kept saying, 'Fuck me! Fuck me! Fuck me! Fuck me!" His cock exploded in her mouth. It began to spasm and jerk. He gave a deep, long growl and began to bang his belly hard against her face. His grip on her hair was so tight she thought he might tear it out by the roots. He roared and growled and his cock kept jerking and jumping and his sauce kept flooding her cavity. She tried to swallow it, but was too afraid of relenting on her efforts. It came bursting from her lips and she began to choke and cough. But he kept going on and on until finally he gave her face one, last forceful thrust, buried his cock deep into her throat, issued a mighty groan and he was done.

She sobbed and sobbed as he eased his cock back and forth slowly now over her lips. His grip on her hair loosened. Carly felt a misery that knew no bounds. She was going insane! She knew it! So many sensations and thoughts and emotions were running through her that she was overwhelmed with grief. Her assailant rapped his knuckles hard on her head twice, causing her to screech with pain.

"Keep those lips tight, you stupid cunt," he snarled.

Carly brought her lips back closed on the softening

shaft. Her body was sick with fear. "Please don't hurt me! Please! Please!" she thought desperately as her sobs went silently on.

Finally, he let his rubbery cock slip from her lips. He patted her on the head. "Not bad, whore," he said.

He picked up her gag. "Jack's right to keep your mouth plugged up all the time," he said as he examined the penis like instrument. "It makes your mouth so receptive. Open up."

Carly parted her lips. He slipped the instrument into her mouth and fastened the straps behind her head. He patted her on the cheek. "Enjoy," he said.

He rolled away from her and she heard him fishing around on the floor. A moment or two later, she heard the flick of a lighter and smelled the aroma of burning tobacco.

He got up from the bed and walked towards the bathroom. She heard water running and assumed he was getting a drink. He came back and just stood there, smoking and watching her for a while. Then she heard him step away again and he sound of the cigarette hissing as it landed in the toilet. And then he was back.

Carly's sobs had subsided and she was left with just her misery. The man came over and rolled her back to her belly. She felt him unfastening her wrists from her ankles. She slowly stretched her legs out and groaned. He undid her hands from each other and brought them over her head. He reconnected them and fastened them to the chain that led from the headboard. He released her legs and told her to get on her knees. Then he pulled on the chain until she had walked herself towards the head of the bed and he tied it off, making it tight.

"Get on your back," he told her. She rolled over to her back and, at his command, raised her knees and spread them apart. Her hands were bound over her head.

"What a pretty, little pussy, whore," he told her. He crept up on the bed. He ran his hand over it. "And nice and juicy," he remarked. "You must like getting your face fucked." He crept forward and ran his hands outward along her thighs to her knees and back. "And such beautiful, soft skin. It's too bad we can't keep you around a little longer. I could get used to fucking you."

He ran his hands back and forth again. Carly felt her pussy rise.

He placed a hand on it and began to slip his thumb up and down her loose and sloppy divide. A rush of pleasure went immediately through her. She moaned and her hands balled into little fists.

He didn't say anything. He just dipped his head down and then dragged his tongue up from the edge of her perineum slowly to the apex of her gash. He tickled her clit with its tip. Carly sighed and her hips moved of their own volition. He brought it down again. She shivered.

"Like that, don't you," Ike asked facetiously.

Carly couldn't answer. In her darkness, she imagined the man smiling evilly at her. Yes, she did like it, to her woeful shame.

A second later, she sensed the man's head lowering again and she felt his lips seize her stiffened bud. He suckled at it gently while he caressed her inner thighs with his hands. She tried to deny the feelings of pleasure he was sending her, but it was useless. She tried to suppress her moan, but it was impossible. The man's tongue now was lapping at her crux, lathering over her love bud. He let it slide downwards, wriggling it inside her and then washing her outer lips all around.

That familiar feeling was building in her. When he seized her love bud again, flicking it with his tongue while keeping a steady suckle on it, she arched her back and groaned. "Mmmmmmmmmmmmmmmmm," she moaned through her gag. "Mmmmmmmmmmmmmmm." His hands slid up and took hold of her breasts, mashing and massaging them. His fingers pulled at her teats while his tongue, pointed hard, drew mesmerizing little circles around her clit. He alternated flicking at it with the tip of his tongue and washing it, lapping at it with his tongue broadened, letting its rough texture abrade her tender organ.

He soon had her lusts at a fever pitch. She had given up resisting him and she let wave after wave of ecstatic sensation flow through her. He brought her near the top, while she panted and moaned and squirmed her hips, only to draw back and pause while she receded from the pinnacle. He did it again and again. She was moaning and begging him in her mind to let her come. "Don't stop! Don't stop! Don't stop!" she would repeat in her head as her lusts swelled to near bursting. When he relented his efforts, she would moan and whine. She spread her legs wider and lifted her hips, seeking his tongue. His tantalizing hands ran over her thighs, her belly, her breasts. "Please! Please!" she thought madly. "Please!"

And then, finally, she reached that plateau that exists just before an orgasm strikes. He held her there for the longest time, just barely touching her with his tongue, floating his fingers delicately across her skin. She groan loudly "...eeeeeeeease! ...eeeeeeease!" she called out through her gag. "...eeeeeeease!"

And then his mouth descended on her pulsing button. He began to suckle and slaver and lick and lather over her pussy. "Uhhhhhhhhhhhhhhhh! Uhhhhhhhhhhhhhhhh! Uhhhhhhhhhhhhhhh!" she called out as she came. Her pussy erupted into a cataclysm of contractions. Her body shook. Her thighs twitched and shuddered. Her heels dug deeply into the bed, sliding up and down frantically. "Uhhh! Uhhh! Uhhh! Uhhh!" she groaned. Her pussy was throbbing hard and fast. His mouth continued its lust driving attentions. Her orgasm kept going and going, way past the point of toleration.

And then, mercifully, she crested. His mouth slowed on her puss, contenting itself to drawing out her residual pulses of pleasure. When he lifted his head, Carly squirmed and writhed her body, needing to shake off the spell he had put her under.

Then he moved up. She felt his thighs brush up against hers. He propped himself up with one hand and with the other guided himself to her crevasse. She felt the round head slide up and down her entrance. "...ooooooooooo! ...eeeeeeeeeease!" she tried to beg. When she felt him slide easily inside her, filling her void, abrading her tender inner self, she moaned and a wave of self pity flowed through her.

When he started his motions, his belly laying atop hers, his chest mashing her breasts, his breath coming hot against her ear, her pussy came alive with sensation. He fucked her slow and steady. The friction against her tunnel's walls, against her swollen clit, were incessant. "Stop! Please! Stop! Stop!" she called out in her mind. "Wait! Just wait! Let me catch my breath! Just a moment! Please! Please!" she prayed desperately inside, knowing that he could not hear her and knowing that if he could he would pay her no heed.

She had no choice but to accept the pleasure he was sending her. Her passions grew greater and greater. She could not hold back. Her pussy erupted again, clasping itself repeatedly against the invading member, sending her fierce rushes of pleasure. She bit down on her gag and moaned and groaned. Her hips writhed and pushed up to meet each one of his downward thrusts. Her hands were clenched into fists. Her heels dug into the back of his shins.

He was groaning too. But she sensed an immaculate control on his part. He would not get carried away. He would not come until he was ready. It was easy for him, in control, in charge. She went past her second orgasm and spun into her third. He was pumping harder now, faster. Her mind tried to grasp the thrusting member, hold it still. Her very powerlessness to do so sent her mind into a whirl. He was using her, using her, she thought madly. "They all will! I won't be able to stop them! They'll fuck me and fuck me and fuck me! Oh, god, please, no, no, no! Please! Please!"

And then, suddenly, he stopped. He slipped from her burning hole. His hands went under her thighs and she felt them being lifted up. He had gotten a chain from somewhere and he fastened one end of it to her right ankle bracelet. She felt the end go through the ring on her collar and then her left ankle pulled down and fastened off too. She was bent back, her ass in the air. He hurriedly spread something cool and oily on her rear entrance. She knew what he was doing. She cringed as the head of his cock probed at her delicate ring. "...eeeeeeeeease ...on't!" she called through her gag. But a second later, she felt her ring expand, her membranes tear, and his cock plunged inside her bowels.

"Oh, yeah! That's nice! That's nice!" she heard him say through her misery. "So tight! Tight and hot! Oh, yeah! Yeah!"

He was plunging in and out with frantic speed. He was atop her, plunging downwards. He gathered her ankles in one hand and began to press them down, down, as far as they would go. His other hand found her crevasse, and he began plunging his thumb in and out of it, running it across her clit again and again.

"Uhhhhhhhhhhh! Uhhhhhhhhhhhh!" she moaned. He was driving her inexorably towards another completion. The cock in her ass was sending a steady, hot, electric current to her sex. His hand was pushing her pussy beyond tolerance. She felt a tidal wave of lust building up inside her. All thoughts but the enjoyment of her pleasure were out of her mind. "Uhhhhhhhhh! Uhhhhhhhhhh! Uhhhhhhhhh!" she groaned. Her assailant was pounding away at her, grunting, groaning, calling out his need. And then he issued a roar. He gripped her ankles as if holding on for life. The digit in her pussy was thrusting madly. She could feel his pulses within her. Her pussy exploded anew. She groaned and cried out and screamed and moaned. Her innards were convulsed in mind wrenching throbs. "Uhhhh! Uhhhh! Uhhhhh! Uhhhhh!" she groaned.

Her assailant's thrusts finally began to slow. Her contractions softened and began to wind down. He was still moaning and she was desperately trying to catch her breath. Her heart was pulsing violently. He was leaning down hard on her as if deprived of all energy. For a few moments, they remained that way. Her mind was spinning and it was hard to return herself to anything close to equilibrium.

Finally, her assailant rose from her. She heard him go into the bathroom to clean himself and then return. He fumbled with something by the side of the room and then came back to her.

A rope was tied around her right knee and then fastened to the side of the bed. He came around to the other side and tied that one off too. "There, that ought to keep you nice and still," he said. He got up from the side of the bed and walked away for a second. And then he returned. She sensed him standing at the foot of the bed looking down at her obscenely displayed loins.

"You're a really good fuck, cunt," he said to her gruffly, "but you've got a lot to learn." Then she felt something dragging across the insides of her thighs. When she realized that it was the thongs of a whip, her body tensed and she began to whimper.

"You know you're not supposed to talk. That's why you're gagged. Nobody wants to hear what you have to say. You should be grateful that I don't want you all marked up when you meet your new owner tonight. This here flogger will hurt like hell, but it won't sting as much as a lash would. So mark yourself lucky."

Carly didn't feel lucky. Her whimpering turned into sobs. It was so unfair! So unfair! "Please don't whip me! Please don't whip me!" she thought frantically.

The strands of the flogger left her skin. There was a pause. She heard them whistling through the air and a half second later felt an intense burning on the inside of her left thigh.

"Ooouuuuuuuuuuuuuu! Oooouuuuuuuuuuuuu!" she cried out. Before she could catch her breath, another blow fell, this across the inside of her right thigh. It burned like anything and she cried out again. She pulled and jerked at her confinements desperately, but she could not get free. She knew where the next blow would fall and she wanted at all costs to avoid it. "Pllleeeeeeeease don't! Pllllleeeeeeease!" she thought madly.

There was the same sound of the leather running through the air and immediately following she felt a rabid burning spring up on the fulcrum of her thighs. The lashes curled around the curve of her body and struck right along her delicate pudendum.

"Eeeeeeeeeeeeeeee! Eeeeeeeeeeeeeee! Eeeeeeeeee-eeeeeee!" she screamed. And then the blows started falling one atop the other. He worked over her thighs, her rear cheeks, her fulcrum, again and again. She screamed and wailed and cried and used everything in her mind she could think of to make it stop. It was like a river of fire was washing over her. Not being able to see the blows, to know when they were coming, to be able to prepare herself for their fall made it ever so much worse. It was like and invisible force had exploded into the room and was washing lava all over her poor, distended, helpless regions.

She was sobbing madly when he finally stopped. He didn't bother to say anything to her, but she sensed him standing there appreciating his handiwork. Then she heard the flogger drop to the floor and he left.

* * * * * * * * * * * * * *

When Ike had left the kitchen, the small crowd broke up until there was just Jack and Stitch left. Jack had taken possession of the bottle of Jim Beam and he poured himself a double shot as everyone was walking out.

"Take it easy, bro," Stitch told him.

"Mind your own fucking business," Jack answered as he threw it back.

Stitch sat down at the table. He took hold of a rocks glass and poured it near full. He lifted it to Jack who matched it with another one of his own.

"Fuck the motherfuckers!" Stitch announced as they clicked their glasses together.

"Fuckin' eh right," Jack replied.

They downed their drinks and Stitch moved the bottle

of Jim Beam out of Jack's reach.

"It may not feel like it right now, Jack, but you're sitting on top of the world," he told him in an avuncular tone. "You can have a hundred girls like the one upstairs. Once you get your deal going with Morales on one of your trips you can pick yourself out something real nice and bring her back to Mexico with you."

"It's not the same," Jack complained.

"Listen," Stitch said calmly and sympathetically, "you and I chose a way of life. We coated our souls with iron and did what we had to do. There's no room in our lives for sentiment. Two weeks from now this girl will just be a memory to you. You feel special towards her because she was your first one out of the joint and you travelled so close together. For you, it was a time of heightened stress. It made you vulnerable. But that's not who you are. You might hate Ike for what he's done, but he's just like you. And he's right, too. For you to make this girl's pussy the center of your life would spell disaster. Sooner or later you would have to make the same decision you made today. And if you chose wrong, that would be an end to you. We're not meant to own anything permanent. We are supposed to have nothing to lose. It's the only way we can live."

Jack knew that everything that Stitch was saying was right. It was difficult to accept, that's all. He had made a connection with the girl and he hadn't done that in a long time. It was a connection that most people in the straight world wouldn't accept, would think as abnormal, even perverted, but it was a milestone for him. He thought of the moments when he might have put her to sleep and the feelings he had then, fear of loss of something important, something vital, came resounding back.

And that asshole Ike was upstairs fucking her right

now! Jack had spent his life angry and that feeling was familiar to him too, the feeling of spiteful hatred, a rage against the injustices the world had visited on him, a determination to acquire revenge, no matter what the cost. It had driven him for years and years. It had allowed him to pull a shell over himself when he was sentenced to life without parole. It had been what had made him sell off that stupid little college kid back in the day, his first real act of out and out cruelty.

He knew that only by concentrating on that kernel of pain inside him, by letting it fester and grow into the pure, unadulterated hatred he had for the world and everything in it, would he survive. And, just as Stitch said, Ike had done him a favor. The girl was poison to him. She had lured him into a realm of feelings and emotion that threatened to erode away all of his strength, all of his power, like some form of kryptonite. And the feelings of sorrow he felt when he thought of what the girl would go through as the sex slave of some Mexican drug lord, well, that would just have to go. He would replace it with anger and hatred.

She was going to get what she deserved, no less. She was going to get what everyone deserved, but especially her, she who had sought to sap his strength with her piteous looks, her needy pouts, her ravenous cunt. He thought of her upstairs, getting her mouth stuffed with Ike's cock, or spreading her legs and being brutally and thoroughly fucked like the lowliest whore in the lowliest whorehouse. That was what she deserved all right. And he was glad, happy, that she was getting it.

The booze was making his mind foggy and thick. It filled him with self-pity and remorse and shame. He knew that these things, this hatred, this anger, were what he was supposed to feel, what he needed to feel. But he couldn't shake the feeling of personal tragedy that was filling him. The girl was his last, best chance at recovering his humanity. And she was gone. Other men would have her. Other men would fuck her and she would fuck them. The thought of it filled him with a deep, deep sorrow. It would have been better to have done the job on her like he had wanted to.

But he couldn't even do that now since this Morales guy would take it as an insult. He would pay the price for it and all this struggle, all the years of planning and endurance, seeking only what he now had proffered to him, which lay at his feet just waiting for him to pick it up, would go to waste.

He would have to go on without her. Maybe, like Stitch said, in a week or two, he could forget her, forget what might have been. Life had handed him another shit sandwich and he had no choice but to eat it.

"Ahhhhhhh, fuck it!" Jack said morosely.

"That's the spirit, Jack," Stitch said. "Hey, I got an idea," he continued, "I got to feed and service the stock downstairs. Why don't you give me a hand? It'll take your mind off of everything."

Anything seemed better to Jack than sitting around mooning about the girl. "Sound's good," he replied.

Stitch got up from his chair and went to pick up the 5 steel, shiny, doggy bowls from the floor, stacking them up on one another. He brought them to the sink.

"I had Maureen all trained to do this stuff, but I don't think we'll be seeing too much of her anymore," he said as he began to rinse the bowls in the sink. "When the new girls come, I'll pick one out to give me a hand with things. Morales will probably be dropping off some Mexican cunt tonight for us to sell down the line. I might just take one for permanent duty here. I'm tired of breaking in a new girl every few months."

He had all the bowls rinsed and stacked in the dish rack. He turned to the stove. There was a big pot there that had been simmering all the time since before Jack came into the room. Stitch picked up a big wooden spoon and gave it a stir. Satisfied, he grabbed two dishtowels and took hold of the handles on the pot.

"Grab two of those bowls for me willya," he asked Jack. "And follow me."

Jack did as was bid. Stitch led him back into the main room and then off to a door on the side. It was large and steel encased with a large, brass dead bolt lock on it. Stitch put down the pot, took a ring of keys from his pocket, picked one out, and unlocked the door. Jack held the door open for him as he picked up the pot and walked through it.

There was a small landing and then a set of coarse, steep, wooden stairs that went straight down. Stitch led Jack down them to the bottom. He led Jack to another door constructed of thick wood planks. It had a big brass deadlock like the other but also a steel plate with a large padlock. Stitch put his pot down again and unlocked them both. He flicked on the light inside the next room from a switch just outside the door. He swung the door open and Jack preceded him in.

The room was large, about 40' by 50'. It had a floor made up of thick slabs of stone. The walls were made of stone too, rough pieces, joined together with cement. The ceiling was about 10' high and crisscrossed by heavy beams. There were no windows.

It was cool inside, almost cold, and damp. The room had a musty smell. There was a row of cages along two of the walls, five in each row. Four of them were filled by blinking, startled, naked women. They were distributed evenly amongst the cages so that no two were adjacent to each other. The women's feet were bound together with a 6" long chain and were connected to their wrists, which had been locked behind their backs. They all wore leather shield gags that covered their faces from just under their noses to over their chins. They looked very unhappy.

Two of the women were very young, 18 or maybe 19. One had midlength, wheat colored blond hair and the other long brown hair that reached below her shoulders. The other two cages contained the woman Jack had kidnapped and the FBI lady. Jack took note of the excellent security. To get out, the girls would first have to figure out a way to undo their chains. Then they would have to figure out a way to get out of their cages. And then they would have to figure out a way to get through the double locked door. They would have to do this in absolute darkness since the light switch was outside the door. The chance of escape was just about nil.

Stitch put the pot down just inside the doorway and took hold of a three foot long pole-like object that was hanging on the wall just to the outside of the door. Jack recognized it as an electric prod. He stepped back into the room and closed the door, locking the deadbolt.

"Now who's going to go first?" Stitch said lightly. He walked over to the cage that held the young, blond girl. "I guess you," he said. He took out the ring of keys again and unlocked her cage. He turned on the prod and it made a 'beep!', signaling it was ready. He swung the door to the cage open and prodded the girl with the pole without pulling the trigger.

"Come on out now, honey," he told her. "Give me any trouble and you'll get a blast from this, understand?"

The girl morosely nodded her head.

The cage was not quite tall enough for her to kneel up

at full length. She rose to her knees, bending her head over, and started to shuffle out. Her skin was pale and she was finely shaped. Her breasts were heavy and they swayed nicely as she moved. She kept her eyes fixed warily on the two men. They were moistened as if the girl was fighting off tears.

When she was out of the cage, Stitch closed the door behind her and then released her wrists from her feet. He then unhooked the chain between her ankles.

"Get up," he said.

The girl struggled to her feet. "Okay, now like I taught you, up and down, up and down until I say stop."

The girl began to a series of slow, unsteady knee bends.

"That's it," Stitch told her. "Feet wider apart."

To Jack he said, "These two have been down here almost a week. I like to exercise them a little so that they don't get all cramped up. Otherwise, when it's time for them to go, you gotta carry them up the stairs."

Jack could see the wisdom of Stitch's routine for the girls. They had done something similar back in the old days in Wausau. Jack counted 20 knee bends when Stitch told the girl to stop. There was an anxiousness in her face which went beyond her fear. She was breathing heavy through her nose.

"Okay," Stitch told her, "over here."

Jack noticed a chemical toilet in the corner of the room. The naked girl scooted over to it quickly. She sat down without waiting for permission and a moment or two later, Jack heard the sound of her water hitting the chemical pool below her. She issued a relieved sigh.

Stitch motioned the girl up with the prod. She stood up from the toilet and, without being told, bent over and spread her legs. There was a roll of toilet paper on the wall and Stitch took out a nice length and wiped the girl's pussy clean with it. "You don't want them to get a rash or anything," he commented in explanation. "I keep 'em nice and clean so that when we turn them over they're in tip top shape. Later, I'll give 'em all a nice enema so that they're all cleaned out for their trip."

Stitch tossed the paper into the toilet. "Okay, now girl, over here," he ordered. The girl walked unsteadily over to a shower head which jutted out from the wall. There was a drain built into the floor underneath it. On a shelf were soap, shampoo, some towels and a pile of washcloths. Stitch turned the water on and regulated its flow until it was coming out warm.

"It'll speed things up if you give 'em a shower while I feed 'em," he told Jack.

"No problem," Jack replied. He handed the bowls he had been carrying to Stitch and then addressed the girl. "Turn around," he told her curtly. She obeyed without question. He undid the straps that held her gag in tight and removed it from her mouth, putting it down on the shelf. He then unlocked her hands from behind her back and, after coaxing the girl under the stream of water with a little push, attached them to a chain that hung down from the ceiling from above the shower head. The chain had enough slack that the girl's hands were held up around her chest.

The water cascaded over the girl. Jack let her get good and wet and then pulled her by the elbow until she was outside the flow of water. He rinsed a washcloth and then soaped it up.

There was a commotion over by the cages that drew Jack's attention. Stitch was speaking harshly to the brown haired girl.

"You're a fucking pig!" he told her angrily. "This is the

second time you pissed your cage!" The girl was still huddling within the cage's confines. Her eyes were large and pleading. Stitch pressed the prod against her belly and pulled the trigger. There was a loud 'crack!' and the girl released a muffled scream. Stitch pushed the prod up against her again. The girl let out a muffled plea for mercy, but Stitch pulled the trigger again. Her body jumped inside the cage and she screeched.

"Once more for good measure!" Stitch said angrily. The girl was curled up and scrunched against the far wall of the cage as far as she could go. She was sobbing. Stitch thrust the prod between her legs. She shouted a desperate plea and a second later the prod spoke again, issuing another loud 'crack!' within the room. The girl's body cringed and she released a horrible wail.

Stitch gave her a few seconds to regain her equilibrium and then ordered her to get out. Weeping and wailing, the girl obeyed. "The next time, there'll be a whipping," he told the girl as she took up a kneeling stance in front of him, her body shaking, tears flowing down her face. "I don't care if it gets you all marked up," Stitch added. "I won't have a pig like you dirtying up my cages!" He pushed the prod against the girl's chest. "Got it?" he demanded harshly.

The girl nodded desperately, cringing from contact with the heinous instrument.

"Okay, then," Stitch said, "as long as we understand each other."

He went to release the girl's ankles from her wrists and Jack went back to his task at hand. The blond haired girl, dripping wet, was looking at him unhappily. Tears had flowed down her face too. Jack reckoned that she and the other girl were friends. Well, that was too bad. They'd undoubtedly be separated once sold off. It didn't due for a girl to have too close a friend where she was going. It fomented conspiracies to escape.

Jack squeezed the excess water from the washcloth and began to wash the girl's body. It was soft and pliant. He spread the soap over her delightful breasts and taut, flat belly. She still wore the evidence of her maturity around her sex and he washed that too, letting a nice lather work up amidst the hairs. He had her spread her legs and washed her crack thoroughly.

He couldn't help think of the girl upstairs and the times that he had washed her. He tried to put out of his mind what she was undoubtedly doing now. He pushed the blond haired girl roughly so that her back was towards him and he rubbed the cloth over her rear cheeks and the split between them, making sure that he probed deep her little rear hole. The girl whined when he did it and he told her, gruffly, to shut up.

When he had finished doing her back and legs, he made her stand under the flowing water again. He watched her as she rinsed off. The girl, his girl, had been blond too when he had first got her, he thought unhappily. Their bodies were similar. This one was maybe a tad taller. He could almost pretend that it was her. Carly. That was her name. He wished that he had not remembered it. Knowing her name, recalling it, would not help him forget her.

He let the girl rinse off and then made sure that she got her hair all wet. He brought her back out of the flow of water and shampooed her hair. When the soap was all washed out, he put her back under and then poured some cream rinse into her hair. He had her rinse that out and then pulled her from the shower. He quickly dried off her head and body with one of the towels and then brushed her hair until it was straight.

He released her hands from the chain. There was a tube of toothpaste and a couple of worn toothbrushes on the shelf. He spread some toothpaste on the brush and handed it to the girl. She looked at him dolefully and then went to work. He let her go one for about a minute and then took the toothbrush away from her. She spat the foamy whiteness onto the drain. There was a cup on the shelf and Jack took it, filled it from the shower and gave it to the girl. Obediently, she rinsed out her mouth and then spat it out. She handed the cup back to Jack.

Picking up the gag, he took hold of the girl by her elbow and turned back toward the cages. Stitch was standing there watching the brown haired girl consume her meal. Her legs were spread and she was bent over with her face into one of the shiny, silvery bowls he had brought down. Stitch had her gag in his hand.

Jack had the blond girl kneel on the floor outside of her cage.

"All right, that's enough," Stitch told the brown haired girl. She brought her face up from the bowl. It was smeared with the brown sauce of the stew.

Jack watched as Stitch slid the bowl with his foot over to where the blond girl knelt. He pulled the pot he had brought down over to it and then ladled another large ration of stew into the slivery bowl. "Okay, get to work," he told the blond girl.

Jack washed the brown haired girl while the blond girl ate. She was thinner and taller than the blond girl. Her tits were smaller, but still firm and ripe. Jack lingered over them as he washed them. Her nipples stiffened as he handled them. He wondered what it would be like to fuck her.

Ultimately, finding a new bitch to fuck and torment on a regular basis was the only recipe for forgetting about his former captive. When he had the girl turn around and did her back, he noticed that her ass was small and a little boney near the hips. It wouldn't be her he would be picking out. He liked them with a little bit of padding back there. But someone would like her and within a few days, maybe less than 24 hours, this girl would be fucking any and all comers, and doing it with sincere enthusiasm if she knew what was good for her. He gave her ass a harsh swat as he ordered her back under the water. She screeched unhappily and obeyed.

When he was done with the brown haired girl, Stitch had the blond girl all bound up back in her cage. The Ramirez woman was out and eating obediently. He had already let her pee. Both dog dishes were on the floor in front of her, one containing her ration of stew and the other about 2 cups of water.

"Enough," Stitch told her. "Now drink the water." The woman looked up at him resentfully but dutifully shifted her attentions to the liquid.

Jack had already stuffed the gag back into the brown haired girl's mouth. He was about to put her back in her cage when Stitch told him to give her a chance to pee first. "I didn't give her any water, so maybe she'll behave herself this time," he said. "But see if she can go anyway."

He took her over to the toilet, now loaded up with yellowish-green fluid and sat her down. The girl strained and strained and finally a thin stream emerged. Her eyes conveyed her relief.

When he brought the girl back, Stitch had the Ramirez woman ready for him. He took custody of the brown haired girl. There was a 5 gallon steel pail on the floor with a strong smelling cleaning liquid in it along with a rag. Stitch unhooked the brown haired girl's wrists from behind her back and told her to clean out her cage.

Sadness in her eyes, the girl sank to her knees, wrung out the rag in the pail and went to work. Jack took the Ramirez woman over to the shower.

She had a mature body compared to the other girls. Her breasts were just a little less firm and her flesh a little plumper and softer, small layers of fat where the other girl's had muscle. There was something about it that attracted Jack. Ike had said that he would suggest to that Morales fellow that Jack keep custody of her until she was ransomed. That might be a very nice thing, Jack thought as he handled her body.

He was getting hornier and hornier from handling all this female flesh. It made him think of the girl upstairs. Everything was reminding him of her. It made him angry. Who was she to have this kind of effect on him? "I should have killed her," he thought. He was probing the Ramirez woman's tiny rear aperture with the washcloth, a fresh one for each girl, and he did it with just a little more force than he did the other ones. The woman cried out.

Jack took hold of her long black hair and shook her head harshly. "Shut the fuck up!" he told her angrily.

"Please! Please!" the woman called out. "My husband will pay! He has plenty of money! Please! Please don't hurt me!"

Jack spun the woman around and slapped her fiercely across the face. It jerked her head back and she screamed.

"I told you to shut the fuck up!" Jack yelled at her. He turned to Stitch. "Give me that prod," he barked. Stitch walked it over to him. The FBI agent was on her knees eating her meal.

Jack took hold of the prod and released the woman. She began to back away from him, her bound hands held up before her, desperately seeking to ward off contact with the prod. "Please don't! Please! Please!" she called out. "I'll be good! I'll be quiet! Please! Please!"

She was backed up against the wall and had nowhere else to go. Her face was a mask of fear. Tears were flowing down her face. Her hands were held up before her.

Jack paused for a second and then thrust the prod quickly towards her. It made contact on her belly, just above her black haired, shrouded sex. "Ahhhhhhhhhhhh! Noooooooooooo!" the woman screamed. Jack pulled the trigger. "Crack!"

"Ayieeeeyahhhhhhhhhhhh!" the woman called out. Her body shuddered and banged up against the wall. She bent over double and then fell to her knees.

She began to wail. Jack shoved the prod up against her again. He pushed it under her chin and lifted her face so that she was looking at him. "Shut the fuck up!" he yelled at her. She continued to wail.

"Now!" he said. "Or I'll give you another one!"

That got her attention. She clasped her lips together tightly and nodded her head vigorously. Her chest was heaving and her bound hands were held tight against it, covering her breasts.

"Put your hands down!" Jack ordered curtly.

She slowly lowered them until they were by her waist. You could tell that she was ready to bring them back up in an instant should Jack threaten to give her another jolt. The prod was jammed up under her chin.

"Learned your lesson?" Jack asked her.

She nodded as well as she could, her eyes pleading hopefully for no more violence.

"Okay," Jack told her. "Get up!"

She rose to her feet. She gave Jack no more trouble. When he was done with her, he brought her over to where Stitch was waiting. The brown haired girl was in her cage. The FBI lady had finished her meal and was kneeling there, brown faced, awaiting orders.

"You can do her," Stitch said. "I'm going to take a little of the edge off."

"No problem," Jack said.

He led the FBI lady over to the shower. He thought twice about undoing her wrists. He realized that she was probably trained in self-defense and apprehension techniques. The rule was for broads like this to always have them confined in some way. If their hands were free, their legs should be bound, and vice versa. And if both were free, she should be chained to something. He could see her eyes flitting about, calculating the odds of this and that. But there was a submissiveness to them too. The boys had had her out last night and had a good time with her. Her body bore the marks of the whip, and pretty fresh too. She had been taught a lesson or two, he was sure. But you had to be careful dealing with a broad like this. He kept her hands fastened behind her back.

It was a pleasure to manhandle her body. Like the Ramirez woman, she was older and more mature. Her flesh had a mellowness to it. "I must be getting old," Jack thought to himself. They used to throw ones like this away in the old days. But now he was wondering what that Morales guy would do with her. It would be fun to train her. She had just the right amount of surliness and inner strength that would make it a challenge. "Fuck her," Jack thought when his thoughts went to the girl upstairs. He could have a good time with this one.

Stitch was getting a blow job from Mrs. Ramirez and was seeming to enjoy it. He was grunting and moaning as he slid his cock in and out of the mouth of the kneeling woman. She had a remorseful look on her face. Jack was sure she would have to give quite a few blowjobs before she was reunited with her hubby. And more, too. She would survive, but sucking a cock was never going to be the same again.

Jack held the elbow of the FBI lady as he waited for Stitch to finish. He concluded with a loud groan and a frantic pumping of his cock into the woman's mouth. When he finally pulled her off, she was crying again. He patted her on the head and said, "Thanks, honey," and then reinstalled her gag. He made her shuffle on her knees over to her cage, fastened her wrists to her ankles and bound them together with the 6" chain. She shuffled the last few feet into her cage and Stitch slammed it shut.

He turned to Jack. "Why don't you knock a piece off of the FBI lady before you come upstairs," he suggested. "I'll leave you the key and you can lock up when you're done."

"Suits me fine," Jack replied.

Stitch took the key chain out of his pocket and, after showing Jack which key was which, handed them to him.

"See what I mean," he said. "There's hundreds of these broads around. And you're going to have your pick of them. Forget that girl upstairs. You would have gotten tired of her in a little while anyways."

Maybe, maybe not, Jack thought. But he was going to fuck this one now.

"See you upstairs," he told Stitch.

"Make sure you bring the dog dishes," Stitch reminded him. "And hang up the prod outside. If one of these bitches managed somehow to get free, I wouldn't want to be greeted with it when I opened the door."

"Will do," Jack replied.

He left the FBI lady standing naked in the middle of the room while he went over to the door and unlocked it so Stitch could leave. The grey haired biker gave him a nod and Jack closed the door behind him. When he returned to the room, the FBI lady was looking at him, dismay in her eyes.

Jack picked up the prod. He raised it and started to approach the woman. She backed away, apprehension now showing. She kept going until she hit the wall. Jack was right behind her. He took the prod and jabbed it against her belly. "We're not going to have any problems, are we, bitch?" he asked.

Special Agent Linda Kramer felt her body shudder. She was looking at the man who had been described to her as one of the meanest men alive. She had seen what he did to the other woman. That was just a sample of what he was capable of. The man pushed the prod up against her breasts, poking them, pushing them back and forth. What did her FBI training tell her to do now? She knew what she wanted to do. She wanted to submit. She had been given a taste of the prod last night when they went to return her to her cage. It was the guy they called Billy Boots who brought her down. She had done nothing wrong. But the diminutive guy had shoved her into her cage and then went at her with it. He must have given her five or six shocks, all in rapid succession, laughing all the while.

Later, in the dark, after he had left, she cried and cried. She knew that the others could hear her. She knew that she should be a strong example of resistance and hope for the other females, but she couldn't help it. What was happening was all too horrible to think of.

She had heard one of the men last night say something about her going to Mexico. She didn't want to go there, but if that was their plan for her it meant at least that they weren't going to kill her. She wanted to live, desperately wanted to live. And she wanted to experience as little pain as possible in the process. But there was something inside her that wouldn't let her surrender. She couldn't give in to this monster. It went against everything she had been taught. For her own self esteem she had to oppose him. She would not give in!

"...uck ooouuu!" she spat out at Jack from behind her gag. Jack just smiled. He dropped the prod down quickly to her pussy before she could react and pulled the trigger. It made a loud noise.

"Oooooouuuuuuuummmmmmmpf!" Linda called out as she collapsed to the floor. It felt like someone had kicked her there. She felt the prod touching her rear cheek and before she had time to move away, the prod sparked again and she was punched in the ass, forcing her to roll over and screech loudly. This time he pushed it against her breast. She wanted to shout, "No!" when the current passed through to her with a jolt. She screamed and rolled over again.

Jack held the prod up. It needed to recharge. The FBI lady was scrambling to get further away from him. She was sobbing and wailing. Jack just followed her, waiting for the prod to reboot. It didn't take long. He backed her into a corner. She stared at him wide eyed as he extended the prong once again. Her urge to rebellion had now dissipated. She was ready to do whatever he said, but she had no way to communicate it to him. "...eeeeeeese! ...on't!" she tried to say. The prod was stuck against her belly. "Crack!"

"Ooooouuuuuuuuuuuuuu!" she screamed. "Ohhhhhhh-hhhhhh! ...on't! ...on't! ...eeeeeeeeeeease!" she tried to yell. "Crack!" Another jolt of electricity made her body cringe and her muscles cramp violently. And then, "Crack!, this time against her ass again as she had rolled into a ball to protect herself. It felt like he had struck her there with a baseball bat. "Ooooouuuuuuuuuu! Ooouuuuuuuuuuuu! ....ease ...op! ...ease op! ..m ...eggin ouuuuu! ....eeeeeease ...op! ...eeeeeeeeeease!"

Jack paused while the prod reloaded. "So, you're going to be a good girl?" he asked her tauntingly.

"...es! ....es! I ...ill! I ...ill!" she replied frantically. She looked up at the man piteously. Her bravery had all run out on her. Surely she had done enough to satisfy convention! Surely her masters at the FBI didn't expect her to go through more than this!

But it was more than her concern about letting the Bureau down that had motivated her revolt. More than the need to put up a brave front for the other women. Last night the men had used her and it had been horrible and degrading and painful and shameful. She had experienced no lust or pleasure at it. But the night before, when Ike had taken her upstairs, that had been different. She had responded then and in a way that frightened her, shook her self-concepts to their very core. And it would be that way again now, she was sure of that.

This cruel, hard man would put his hands on her and bring her feelings and desires that were repugnant and shameful. How would the other women think of her? How could they ever have trust in her if she was somehow to lead them to freedom, as remote as that possibility was? And how would it seem to her superiors if they ever did get free and these women told them what they had seen her do and how she experienced it?

But that all paled from the reality of the fact that Blackjack was willing to induce as much suffering as it took to force her to comply. Whatever her power of resistance, his power would be stronger and last longer. There was no way she could win. She surrendered to her fate.

Jack let her lie there a minute or so. Then he told her to get up. She rose wobbly to her feet, casting dark, hateful glances at him. He pushed her with the prod until she was in the middle of the room, facing the cages. Hooking the prod into his belt, he stepped behind her. Her bound hands were sitting on the top of the rise of her rear cheeks. He released his hardened cock from his pants and he pressed it against them. "Take hold of it," he ordered.

Her hands were fastened palm to palm and she was able to open them enough to let his rigid manhood to slip in. She whined as she felt his rigidness, his heat against her hands. He circled his own hands around her chest and took hold of her breasts. He started massaging and caressing them. Linda felt the vibrations of her nascent arousal immediately. She looked out and she could see that the eyes of the other women were on her. She whined and her body shifted. The man's hands clasped tightly around her breasts.

"Hold steady, bitch," he told her. He took hold of her nipples and twisted them. She cringed in pain. She stilled. The hands went back to work.

They explored her breasts and belly, travelling lightly over her skin, spreading their warmth. But they always came back to her breasts, kneading them, massaging them, caressing them, pulling on her teats, circling them and squeezing them tightly. All the time his cock was in her hands. His weapon, his meat, his prick, and the sensation of holding on to the object that would enter her, provoke her passions, drive her lusts, was shameful and so, so exciting.

He gave her breasts a squeeze and took hold of her nipples, stretching them from her, pulling her breasts out as far as they would go. The tension on her flesh was too much to take. She issued an unhappy moan. She had closed her eyes long ago, but now shut them harder, trying to block out what was happening to her, trying to erase the image of her standing before the other women as she succumbed to the man's attentions.

Then, while one hand continued to caress her breasts, the other dropped ever so slowly over her belly and down to her loins. It brushed across her sparse growth and delicately flitted over her pudenda. She shivered and suppressed a moan. When a long, thick finger slipped from the base of her divide slowly, slowly to the top, burying itself deeper and deeper into the channel between her love lips, she did moan and she regretted it fiercely.

The man soon had her crevasse dilated and mushy. He had leaned her over just a smidgeon so as to reach her loins and her breasts were swinging free from her body. Her hands had grasp of the man's meat and were caressing it mindlessly. When she moaned again, the hand in her loins driving her to distraction, he slipped his hand free from her now steaming sex and slipped his cock free of her hands. He took hold of her neck and pressed her forward. "Spread your legs," he told her. She swallowed a sob and spread them.

He had her half bent over. His hand was coming in from behind her now and he was able to thrust two fingers deeply inside her with ease. He ran them back and forth for a while, making her moan and shift her hips. And then he stepped forward. His left hand had hold of her neck and pressed her down even further, until she was almost tipped over. His right hand guided his steely shaft to her crevasse. It bumped up against her swollen love lips, pushed for a moment against her perineum, and then, finding her hole, slipped right in.

Linda Kramer of the FBI, Special Agent, top of her

class, rigid devotee of the Bureau, issued a deep, satisfied sigh. She hated herself for it, but there it was. When the man's motions began, she groaned and began to ease her hips back and forth to meet him.

Jack sighed too as he plunged deep into the woman's divide. Its walls seemed to grasp him firmly. Her interior was hot and soft. His cock glided along, in and out, happily. He bent the woman over even further, holding on firmly to her hair and prodded her legs further apart. Now he was truly buried deep inside her. His thrusts were long and hard. He could feel the tingling which presaged completion and he suppressed it, enjoying too much the feel of gliding over her velvety interior back and forth again and again.

Linda whined as her hair grew taut. She couldn't move her hips now with them all distended, but she received each stroke of the man's cock as if it was a gift. She had felt his immensity and length with her hands, his shape, his contours, and she was able to imagine his instrument as it plunged along her crevasse driving her closer and closer to explosion with each thrust.

Her face was tilted upwards, facing the cages. She opened her eyes for a moment and saw the stupefied faces of her sister captives staring back at her. A wave of humiliation passed through her. It was soon negated by the ever increasing passions that the man was producing in her. She felt her need rising and she began to utter little, impassioned groans each time the cock buried itself within her to the hilt. "Ugh! Ugh! Ugh! Ugh!"

The man's thrusts were coming harder and faster. His grip on her hair tightened. Her loose breasts were swinging to and fro. It was coming! It was coming! She couldn't do anything about it! "Oh, stop! Stop! Stop! Please! Please! Pleeeeeeeeeeease!" she thought madly.

And then it hit her. Her body shuddered and her pussy clenched tightly. The man behind her released a deep, urgent groan. His other hand had been on her hip, but now circled her and took hold of a breast, squeezing it hard.

"Mmmmmmmmmmmmpf! Mmmmmmmmmmmmmmmmmpf! Mmmmmmmmmmmmmmmmmpf!" she moaned as her pussy delivered a series of hard, intense jolts to her. Pleasure washed through her. She screamed and moaned.

Jack was holding on tight. His cock was dancing and jerking and pulsing deep in the woman's cunt. "Oh, yeah! Yeah! Yeah!" he thought. This was the thing! This was the thing to make him forget her! "Ahhhhhhhhhrgh! Ahhhhhhhhhhhrgh! Ahhhhhhhhhhhhhrgh!" he groaned.

And then his spasms began to wind down. He slowed his thrusts. The woman's pussy was still giving him pleasurable squeezes, but ever softer and softer. He let his cock give him a few more twinges of delight and then he stopped. He paused a moment and then slipped his softening meat from its home. The girl issued a deep sigh. He pulled on her hair until she was standing up. He gave her breasts a couple more satisfying squeezes and then ordered her to her knees. Still holding her hair, he made her shuffle over to her cage. He then connected her ankles to each other and then to her hands. He ordered her in.

"Yeah, this one would be fun to train," he thought. Maybe giving up the girl wouldn't be so bad after all. When the FBI lady was in the cage, he slammed the door shut and locked it.

He picked up the dog dishes and checked the room one more time. He went to each cage and double checked it to make sure that it was locked. He went to the door, took out the keys Stitch had given him and opened it. Before he turned out the light, he took one more look around the room. The woman was curled as much as she could into a ball, her eyes jammed shut. The other females were staring at him with fear. "See you later, ladies," he said to himself and he shut the light and closed the door.

Linda welcomed the pitch darkness. She heard the locks being closed on the door. A moment later there was silence. All except for her doleful sobs.

CHAPTER TEN

Jack still felt a little woozy from all the booze and the dope he had smoked. He found, too, that having fucked the FBI lady hadn't taken his mind off of his captive for very long. He trudged up the stairs from the cellar with a feeling of foreboding. By now, he assumed, Ike had finished fucking her and he would have to decide whether to go upstairs and examine the fruits of his abuse, or to sulk for the rest of the day downstairs.

He came up to the ground floor and entered the main room. Big Betty was standing near the door getting ready to leave. A very morose looking Maureen was there. She was dressed in a pair of cut off denim shorts and an orange tube top, the clothes, Jack presumed, that she had been captured in. A pair of flat leather sandals was on her feet. Her hands were bound behind her. She was wearing her head harness and had the harsh gag in her mouth that Jack had seen Big Betty adorn her with in the kitchen earlier. She looked more forlorn than she had been when she was naked. Somehow being in her own clothes highlighted the freedom and rights she had lost. Jack had no doubt that it was the last time she would wear them, maybe wear any clothes at all. It was a poignant sight.

The girl, Vida, was dressed in her yellow sheath dress and wearing a pair of high heeled sandals. She held the chain that led to the gag in Maureen's mouth.

Big Betty was dressed in her expansive, dirty blue jeans and a denim vest over a black t-shirt that had white lettering on it that said, "If I Had Balls, They'd be Bigger Than Yours!"

"That just might be true," Jack thought.

"Hey, Jack," Betty called out. "It was great to meet ya!" She stretched out a hand towards him. Jack took it and shook it. She had a grip like a man's.

"Next time you're up here, you'll have to stop by my place," she said. "Anything you want."

"Thanks," Jack replied.

"And I'll pay top dollar for any good pussy that comes your way. We go through 'em pretty fast."

"I'll keep that in mind." Jack answered.

"Well, see ya. Maybe I'll get down to Mexico one of these days and we can party."

"I'll be looking forward to it," Jack replied dully.

Maureen's eyes were brimming with tears. As Betty started to the door, Vida gave the chain a little tug. Maureen's eyes widened and she whined and hurried off to follow, the heels of her sandals clickety clacking on the floor.

Jack followed them to the porch. He watched them go up to a dusty, dark red El Camino. They pulled the girl up onto the bed behind the cabin and made her lie down on her belly. They used a series of straps to fasten her down and then pulled the vinyl cover over the flatbed and snapped it down all around. Betty got into the driver's side and Vida the passenger's. A few moments later, Betty backed the car out of the little cut out which hid all the vehicles, turned and drove away in a cloud of dust.

There were a couple of the boys on the porch drinking beers. Jack just nodded to them and went back inside. He was putting off going up the stairs. Stitch came out of the kitchen and he gave him the keys.

"Everybody locked down tight?" he asked Jack.

Jack just nodded.

"Morales will be here about 9 tonight," he told Jack.

"Dinner'll be around 7 or so. I'm makin' chili. We don't feed the girls dinner on nights they're going to travel."

"Okay." Jack said automatically. He looked around for Ike. The last thing he wanted to do was to go upstairs while he was still humping away at the girl. Stitch read his mind.

"Ike left. He said to tell you that the girl was more than all right and that he'll try to get the 25 grand you want for her from Morales. He'll be back later."

Jack didn't know whether to be happy about the news regarding the 25 grand or not. The way he felt now, he really didn't care.

Stitch went back into the kitchen. One of the biker boys brought the blond haired girl down the stairs and put her in a cage. She looked worn out. Jack wondered how many guys had fucked her today. He turned and went up the stairs. He had lost the whiskey and pot high he had had and was feeling drawn and tired himself. He walked slowly up the stairs until he reached the landing and then went to the door to his room. The key was hanging on a hook outside. He took hold of it and hesitated. He didn't know what he would find on the inside. He took a deep breath and put the key in the lock. He turned it and entered the room.

When he flicked on the light, he saw the girl on the bed. Her hands were stretched out above her and her knees were brought up towards her chest and then tied off to the sides of the bed. She was still wearing her blindfold and her gag. He shut the door.

The whip on the floor told Jack that she had been punished. For what, he didn't care. He picked it up and then slipped the thongs over the girl's belly and over her presented pudenda. A swell of anger arose in him. It was her fault that he was feeling this way, her fault that her beauty had incited Ike to want to fuck her. He envisioned in his mind the brutal biker mounted upon the girl, slipping his cock in and out of her, and her, overcome with distraught ecstasy, moaning and groaning with pleasure.

"You fucking cunt!" he thought dismally as the ache rose inside him. An urge came over him to make the girl pay for bringing these feelings out in him. He saw himself, in his mind's eye, belaboring her flesh with the flogger, hearing her screams and cries of pain, watching her skin get redder and redder. He had seen a long pony whip hanging on the wall. It would make long, bright red stripes on her flesh and would burn like fire. His grip tightened on the flogger. The girl was whining and crying as she experienced the leather thongs drifting across her skin. He saw a flash of red before his eyes. He planted his feet and drew the flogger back.

And then, all his anger just went right out of him. What good would whipping the girl do now, he asked himself. It would just highlight how powerless he was. And besides, the girl wasn't really to blame. It was himself. He was the one who had gone soft. He was the one who had lost himself in a romantic fog. What had he ever been thinking? He tossed the flogger aside.

He was tired and wanted to rest. And he didn't want to lie down on the bed next to the girl. If he got close to her, if he rubbed up against her naked skin, there was no telling what he would do. He didn't want to fuck her. That was all over. But he might become so overwhelmed with emotion that he just might strangle her. Then where would he be?

Remembering what Stitch had told him about the cage in the closet, he opened the closet door and looked inside. There was a 3' by 3' cage in there, just like Stitch had said.

He went to the bed and untied the girl's knees. Then he undid her wrists from the chain at the head of the bed. The girl was crying and her flesh was hot and inviting.

"No!" Jack said to himself. The contact with the girl was making his lusts grow. "No! I'm not going to do it!" he insisted in his mind. Fucking the girl now would make handing her off to the Mexican all that much harder.

He made the girl roll over and connected her wrists behind her back. He took hold of her rust colored hair at the back of her head and pulled on it until she rose up onto her knees. Then he led her off the bed. He took her into the bathroom and let her pee and then brought her over to the closet. He forced her to her knees again and told her to move forward. She shuffled over to the cage. When she reached it, he pushed her head down and told her to keep going. The bottom of the cage was padded and she crept onto it. Her body just about fit inside. He shoved her until she was fully within and then closed the gate. She was sobbing.

"Too bad!" he thought. He took a long look at her. She was trying to turn her body so that it was facing him. He heard her make a sound like she was trying to say something. He ignored it and shut the closet door. It cut off all sound.

Kicking off his boots, he then shut off the light. There was still just a little bit of sunlight coming into the room from the gaps between the boards over the windows. It made the room look yellowish and foggy. He lay down on the bed. He could smell the odor of the girl on the sheets and the odor of semen and sweat. A wave of self-pity flowed over him. "Fuck her and fuck everybody," he said to himself. A moment later, he was asleep.

Carly could not stop crying. She had known it was

him at the door. She would know his footfall anywhere. When he came into the room, she wanted desperately to run and hide, but, of course, she couldn't. She knew that seeing her this way would remind him that she was now soiled goods. When he stood there and looked at her, she could feel his eyes traverse her body, looking at her sexual divide, imagining the cock of the other man piercing it, using it, soiling it.

When she felt the thongs of the flogger drift across her belly and sex, she shivered with fear. She didn't want another whipping. She knew that if he started beating her, that he would find it hard to stop. "Maybe that would be for the better," she thought miserably. Maybe it would be better that she suffer physically for her sin of letting the other man have his way with her, though she could have hardly refused. The physical pain would help blot out the psychic wound.

And now that she knew that she had been sold, that she would be departing the relative safe haven of his care, custody and control to go to some awful fate, maybe it would have been better if he had killed her. Maybe eternal sleep would be better than what she knew she would suffer, whether it was going to be at the hands of that bruiser of a lesbian who called herself Big Betty, or to a Mexican whorehouse.

When he had untied her knees, something inside her had begged for him to take her, yearned for him to grant her ablution for her sins, the sins of being powerless and wanton, of being helpless and fearful, of being slavish and obedient, of not being sufficiently desirable for him to assert his preeminent claim to her. But he did not plot himself between her knees. He didn't rip out her gag and take her mouth. He didn't take ownership of her though all of her begged that he would.

She obediently allowed him to take her to the bathroom and pee. And even then, when they headed back towards the bed, her hopes rose. But he did not take her to the bed. He shoved her to her knees and ordered her forward. She had heard him opening the closet door and now she remembered what was in there.

"Please don't! Please don't!" her mind screamed sorrowfully as she edged her way to her newest, harsh imprisonment. She wanted desperately to plead and beg with him not to put her there, not to blot her out of his presence, his vision. She broke out into sobs. When he shoved her body in, his hot hands on her flesh, and when she felt the cage door close up against her skin, she tried to turn and face him. She couldn't hold back any longer even though she knew that speaking out to him was the gravest of sins. "...eeeeeeeeease ...on't! ...eeeeeeeeeeease on't! ...eeeeeeeeeease!" she whined piteously. And then the closet door shut and she was alone.

She sobbed and sobbed and sobbed. All was lost. She cursed him, cursed everyone. Cursed the FBI who had failed to find her, cursed Randy, her boyfriend, for not saving her, cursed the world for being indifferent to her plight.

She had already spent most of the day in darkness because of her blindfold, so it was not the darkness of her confines that oppressed her. It was knowing that he was outside, not more than three or four feet away from her, callous to her fate. It was the cold hard steel of the cage's bars that pressed up against her skin. It was the feeling of being stored away, cut off from all contact with the world, knowing that the next time she saw the sun, she would be far beyond any help that anyone could give her.

The gag in her mouth, she had worn that most of the day too, was an offensive reminder that her mouth was no longer her own, that strange men would use it, dozens, maybe hundreds of them. She bit down on it feverishly. She would rather die than face her fate. "Maybe if I can chew it off and swallow it I can choke to death," she thought miserably. "Then, when he opens the door and sees me gone he'll be sorry. They'll all be sorry!" And she would have outsmarted them. She would have shown them that she was not powerless. She had the power to say 'No!' She had the power to deny them her essence. She bit down hard, hard, hard, but it was no use. She couldn't rend the hideous object. She could do nothing. She was as powerless as a worm. They had all the power and she was helpless before them.

There was nothing to do now but endure. But there had to be a way to recover her freedom! There had to be a way out of this! There just had to be! "Oh, please, God, let there be! Please! Please!" she thought madly. And then, hearing no answer to her prayer, she descended into a dreary, soul wrenching torpor.

Jack awoke with a start at the knock on the door. "Dinner's ready," came the voice outside of it. Stitch's voice. It had taken him a moment or two to remember where he was. The sheets were all tangled and sweaty, his smell now mixed with hers. He looked frantically around the room. Where was she? And then he remembered. He looked over at the closet door. It was silent and cold. She was behind it. She who would be lost to him forever before the day was done. He felt an urge to draw her out of her imprisonment and give her one more delirious fucking. But as he thought of it a sourness came over him. No, that would just be torturing himself, he thought. Better that she remain out of sight and, to the extent possible, out of mind, until the time came to turn her over.

The room was swathed in only a dim light. He sat up from the bed and searched around the floor for his boots. He found them and put them on, tying them tightly. He got up and headed for the door. They key was in his pants. He took it out and unlocked it. Before he pulled it open, he took one more look at the closet door. He imagined her all scrunched up and helpless on the other side of it. Good, he thought. "That's what you deserve." He opened the door and stepped out into the hallway.

Coming down the stairs, he saw that the black haired girl and the blond were ensconced in their cages. Their hands were bound behind them and they were wearing gags. There was the sound of a happy crowd coming through the door to the kitchen. He pushed against the swinging door and entered.

The crew from this morning, absent Big Betty and her slave girl, were at the table along with a couple of other guys. Stitch was walking around the table ladling out steaming chili from a pot. There were crackers and bread on the table along with butter and a bottle of hot sauce. Ike, as before, was sitting at the end of the table furthest from the door. His head went up when Jack came in.

"Sleep well?" he asked him.

"Well enough," Jack answered morosely.

"Your girl sure knows how to fuck," Ike commented. "It's too bad we can't keep her around here for a month or two."

Jack's eyes burned and his belly tightened. There was a long, serrated knife by the loaf of bread on the table. He thought, for a moment, of thrusting it into Ike's heart. But then Stitch nudged up beside him.

"Have a seat, Jack," he said, "and have something to eat."

Jack looked at him, remembering the talk they had

had. Stitch was paused, waiting for him to take a chair.

"Okay," Jack said morosely. He sat between the guy they called Killer and another guy who he had seen earlier hanging around the house.

The men laughed and jawed each other up as they ate. Someone had tapped the keg from the night before and placed it in the corner. Every once and a while, one of the men would go over to it and fill a large, glass pitcher with it and return to the table. Someone poured Jack a mug of the amber brew.

A clock on the wall said it was 7:30. The men seemed a little edgy as the time to receive the Mexicans approached. As they finished their meals, a joint came out and was passed around. Jack had finished his second mug of ale and took a hit. The chili had been hot and delicious. He thought, for a moment, of the fact that it was too bad that Stitch was a wanted man. He could probably open up a nice Mexican restaurant and do well for himself.

The gray haired caretaker had taken a seat across from Jack. He kept giving Jack knowing looks. At one point, Ike addressed him and asked if the "broads" downstairs were all ready for their trip. He answered affirmatively.

To Jack he said, "The girls will be leaving tonight on the plane with Morales and his boys. You'll be taken across in a day or two through the tunnel. You can help Stitch break in the Mexican girls Morales will drop off tonight. That should keep your mind off things."

"Yeah," Jack answered dully. There was no sense fighting anything. He almost wished they would drop him off in town somewhere so he could shoot it out with the cops. He wondered if the ache he felt inside would ever go away. The joint passed his way again and he took another hit.

When dinner was over, Jack helped Stitch clean up. The he went out to the porch to smoke a cigarette. A couple of the boys were already there. One of them had brought out a bottle of Jim Beam and Jack took a couple of tots from it as it was passed around.

Night had fallen. It had turned a little chilly. Jack sat in a high backed deck chair and watched the stars. They were brighter than he had ever seen them. The boys were mostly silent. It was peaceful and calm. His thoughts kept going back to the girl upstairs and what a time they had had. It seemed a long time ago that they had spent the day in their snowbound cabin although it was only the day before yesterday. He thought of the way she squealed when he had first penetrated her rear entrance, the sight of her face with her lips pursed around his cock, the little strip tease he had forced her to make their first night together. He thought of the letter he had found in her purse, the one to her mother.

Carly, Carly, Carly. For three days he had not been able to remember her name and now he couldn't get it out of his mind. He wondered if he would ever see her again in Mexico. That guy Morales might keep her all to himself, at least for a while. And when he got tired of her, who knew what he would do with her. He might sell her off to one of his business associates or put her to work in a whorehouse. He thought of the sight of her widespread thighs, the divide between them glistening with arousal, her eyes looking up at him imploringly, her mouth shielded by the leather of her gag, her arms bound up behind her.

"Shit!" he exclaimed to himself. When was that Morales guy going to get here? He dreaded the moment of handing the girl over to him, watching him put his paws on her, claiming her, a toothy smile on his face, the girl cowering in fear. "Shit! Shit! Shit!" he said silently. When the bottle came around again, he took a big swig.

"There they are," one of the men said. Jack looked out into the desert sky. A pale form was sweeping over the darkened landscape. Off in the distance, maybe a half mile or so away, two lights appeared, marking, no doubt, the dirt runway for the low flying plane.

Ike had wandered out onto the porch. "Billy," he told the diminutive biker, "get the pickup up to the strip." And to Jack he said, "Better get your piece of ass ready."

You could just hear the drone of the aircraft's engine. Jack rose to his feet. He was a little unsteady. He had done a lot of drinking for a guy who never touched the stuff before he went to stir. "Maybe I'll drink myself to death," he thought. He turned and walked into the house.

The two girls from the cages were outside of them now. They were kneeling in the middle of the main room, their knees spread and looks of misery emanating from their eyes. Stitch and two of the other guys were going through the door to the basement to get the four women stored there. Jack turned to ascend the stairs.

When he reached the door to his room, he paused. Was it too late to grab the girl and make a run for it? He could steal one of the bikes outside and be off in a second. But where would he go? What would he do with her? And then he thought, "Yes, it's too late. Too late for everything." He had to go through with it. And, after all, wasn't this what he had wanted, a chance to live the high life once more? The girl was his ticket to it, the price he had to pay. That's all. And fuck her anyway.

Three days ago, he hadn't even known her and he had been all right then. He could do without her, would forget her like he had forgotten all the others. She was just a piece of ass, a cunt. Like all the rest. And it was stupid for him to feel this way about her. She didn't give a shit about him, would betray him at the first chance she got. She deserved everything she got. They all did.

He turned the key and pushed the door open. He flicked on the light and closed it. He looked at the closet door. She was behind it, silent and blind, awaiting her fate.

He put his hand on the doorknob. Something was making him hesitate to turn it. He thought again of her flesh, its warmth, its softness, her breasts, her lips. All gone forever. "Fuck it!" he declared audibly. He turned the knob and opened the closet.

The light from the room illuminated the small space. The girl's head was uplifted, as if seeking out whoever had opened the door. He knelt down and unlocked the cage and then swung the door open.

"All right," he said. "Get out."

The girl moved slowly. She was whining. He ignored her unhappy sounds and when she had cleared the cage, took her by the hair behind her head and brought her to her feet. She was unsteady and she moaned. Her breasts moved enticingly. He took hold of one and squeezed it. "Goodbye," he thought.

Releasing her breast, he dragged her into the bathroom where he made her pee for the last time. After, he brought her back into the room and made her stand in the middle. He went to one of the bags from the car and pulled out the girl's purse, her dress and the yellow high heels she had been wearing when he had captured her. He made her lift her feet one by one as he slipped the shoes onto her feet. She wobbled on them unsteadily. Then he turned her around and released her hands from behind her back. He took the dress, scrunched it all up and drew it over her head. The slinky, yellow thing descended over her shoulders and then draped itself over her body. He pulled it down over her hips and then stood back.

She was a sexy bit of fluff, he thought. The slinky dress emphasized her graceful hips. He made her turn around and looked at her from the front. She was still wearing her blindfold and gag. Her hands, loose for the first time all day, hung by her sides limply. Her breasts filled the bodice of the dress nicely. It was a little wrinkled from being stored up in a bag for almost four days, but it still looked nice. All that was wrong was her reddish hair.

Her high heels made her breasts and ass push out just enough for emphasis. The dress came down to about mid-thigh, what lay beneath it tantalizingly hidden away. All you had to do was slip a hand up it and you would find her treasure, he thought. The dress almost invited it, especially if you knew what he knew, how passionate and obedient she was.

He stood looking at her for a moment. She was shaking and crying silently. "Fuck you," he said to himself. He resisted the impulse to strike her. "What good would that do?" he thought.

Reaching around her, he released her gag. Her breasts pushed up against his chest. He pulled it from her mouth tossed it on the bed. Then he drew the blindfold off of her head.

Her eyes were full of tears and her lips were trembling. She looked at him dolefully. He ignored it. He picked up her small, matching purse and handed it to her. "Take out your makeup and do your face," he told her. "And stop crying. If you don't, I'll whip you till you scream. Understand?"

She nodded at him and took the purse. Without comment, without resistance, she went into the bathroom and opened her bag. She pulled out a compact with some blush inside it, a tube of lipstick and her eyeliner. He watched while she put it on, entranced. "Will this be how I'll remember her?" he thought to himself. She looked more human than she had in days, since he took her, more like a regular girl. She was leaning over the sink, applying her eyeliner, carefully watching her efforts in the mirror. She was sniffling, but had stopped crying. He wondered how much she knew about her fate. They had talked pretty much openly about it when she was around. It was impossible for her not to know what was happening.

What was she thinking? Was she thinking that it was better to be shut of him, regardless of what fate awaited her? Was she sorry, just a little to be leaving him? This morning, when they had fucked, and last night too, he had felt something special between them. Had she felt it? He had thought she had. But maybe that was just his wishful thinking, his imagination. How could she feel anything for him after what he had done to her, taken her away from everything that she knew and loved? She would probably think nothing about stepping over his dead body. So why did her feel this way about her?

Carly had finished her eyes and cheeks and was putting on her lipstick. Her hand was shaking. She was trying ever so hard not to cry. She was so scared her body was chill. Being dressed in her clothes, wearing her heels, making up her face as she had done a thousand and one times before, was so incongruous to her surroundings, what she had gone through, that it made her belly twist into a knot.

She had spent a long time in the cage. A long, miserable time. It had been horrible to be in there and she had yearned for the man to come and set her free. At the same time, she had been praying never to hear his feet outside the door, to never hear it swing open, because she knew that those would be signs that she was soon to be delivered to her new owner. And now, it was perhaps moments away. "Oh why, why, why is this happening to me?" she thought miserably. "Please don't let it happen! Please don't let it happen!" she prayed.

When her lips were covered in red, she quietly put her makeup back in her purse. Then, dutifully, obediently, meekly, she turned and handed it back to the man. He just tossed it aside. She watched it land on the bed. All of what she had left of her life was in there, she thought. And now she would be leaving that behind as well.

The man was staring at her. He was no more than a foot and a half away from her. She felt compelled to look him in the face as he towered over her. What was that she saw in it? Was it cruelty? Was it harshness? Was he thinking about the $25,000 he would demand for her? And what would happen to her if he didn't get it? Would he take her out to the desert and kill her? Or would they kill him and take her anyway?

Or was that sadness she saw in his face? What did he have to be sad about? He would be free. He would be able to do anything he wanted. He could kidnap and rape until his heart was content. She thought of his cock between her legs and his hot tongue in her mouth. She thought of the ways he had made her come, shouting out her passions. Had something happened?

She had felt, in the last 24 hours, drawn to him like she had never felt drawn to anyone before. He had pierced her inner self, shown her things about herself she had never known. If she ever got free and met him again, what would it be like? Would she surrender to him, give herself over? Would she kneel before him and place her forehead on the floor as he had made her do so many times? Would she strip herself and open herself to him, take his cock in her mouth, her pussy, her rear, willingly, wantonly?

Out of the corner of her eye, the empty bed loomed. "Fuck me!" she thought. "One more time! Please! Please! Fuck me until I die in your arms! Don't send me away! Please! Please!" But she dared not speak. She could tell he wanted it too. "Let's die together, here! Now!" she thought. "Please don't send me away! Please!"

And then his face clouded over. The hardness she had seen so often came back into his eyes. It was the same hardness she had seen the day he put the gun to her head out in the woods that day. He was going to do it! Sell her! Doom her! "Oh, please don't do it!" she begged with her eyes once more. "Please!"

"Turn around," he growled. She hesitated, and then obeyed. She was struggling mightily not to break out into sobs. She felt him grab her wrists and put them together, linking the rings in her bracelets. Then he made her turn around again. He had the blue ball in his hand. It was her last chance to speak, to beg, to plead, to tell him how much she wanted him, that she would obey him an all things, forever and forever! All of her wanted to. She couldn't find her voice. She had been silent for so long that she couldn't make the words emerge. The idea of speaking to him seemed like the violation of the worst and strongest taboo. She just couldn't do it.

He didn't tell her to open her mouth. He just shoved the blue rubber ball against her lips and forced it in. It filled her mouth, stretching her lips, silencing her. "It's too late! It's too late!" she thought with despair. "It's too late!" A second later, he placed the blinder back over her eyes. She was in darkness once again. His hand took hold of the hair behind her head and he marched her towards the door.

It had taken all of Jack's strength to finish getting the girl ready. She had a look of deep sadness and despair across her face. Her lips were trembling and her eyes had begun to fill with tears. He had wanted to speak to her, to tell her something, anything that would make it better. But he had nothing to say. What could he say? He was selling her into the most abject bondage. She would never have another free day the rest of her life. The men would use her until she was all used up and then throw her away. She would be owned by men who would have no more thought of her than if she was a horse or a dog. They would inflict brutalities upon her so dire that she would beg for death. "What am I doing?" he thought miserably. "Why can't I stop myself?"

Then, with a surge of determination, he had pressed the blue ball into her mouth. He had covered her eyes. He marched her to the door and out. She issued a little whine but gave him no resistance. Slowly, carefully, he brought her down the stairs.

The main room was filled with cold, hard men and terrified, helpless women. A line of small statured, black haired, brown skinned women, dressed in colorful short skirts and dresses were standing in a line, front to back, along one side of the room. Their hands were all locked behind their backs and they wore leather collars with chains that led from one to the other. They were crying and whimpering, looking frantically around for some way to escape their fate.

Alongside them were four men with shaggy black hair, dressed in tight denims and dark t-shirts holding what looked like electric prods in their hands. They had pistols strapped to their waists.

The females from downstairs had been brought up

and they were kneeling down next to the other two girls, Julie and Camille, their unhappy glances mirroring those of their dark skinned sisters. They were naked. Two sharply dressed men were examining them. The woman Jack had kidnapped, Mrs. Ramirez was standing and having her breasts examined by one of the men. Her gag had been removed and she was squealing and crying as the man assessed her mammaries. After a few seconds of this, the man hauled off and slapped her across the face, turning her head and yelled, "*Silencio, tu pinche cabrona!*" The other man laughed and said something in Spanish.

Ike and the boys were strewn about the room. Ike and Mouse were standing near the well dressed men and Rocker, Billy, Stitch, Chaz and Killer were watching the other Mexican men warily, watching them. The biker boys were all armed.

Ike turned and looked at Jack descending the stairs. "Here he is now," he said.

The two well-dressed men, one older, mid-fiftyish, a little on the heavy side, and the other, slim, fit, maybe 30 or so, turned to look at Jack. Their hair was well trimmed. They both wore full, sculpted moustaches. Their skin was lighter than their underlings', more of a dark tan than brown. They had an air of authority, wealth, power. The older one was dressed in a well tailored, buttoned, black suit with very faint and narrow white pinstripes. His tie had soft pastel colors reminiscent of a Monet.

The younger one's suit was a light metallic blue, slick and shiny, almost iridescent, cut to complement his muscular chest, wide shoulders and almost girlish hips. He wore no tie and his suit and pale green silk shirt were open, revealing a thick neck and a hairless chest. While the older man's hair was cut short, businesslike, the younger one's was a little longer, down over his ears and modish. They both wore large golden rings on their left hands. Their shoes were black and shiny, almost certainly custom made. When they saw Jack, the older one smiled. The younger man sneered.

Jack walked the girl down to where they stood. The men eyed her salaciously. The older man stepped forward and held out his hand.

"*Hola,* Signor Blackjack," he said in heavily accented English. "I am honored to make your acquaintance."

"Jack, this is Mr. Morales," Ike said as Jack took his hand.

"Pleased to meet you, Mr. Morales," Jack greeted him.

"And this is my son, Lorenzo," Morales stated. Jack shook his hand too.

"I was just admiring this nice piece of merchandise you have brought me," Morales continued. "Your *policia* are looking high and low for her. I hear that her husband has put out a $100,000 reward."

"That's good news," Jack answered.

"But, I think he will pay a lot more than that, don't you?"

"If everything I've heard is true," Jack replied.

"Oh, it's all true," Lorenzo interjected. His English was more cultured than his father's, but whereas the father's voice was smooth and velvety, Lorenzo's was harsh and nasal. His features were sharper too, shark like. There was an aura of cruelty about him. While the father was apparently unarmed, Lorenzo had a Glock attached to his belt.

"He's going to have to pay through the nose if he wants his little *conchita* back," Lorenzo continued. "But first I think that she will have to become acquainted with a few of our customs," he said, smiling. He took hold of the woman's nipple and gave it a sharp twist that made her shriek. He slapped her again, harshly.

"*No mames, puta!*"he yelled at her.

She was crying fiercely. "Please…." she started to say. Lorenzo slapped her again and rattled off something harsh in Spanish that made the woman cringe.

"I think this one will need a good whipping when we get home, Papa," he said.

"Now, Lorenzo," the father replied, "I think we should give the poor woman a chance to show her obedience first. You've frightened her." He turned to the woman and tapped his hand on her cheek. In English, he asked her, "You'll be a good girl for us, won't you Signora Ramirez? As long as you keep your legs open and your mouth shut you'll be okay. In a few months, who knows, maybe a year or so, we'll return you to your loving husband just a little bit worse for wear."

"Ohhhhhhhhh!" the Ramirez woman moaned. Jack could tell that she wanted to beg and plead for her freedom, but she gave the junior Morales a frightened look and held her trembling lips tightly together. There was a spot of blood on them where Lorenzo had slapped her.

Morales nodded to Ike and Ike to Mouse. Mouse had been holding her gag and he shoved it back into the woman's mouth forcibly. She issued a muffled cry and then he locked it up behind her head.

"Back on your knees," he told her curtly. The woman sank down obediently, tears streaming down her face.

Morales turned his attention to the girl.

"And I understand that you have brought me something special," he said to Jack.

A wave of anger passed through Jack, but he held his temper. He had to stay on course. This man was the key to his freedom. All depended on his good will.

"Very special," Jack replied. "All the way from Wisconsin." He pushed the girl towards the two men so that they could get a better look at her.

The men took their time examining her. Her dress and makeup accentuated her beauty and desirability well. Her plump, red lips were pursed around the blue rubber ball in her mouth. Her stiff nipples, atop her solid, ample breasts, could be easily discerned through the fabric of her dress. Her legs were long for her body and the high heels complemented their gracefulness. Jack knew that she would be hard to resist.

"I understand that you want $25,000 for her," Morales said after a short while. "That's a lot of money for a whore."

"Don't worry, she's hot, Mr. Morales," Ike said. "I tried her out personally. You won't be disappointed." Jack gave Ike a bitter glance.

"That's too much, Papa," Lorenzo spat out. "She's just a cunt like all the others."

"It is a lot of money, Signor Jack," Morales said smoothly. "Can I see her first?"

"That's no problem," Jack replied. Keeping his hold on the girl's hair with one hand, he reached down with the other and took a hold of the hem of her skirt. He pulled it up over her belly, her breasts and then over her head. He let it drape down over her bound wrists. The girl gave out a squeal of unhappiness. He shook her head and told her to shut the fuck up. He pushed her a little bit closer to the older Mexican so that he could get a good look at her, arching her back so that her bare breasts stood out to good effect.

"*Muy bonita,*" Morales said admiringly. He reached out and took hold of a breast. "Very nice," he said again. He let his hand slip from her breast and over her belly.

"Nice and tight," he commented. "And such nice hips. Tell her to spread her legs."

Jack shook the girl's head sharply. "Open your legs," he told her harshly.

Carly was too scared not to obey. She had felt the Mexican man's touch and she had recoiled, her stomach churning. These were cruel, hard men. She had heard the slaps they had given the other woman and her cries of pain. There was an older man and a younger, she could tell from their voices. The younger one, the one who had called the other man "Papa," had a voice that sent a chill down her spine. It was cold and mean and heartless.

She spread her legs unhappily.

The man's hand took hold of her pudenda. It was hot. His fingers tickled her there, and one of them slid along the line of her labial divide. It made her jump and her captor shook her head again harshly. "Keep still, cunt!" he told her.

The finger kept probing until it had insinuated itself between her love lips and found her entrance. "Ohhhhhhhhhh! God, no!" she moaned inside.

The finger probed deeper. His handling of her puss had made her sex lubricate defensively and the finger slipped right into her receptive channel. "Mmmmm-mmmmm!" she moaned in dismay.

"And a very nice cunt," Morales said. "But I can't see her face well with the blindfold on. Would you mind removing it, Signor Jack?" he asked.

"No problem," Jack replied. He slipped it from her head.

Carly looked quickly around her. The man with his finger in her quim was only a few inches away from her. His face was round and slightly slovenly. There was steel in his eyes bespeaking hardness. His lips were fat and soft, holding out his hand. Jack held his own out numbly. They shook.

"Well, that settles that," the older man said.

Carly panicked. She tried to pull away. "...ooooh! ...ooooh!" she screamed through her gagged mouth. "...oooooooh!"

Instinctively, Jack tightened his grip on her hair. She pulled and yanked and screamed.

"You see," Morales said to his son. "A tiger."

Lorenzo's face broke out into a sinister smile. He stepped forward and snaked his hand under Carly's chin, taking hold of the ring on her collar. "I'll take her," he snarled. Jack released the girl's hair. The man pulled her towards him. He slapped her face hard, twice. Carly screamed. He said something to his men. They jumped into action.

The Mexicans had brought a small trunk in with them. One of the men opened the trunk as the other approached Carly holding out his electric prod. As he shoved it between the sobbing girl's legs, Lorenzo released her. A loud, 'crack!' filled the room and the young girl doubled up and fell to the floor screeching wildly. The men were atop her in an instant. One of them held her down on the floor while the other reached into her mouth and removed the blue rubber ball that Jack had placed there. When her mouth was free, Carly began to call out.

"Don't do this! Please! Please! Don't do this! Please! I'm begging you, please! Please!"

The first man had a shiny black leather object in his hand with a long, wide, leather prong at its end. Together, the men forced Carly's jaws apart. "...ooooooooooouugh! ...oooooooooough! ..ooooooooough! ...oooooooough! ...ooooooooooough!" she screamed as she twisted and turned her torso in desperation, her legs flying this way and that.

And then her sounds were abruptly cut off. The men had forced the prong between her lips and shoved it home. The prong was attached to a hood and they quickly pulled it over her head. She struggled, her muffled pleas and screams emerging from behind her gag. The hood went completely over her head and was connected in the back by a series of clasps. The men pulled it tight, sealing her head in leather. There were little eyelets by her nose for breathing and flaps by her eyes that could be lifted for limited sight. For now, they were closed.

"Uuuuuuuuugh! Uuuuuuuuuugh! Uuuuuuuuuugh!" Carly cried out as she struggled to throw the men off her. She was the center of attention in the room now. All of the men had drawn closer to witness her subjugation and enjoy her distress. It wasn't often that you got a girl who actually resisted.

One of the men unhooked her wrists, tossing her pretty, yellow dress aside, and held her arms still while the other one said something to Lorenzo. The evil looking drug lord held his hand out to Jack. "The keys, signor," he said.

Dully, Jack reached into his pocket and withdrew the key to Carly's bracelets and collar. Lorenzo snatched it out of his hand and tossed it to one of the men. He proceeded to unlock the bracelets while the other man drew another object from the trunk. It was a leather sleeve. Carly squirmed and twisted her body in an effort to frustrate the men, but they were too big and too strong and too experienced for her to delay them for too long. One of the men held her down in place while the other fitted first one arm and then the other into the sleeve. It forced the arms together, parallel to each other, wrist to elbow across the lower part of her back. It drew her shoulders back painfully and Carly screamed again. There were buckles on the sleeve and the men used them to pull it tight.

"Mmmmmmmmmm! Mmmmmmmmmmmm!" Carly cried out piteously. She was rapidly losing her battle.

The leather sleeve covered her arms from elbow to elbow, her useless hands, clasped into little fists, sticking out of the end. The men drew her to her feet. There was a ring on the hood just over the gag and one man held her still by it, lifting her up until her tip toes just touched the floor while the other released her collar and threw it away. He then took a new one from the trunk and, while the naked girl whined and sobbed, circled it around her neck. It was made of thick, black leather with golden colored rings front and back. It had a large, scriptive, blood red '*M*' embedded in the front. It clicked closed around her neck.

The Mexican removed her yellow high heels and her ankle bracelets. He attached instead two shiny steel manacles, one to each ankle, connected by about 12" of chain. Then he stepped back and signaled the conclusion of his efforts to Lorenzo. The drug lord stepped forward and took from the other man the electric prod that he had used on the girl a moment ago. He pressed it between Carly's legs. She shrieked, knowing what was coming and then shrieked again as Lorenzo pulled the trigger. She collapsed to the floor. Lorenzo crouched down next to her, placing his hand hard on her neck, pushing her leather encased face onto the rough carpet.

"Now, you'll be quiet, my little *putita*," he snarled evilly, "or the prod will bite you again. Do you want that?"

Carly sobbed a muffled answer, "...ooooough! ...ooooooough!"

Lorenzo laughed. "For now, I'll take that as a no.

Don't be so sad, whore," he told her. "We're going to have a lot of fun. Believe me. And the more you resist and the more disobedient you are, the more fun it will be for me. Understand?"

"...ooooooough!   ...ooooooough!" Carly sobbed through her gag.

Lorenzo got up. He looked at his father. "Let's finish up. I can't wait to get this one home," he said.

The other women in the room were sobbing, the Mexican girls too. Morales, Sr. completed his inspection of the other *gringas*, noting especially FBI Special Agent Linda Kramer, and a price was agreed upon for all. An inspection of the Mexican girls followed with the lifting of their skirts and the opening of their bodices to inspect their tawny colored breasts. Jack watched dully. Carly was lying on the floor, sobbing quietly. The Mexican girls cried and sobbed miserably, requiring a fierce slap now and then to moderate their effusions of dismay.

While Stitch and Ike looked over the Mexican flesh, Morales's men began to accouter the *gringas* in the same confinements that Carly now wore. When they were all done, Stitch and Rocker and two other of the bikers led the unhappy *senoritas* through the door that led to the basement and the disconsolate, faceless *gringas* were all stood on their feet.

A bottle of tequila appeared with some shot glasses. Toasts were cast all around by the satisfied men. Out of the trunk came a large briefcase. While the naked *gringas* stood around bound and hooded, sobbing lowly, awaiting their fate, the valise was opened and several large plastic bags of white powder emerged. It looked to Jack to be about five pounds worth. The men sat around one of the coffee tables and a random one was opened. Mouse sampled it and then nodded to Ike. A scale was produced and the bags weighed. Jack had been right. 5.25 lbs.

At that, everyone shook hands. A briefcase full of cash was handed to Lorenzo. He opened it, counted the bundles of 100's and smiled. He nodded to his dad. The price of the four *gringas*, Mrs. Ramirez and Special Agent Kramer excluded, added up to a little bit more than the seven *senoritas*, supply and demand being what they were, and Lorenzo pulled a bundle or two of 100's from the briefcase and handed them back to Mouse. Ike and Jack would get paid when the ransom came through for the Ramirez woman and as to the lady FBI agent, well, she was just a bonus.

At his father's insistence, Lorenzo removed 5 bundles of 100's from the valise and handed them to Jack. $25,000. Mr. Morales smiled and shook his hand. "I'll see you in Senora in a few days, *mi amigo*," he said. "There's a nice *casa* in our compound I've got all picked out for you. When you get settled, we'll talk. Okay?"

"Okay," Jack replied morosely. His eyes were on the girl. Her shrouded head was swaying back and forth. Her full, naked breasts were trembling enticingly, giving Jack a pang of sorrow. She was still sobbing. He could tell. The large, red 'M on her collar told him that she was no longer his property. "What have I done?" he thought miserably.

There was another round of shots of tequila and *adios's* and handshakes were exchanged. A moment later, the underlings began to escort the girls towards the door. Lorenzo took hold tightly of Jack's former captive's arm and led her away. The naked girls all shuffled slowly out, sobs and moans emerging from their gags, breasts swaying, chains clinking. With the black hoods over their heads, they all looked almost the same, except for a bit of hair that had escaped here and there.

Jack followed them out to the porch. The women were loaded up on the back of a pickup truck and made to sit. The guards got in with them and the rear gate was shut. Morales and his son got into the back of a topless, black SUV, the unfortunate Carly in tow. The engines fired up and the vehicles pulled away. Jack watched dismally as the girl disappeared into the night.

About 10 minutes later, he heard the sound of the small turboprop the Mexicans had arrived in come to life in the distance. A minute or two after that, he listened as it revved its engines and took off down the small runway. He saw it as it lifted off, just a small smudge of grey amidst the speckled stars. It faded away within a few seconds, flying low in the night sky, south, towards perdition.

To be continued.